Society of the Machine

Justin Smith

To Joey

Justin Smith

ISBN: 1466295597
ISBN-13: 978-1466295599

DEDICATION

Dedicated to my loving family, and all of my friends who
supported me during this endeavor. Also, to all of my teachers
who encouraged me along the way.

ACKNOWLEDGMENTS

Thank you to my parents and brother for being supportive and thank you to Kashmeel and Ricky for encouraging me.

PROLOGUE

The year is 2689, and this isn't the future most people predict. It's a future of failure. It's a future of corruptness. It's not the future where everyone has high-tech lasers, jetpacks and ray guns. It's a Marxist future: a struggle between the haves and have-nots. So when people ask where the technology is, it's either banned, or not here yet. Some bans, like the one on lasers, were well intentioned. Fewer lasers, like fewer atomic weapons, meant fewer deaths in war. The effect of this relative backwardness however, was about to make itself felt.

A select group of individuals is just beginning to unlock the secrets of the galaxy. Most people simply refer to these people as *them*: the eternally unknown, but spoken of, *them*. The public however, is still unaware of many things, including intelligent extraterrestrial beings. Trade had been taking place between humans and other beings for nearly two decades, and the secret is now in danger.

It's possible everything could have continued to function normally, except for two events. The first was the conclusion of World War Four. A new type of unity was established which would allow for increased exchange of information. The second event was the outbreak of a civil war in the galaxy, which allowed for the rise a ruthless robot named Sudokus as a leader.

By this year, Earth was the only planet not under Sudokus's control. The important players on Earth could control certain things, but a war was out of their control. It would take more than human ingenuity to stop the enemy. Enemies were turning to allies, and allies were turning into enemies and Earth would need a hero to stop a seemingly unstoppable army. However, even if anyone can stop the army, Earth also needs someone to save it from itself.

PART I

CHAPTER ONE

After World War Four, a treaty politically divided Earth into four sections: Northeast, Northwest, Southeast, and Southwest. Winston is the leader of the Northwestern section of the world, which is comprised of North America and the Western part of Europe. Each Section scuffles with the others in places like Africa and Antarctica hoping to gain control of disputed regions and any resources they would offer. However, relations between these four powers are not hostile, but in fact quite peaceful. There are never wars, only disputes. Citizens of one section can travel to any other section freely. However, supplies are beginning to run low in the different sections. This has caused an increase in illegal trafficking of certain products that have become profitable (Gasoline would have been one of these products, except it became scarce twenty years ago and a new form of fuel called ogelan replaced it). Crime enforcement has stepped up to meet the problem in the form of a new kind of officer. The police officers of the past have been done away with, and the new standards for crime enforcement are Ginyu Guards. They wear a metallic suit of full-body armor and even have a bulletproof visor to cover their faces. The Ginyus are a shoot first, ask questions later type of crime control. It needs to be that way since the jails are starting to get overcrowded. Even if the person was innocent, it would just be another person using valuable space until their trial.

Leon is not a Ginyu guard. He is just one of the many people who dislike them. The Ginyus took both of his parents when he was seven years old. They took them away and he never saw them again. Ever since then he fended for himself.

However, life at this point was much safer than it had been in the past so long as you avoided the Ginyus; so it wasn't terribly difficult for Leon to grow into a young adult. Alcohol didn't exist any longer and neither did any type of drug except for pharmaceuticals. The government still tried to sell generic cigarettes and liquor but the cigarettes were only filled with leaves which had no effect on a person and the liquor was merely water with a chemical in it to make it taste bitter; to drink it was almost a show of toughness, or maybe a throwback to the old days. Leon chose not to drink it because it didn't have a particularly good taste and he didn't want to waste money on it.

Most people did drink it however, so that was one thing which distinguished Leon from the masses, but other than that, Leon was just an average person. He worked as a military test pilot, although he didn't know exactly why. The way things were going right now, there would never be another war. In his high school history classes, Leon learned that World War Four was the final war in the history of humanity. As soon as they signed the treaty at the end of the fighting, warfare became an ancient and barbaric practice. But Leon was still a test pilot for some reason. He never questioned anything, mainly because his pay was very good. He knew his job could call him into work at any time, but this was just the nature of his occupation and he accepted it.

Leon finished another test at work and was on his way home. He usually walked to and from his house and today was no exception. He walked instinctively through the streets, not even taking the time to admire the tall, shining glass buildings around him, or the cars hovering just a few feet above the ground in the streets that surrounded him. He saw this every day, and it was normal to him.

He even managed to ignore the Ginyu Guards who were seemingly on every corner of every street. Their armors varied in color between red, blue, and yellow to distinguish their rank and status amongst other Ginyu Guards. They looked almost like robots in both their appearance and mannerisms. Tinted visors concealed their faces, and every motion they made seemed planned and coordinated. Nothing about them was human or natural.

Leon was nearly home when he passed by an alley between two tall buildings. He always passed by this alley on his way home, but today something made him stop there. He thought he could hear faint murmurs coming from inside. It sounded like whoever was making the sounds was in distress, but there were too many shadows to see anything. Leon walked into the alley cautiously. This wasn't something he normally did after work, but he figured he had some responsibility to help someone if they were in distress. He didn't realize how much this decision would affect him in the future.

"Is anyone here?" There was no response other than an audible moan. Leon continued walking into the alley until he could faintly make out something moving. "Do you require assistance?" As far as Leon could tell it was a man lying there, but he was under a blanket.

"What happened?" asked Leon.

The man responded, but it wasn't anything Leon could make out. It didn't even sound like real words.

"Tomo lo fargled," he said faintly.

Leon thought something might have happened to the man to make him unable to speak clearly. Those certainly weren't actual words that he said. Leon decided to bring him back to his home since the nearest hospital was over an hour away by car and there were long waiting lines anyway.

Leon arrived at his tiny home on the outskirts of town. It was nearby a huge patch of sand, which, from his understanding, used to be a forest. Leon wasn't sure if that was true, but he knew that before the war, New Mexico was the name of the area that he lived in. Now it was just section 14427 of the Northwest. Even country names were only to identify ethnicity unless there was some emergency that required their usage.

Leon's home was just one room with a desk and a hammock held up by nails in the adjacent walls. There was also a bathroom added on to the back of the house. It looked like an outhouse, but there was running water.

Leon sat the man down on the hammock, but the man didn't seem like he wanted to rest. He was trying to say something to Leon, but he was too incoherent. Leon tried calming him down, but nothing he tried worked. Leon could swear he just kept repeating the same three words, "Tomo lo fargled."

Meanwhile, on the planet of Jupiter, a robot was watching Leon. Not just any robot, but a robot named Sudokus. No one knows exactly how he was built, but there were always rumors. Some say he's the brain of an alien with the body of a robot, some say he can steal the minds of others to use for himself. In truth, whoever built him dabbled in a power too strong. It was a new type of technology, which allowed a completely artificial mind to learn and feel certain emotions. Sudokus's mind was almost identical to that of a human. Only he was much smarter and not bogged down by emotions such as love and sadness. He only had the feelings of satisfaction, dissatisfaction, greed, and ambition. That's all any successful being needs. Sudokus had one other thing going for him, like most other aliens, he could read the mind of whoever he so pleased, but he could also see things in the big red eye which was planted right in the middle of his face. He could see things that were happening on different planets.

Sudokus proved to be a ruthless killing machine, even killing his creator. In this way, he gained a following of soldiers and was able to take control of a weakened galaxy. He was a powerful robot in terms of strength. He had some of the features of a human, two arms, two legs a head and body, but he also had other not-so-human features. He had two golden pincers, like crab claws, on his hands. His chest had just an intricate working of pipes, bars and cables. In the middle, you could see his heart. Not an actual heart, but a beating engine. The creator designed it in such a way that it did not require an energy source other than the energy that just floated around in the air. Once the shock of energy started up Sudokus all those decades ago, he was a self-sustaining machine with only the purpose of gaining power.

So Sudokus sat in a room, with his advisors and guards, watching Leon in his eye. He could see Leon in his home, as he was struggling to understand his visitor. Sudokus was more interested in the visitor than Leon. Leon hadn't taken a man into his home; he hadn't even taken in a human. He took in an alien named Harem. Leon sealed both of their fates by doing this. Sudokus recognized the alien as Harem, the leader of a rebellion group on Mars that tried to stop Sudokus's army from taking over the planet. They of course failed miserably in their rebellion, and now Sudokus intended to personally kill Harem; however, he escaped. Now he knew where he was and he planned to send the two best assassins he had to eliminate Harem. Those assassins were Gako and Lada.

Lada was a tall, sleek alien. She was blue with no hair or any distinguishing features except for one big black eye. She had two arms and a body, but rather than legs, she had a tail she slithered on. Her training was in the art of long-range assassinations. Gako was a very large alien with muscular arms that he walked on rather than his tiny legs. He had a large lower jaw with sharp, tusk-like teeth being the only thing you could see of his head due to the large amount or hair covering his face. He preferred close range assassinations, although not hand-to-hand combat.

Sudokus sent these two to kill Harem to punish him for leading the rebellion. Plus, he didn't want him trying to start another rebellion on Earth. Sudokus gave them a down payment for their service and they set off for Earth.

"This is the thirteenth alien we've had to assassinate this week," said Lada.

"It won't be the last either," said Gako. "You should know by now, whenever there's a war, the rebellious ones have to be assassinated one by one. It's the only way to ensure victory."

"Sudokus hasn't even technically won yet. Earth is still a hostile planet for us—which reminds me; don't forget to use your cloaking device. We don't want a repeat of what happened on Venus."

"I told you, I don't need my cloaking device against those weaklings when I have my baby," said Gako stroking his gun.

"Well, the Earthlings aren't quite as weak as the ones on Venus."

Within half an hour of taking off, they reached Earth and activated the invisibility feature on their ship. Lada was the first to get out of the ship followed by Gako.

Back at Leon's home, Leon had gone out, leaving Harem alone. Leon went to go get some water from the local corner shop, thinking maybe his guest was dehydrated. He had tap water, but its purpose wasn't really for drinking. Sudokus had previously given Gako and Lada the coordinates of Leon's home, so it was just a matter of time before they would arrive to find Harem alone there. Their cloaking devices allowed them to look enough like the other humans, that no one who might have seen them would have paid any attention to them.

Gako was the first one to walk up to the door. He punched it open with his powerful arms. He held up his gun and pointed it at Harem. Lada closed the door behind them and put a steel bar across it to prevent anyone from entering. Then Gako and Lada uncloaked to reveal their true forms.

"It was only a matter of time," said Harem in his native tongue. He knew the risk of trying to lead a rebellion. Harem didn't try to fight back; he couldn't escape from the assassins who now stared him down. Harem deactivated his cloaking device to reveal his actual appearance. He was a fat, slimy red blob. He had no legs, just two scrawny arms. He had three eyes on stalks attached to the top of his head. He had no mouth but could communicate telepathically with them.

"Any last words?"

"You may kill me, but not the rebellion."

Gako pulled the trigger on his gun and fired into Harem. Harem didn't scream; he didn't have time to. The specially designed bullets shut down all his vital organs as soon as they penetrated his oozy skin.

Sudokus could feel it when Harem died. He could feel the life force which was inside of Harem disappear. The death triggered his satisfaction sensors. It was one more rebel off the list, but there was really no impact on the actual rebellion. Sudokus knew the logic of this, but the concept involved aspects of the mind that were beyond him. A rebellion isn't just a person, or a group of people: it's an idea. The general feeling that things aren't what they should be.

There was still a rebellion on Mars, but they were underground. They were desperate, so they sent out two things to try to save themselves. The first thing they sent out was an encrypted radio transmission of their coordinates and some other information. The second thing was a flying saucer. It was a tiny saucer, small enough to fit in someone's palm. Inside of it were three aliens who, combined, knew nearly all the secrets of the universe. They travelled slowly, waiting to stumble upon the right individual who they could trust to lead a successful rebellion.

This was the present state of the galaxy. Change was coming quickly, and with that change, came turmoil. The pieces were all in place for a struggle of epic proportions, where self-preservation would be the only guiding force.

CHAPTER TWO

Leon arrived back at his home to find no one there. Gako and Lada had long since left, taking the body with them as evidence of their work for Sudokus to see. Leon looked around his house for any sign of the man, but there was no sign he'd ever been there. Leon simply assumed that he'd decided to leave for some reason, which he'd never know. Leon set the water down on the desk. Water—something that couldn't be watered down in these times. Everything else was turning blander, more diluted, and less effective.

Leon was ready to lay down for a nap, already starting to forget about the strange man he'd met, when he heard a ringing noise. It was his communicator. He pulled the circular device out of his pocket and flipped it open. A holographic image of the person on the other end of the call popped up. It was the CEO of the facility where he worked, or in other words, his boss.

"Hello, Ashley," said Leon.

"Leon, I need you down here as soon as possible. There's a new engineer we hired—supposedly one of the best in the Northwest. Anyway, he has a lot of ship designs, they look better than anything we've had before, and since you're the best pilot we have, I want you to be the first person he sees. You're pretty well known in this industry, maybe he's even heard of you before." "Sounds great, I'm on my way now." Leon stuffed the phone back into his pocket and headed out. It was annoying to have to go back after just being there, but the pay made it all worth it.

When Leon arrived at the testing facility, he looked over to see a young man with oil and grease stained clothes standing near a ship. He was a bit on the short side in terms of height, but didn't have any other differentiating features.

"Are you the new engineer?"

"Yup, that's me. The name is Scott, Scott Winchester."

"I heard you're one of the best engineers around."

"My work speaks for itself. Try out this ship." Scott pointed to a one-man ship a few feet away. It was black and sleek. From past experience with ships, Leon knew it would be fast with relatively weak artillery.

"This isn't like any other ship you've flown. Not only can it achieve high speeds, it also has enough firepower to take down a ship twice its size. It's made possible by a new light weight type of metal."

"Fast and powerful? You really must be the best engineer."

Leon hopped into the ship and took it out to the designated test flight zone. Sure enough, the ship was fast and handled well. It was actually a pleasant flight and Leon didn't want to come back down. Eventually, he did return with only good reviews. Leon started to head back home for the day having completed his job. However, Scott stopped him just as he got outside.

"Hey, Leon—that's your name right? How would you like to be my personal test pilot?"

"You mean leave my job to work exclusively for you?"

"Well eventually, yes, but you could continue to work for her—Ashley, I think she said her name was—for now if you want. I didn't come up to this facility to work here, that's just what I told the girl."

"Why would you want me, you could get whoever you want."

"And I want you. Pilots have been scarce since the end of the last war—especially good pilots. So what do you say?"

"I'll think about it, but we have to work out the specifics before I decide on anything. You've sort of caught me off guard here. Right now, I have to get home before it gets too dark out. I'll meet up with you again the next time I get called in for work."

With that, Leon walked back home in the fading light, wondering why Scott had any interest in him, and wondering if this day could get any stranger. He passed by the alley where he'd found the man and thought it was ironic how the alley was dark during the day, but at night there was a street lamp placed in just the right position to allow someone to see almost all the way through it.

Leon arrived home and turned on a little radio he had on his desk. Not many people had radios anymore. The one Leon had could've been considered an antique, but it still worked fine. Leon tuned through stations until he found something that caught his ear.

"Due to an increase in the amount of air traffic around the moon, an investigation has been demanded by its inhabitants. A number of people have reported seeing a growing number of ships flying around. They've even seen them flying around restricted air space over the city of Gurriligan. A former World War Four army commander known to most as Captain Willy, has assured them they are in good hands. He is looking for a few more pilots, preferably from the Northwestern section where he is visiting, to assist an investigative mission. The main thought is just that a few marauders are planning an attack. Willy has declared that if this is the case, the problem can be easily solved."

Leon looked out his window at the moon. It was always a full moon because of the light from the cities on it. Even the oldest people on Earth could not remember the moon as anything else but full. No waxing or waning. No crescent or gibbous. Leon tried to look for ships buzzing around, but even if they were there, they were too far away.

Leon lay down in his hammock to go to sleep. There was so much to think about. Should he go work for Scott, should he join Captain Willy's search mission? Leon stayed up a few minutes pondering these things before he finally decided to go to sleep.

CHAPTER THREE

Leon woke up the next morning having made one of his two decisions. He decided to go to the moon to investigate. What was the point of being a pilot if you never applied your skills? The only question now was where to sign up.

Leon left his house to go look for an electronic poster on a wall somewhere, or anything that would give him a clue. He didn't have to go very far to find his answer. Leon was walking down the sidewalk toward the main part of town, when he saw a line of people. He followed the line with his eyes until he got to the front. There was a big tent in the middle of the plaza. A sign on the tent read "Pilot sign-up". Leon got into the line and waited until he got to the front. There was an elderly woman who asked Leon some general questions, like age, name and so on. If it was a test, Leon passed because after all the questions he received a card stating the time and location of the departure. It was tomorrow at five a.m.

Leon had a whole day to kill. He decided to walk around town, unaware of the eye that watched him. Sudokus waited in a room, tucked away beneath the clouds of Jupiter. A special type of plastic, which circled around the spheroid covering most of the planet, supported the building, which was many miles above the metal core.

Sudokus had a feeling about Leon just outside his range of emotions. He was actually feeling a sensation of uneasiness. He had no reason to fear any individual, but he could sense something within Leon. Ever since he had first made mental contact with him, he was unable to stop watching him. Yet, there were millions upon millions of miles separating the two, and Leon had no clue Sudokus even existed, so there shouldn't have been any reason for Sudokus to be watching him anymore; yet, he was.

Gako and Lada walked in through the door to Sudokus's office. They carried what was left of Harem, the cloaked alien whom Leon had mistaken for another man, with them. He had shriveled up during the flight, but Sudokus could still clearly tell who it was.

"We did what you asked, now complete the payment," said Lada.

"Of course," said Sudokus, "I have the money right here." He handed the money to Lada and she counted it, making sure Sudokus wasn't cheating them. It was so much easier when they were dealing with weaker minded individuals. Then Lada could just peer into their minds to see if they had the correct payment. There was no telling with Sudokus however. Once Lada was finally satisfied they that they had right amount, she left with her partner, leaving the dead body in Sudokus's office. One of his assistants came over to take it out of the room. They put in the incinerator where all the other assassinated rebels went.

Sudokus now had to make plans for his next move. He had already organized a takeover of Earth's moon, hence the ships flying around it, but now he had plans to assassinate one of the leaders on Earth. He wasn't sure who the leaders were yet, or the best way to go about it, but Gako and Lada were always on stand-by when he figured it out. They killed the leaders of the other seven planets in the galaxy, and Earth should be no harder.

Sudokus reclined back in his chair. He looked around at the different monitors around. Some were for security and others were for observing the daily processes that occurred around him. He looked at one monitor showing the slaves working in the fields. The slaves were ugly aliens that were outcasts from society. Most aliens wouldn't even think of them as aliens because they looked so different. Nevertheless, they were the backbone of society. They were the only ones not concerned with war. They just needed to make the food and make sure things were stable for the Golden Age of Sudokus as soon as the war ended.

Sudokus looked at a different screen. It was a shot of the moon of Earth. Ships were buzzing around, looking for the weakest point. They needed a weak point to infiltrate, but they also needed a secure spot to set up camp once they did infiltrate. They couldn't rush into anything because this was going to be the first battle with Earth. The first battle was always the most important to Sudokus. It was the first step towards the end. Sudokus could sense a disturbance however, as if the inhabitants of the moon were growing suspicious. His army would have to make a move fairly soon or else. Sudokus wasn't sure what the "or else" was, but the image of Leon popped back into his computer-controlled brain as he was thinking those words. Could one person really cause a big problem for him? Maybe he would have known the answer if he had the right emotions to figure out why he was concerned with Leon.

Sudokus looked toward another screen that showed engineers. They were working on prototypes for robots that could fight in wars. They were having little success, but Sudokus couldn't do anything about it; they were the best engineers in the galaxy. If they couldn't solve the problem, no one could.

Sudokus, however, still had faith in the robots his engineers were building, and in cities all over the galaxy, he had electronic posters put up declaring that the new age of warfare was here, and that the ultimate security of the future would be robots. But so far, the robots were duds.

Not too far away, the three aliens in the tiny space ship were starting to get dangerously close to Sudokus. Fortunately, they had the strongest minds in the universe. No one had any way of detecting them without seeing them. They would have to turn back eventually though. The further out they went, the more hostile the life became. So far, there was no sign of the one they were looking for. They knew somewhere in the galaxy, there was someone who would lead the rebellion which would finally stop Sudokus's reign. But what they were looking for wasn't here; they would have to keep searching.

CHAPTER FOUR

Everyone who was alive when the war started on Earth remembered it. It started at night, and though no one on Earth felt it, they saw it.

It was a full moon, just like it was every night, but then something strange happened. People described the moon as having a very strange crescent shape. No one had ever seen part of the moon missing. No one knew that it was only shadows causing it to appear as if part of the moon fell off. There was some chaos of course. They thought part of the moon had fallen off, and if part of the moon fell off, then surely it would land on Earth and crush some people. Everyone was looking for a safe place indoors, but there was nothing to fear. The only people with something to fear were the people actually on the moon. The alien ships were starting to bomb the surface relentlessly. They made sure to hit the main power grids for each of the major cities. Now, from Earth, the moon looked as it hadn't looked for over a hundred years: a crescent.

It was only three a.m., but Leon decided to head down to the location stated on the card. He had plenty of time so he decided to walk, but he soon regretted that decision. Everyone was scrambling around in their hover cars, trying to get to a spot where the moon wouldn't crush them. Leon was concerned about the moon too, but he just wanted to get to the designated location so he could take off and figure out what was going on. He figured even if part of the moon fell off, it would just be floating in space somewhere, not hurtling like a meteor towards Earth.

Leon was the first pilot to arrive. Willy had been there for half an hour already. Leon never saw Willy before. It was difficult to make him out at a distance. His dark skin blended in with the dark night. Normally the nights would've been brighter, but the moon wasn't full. Leon got closer and saw Willy had the body of a professional weight lifter, or ruckle-ball (A sport invented one-hundred fifty years ago similar to American football) player. His biceps were bigger than Leon's thighs. He had the generic hair for people of his race: black and curly, similar to Leon's hair. His haircut was low to his head, almost invisible on this dark night.

"You must be Willy," said Leon. Willy looked up, somewhat caught off guard. They were in a big room near a hangar—though it was more like a garage—and Willy hadn't noticed Leon walk in.

"Yes, I am." Willy looked back down and continued filling out some paperwork.

"I think we might have to leave sooner than we thought. The moon has a really weird shape tonight. I don't know what happened to it."

"You're too young," said Willy. "Haven't you ever seen an old picture of moon phases?" Leon gave him a strange look. He'd never heard of moon phases. "Forget I mentioned that. Just sit tight, we'll leave when everyone gets here. What's your name, son?"

"Leon Dudley, sir."

"Ah yes, I looked you up on file. You're ship is waiting in the hangar."

Leon walked out into the hangar to discover Scott working. By coming in so early, Scott showed he was dedicated to what he did, so Leon decided at that moment to agree to let

Scott be his personal engineer. He would figure out what to do about his old job later.

"I've come to a decision," said Leon as he approached Scott in the hangar.

"A decision about what?"

"I want you as my personal engineer. You have a lot of dedication. You seem like a good guy."

"Thanks, you seem like a pretty good man yourself. As for me being your engineer, you didn't have to agree to it. I wasn't going to leave you alone anyway." Leon could tell he was joking by his facial expression and let out a quiet laugh.

Pilots began flooding into the hangar. Leon recognized a few of them who worked in the same facility he did. However, the vast majority were new faces for Leon. It wasn't necessarily safe to go out with a rag-tag group of pilots—friendly fire and what not—but they didn't intend for this to be a difficult mission. They were just going to chase away a few marauders and then return home.

Five o'clock rolled around and Willy entered into the hangar. Everyone quieted down when they saw him. He was the type of man people naturally respected. He looked out to the pilots. He was preparing to say something to them. He'd given plenty of pre-battle speeches in his fifty-five years of life. This one was no different for him. It just wasn't supposed to be a true battle, only a skirmish at most.

"Don't ever assume anything will be easy. That's the formula for failure. When you get out there, be ready for anything." Willy looked out to their faces again. He could already tell most of the people were losing focus. "You have two missions while you're up there. One is to get those unidentified ships out of the restricted areas. You're second is to restore power to the moon. I'm sure you're all aware of the power outage by now. I want to see the moon as a full circle when you come back down. If for some reason you are only able to complete one of these missions, make sure it is the first one I mentioned. Coordinate your departure and leave in exactly three minutes. Good luck to all of you."

The men all got into their ships and faced forward, staring through the exit of the hangar out into sky. With a minute left before take-off, and the clocks all synchronized, they started up their engines. Finally it was time to leave, and they accelerated out of the hangar in organized rows. The first row left, quickly followed by the second row and so on.

Their arrival into the firing range of the aliens' ships marked the first unofficial battle of the war. It was really no contest however. The aliens had laser beams they could fire with deadly accuracy. The ships from Earth only had metal artillery, which didn't seem to have an effect on the ships. Not that they couldn't use lasers, it was just that governments around the world had banned lasers for combat, even in space. It also seemed that the alien ships had more effective aerial moves and could better avoid enemy fire. The alien ships had such tinted windshields, that no one could see through them from the inside or outside. It should have been the first clue for Earth they weren't fighting any normal humans, but no one thinks about that kind of a thing during a battle.

Leon didn't know what to do at first. This was supposed to be a relatively easy assignment, but now they seemed back on their heels. Should they retreat to Earth or attempt to land on the moon to investigate the power outage? If they did the second option, some people would have to stay engaged with the enemy to buy time for the people who left the battle to investigate. Leon began to realize the situation was nearly hopeless and decided to go on a solo mission to minimize the failure.

He was able to sneak out of the battle and touch down on the moon. He could see the aliens quickly gaining an edge in the battle. Soon, they would shoot down all the human ships and there wouldn't be anyone left to retreat. Leon had to try to turn the power back on before the battle ended.

Leon was sneaking around on the surface. He was in one of the major cities. He noticed the people who inhabited the moon converted some of the buildings into makeshift bunkers. The people on the moon were preparing for the worst. Leon continued walking through the streets until he saw a fenced off area. He saw two giant generators within the enclosure. He was able to climb over the fence with only minor difficulty. The fact that he had his space suit on is what offered the most hindrance to his mobility, although now-a-days, space suits were more streamline than they used to be. Once inside the enclosure, he was able to make his way over to the generators. There was extensive damage to both of them. Leon looked at different cords, buttons and panels and they all started to blur together. Leon realized he didn't know nearly enough about repairing things. Leon calmed himself down and started looking for a different way to restore power. He saw a small sign hanging on one of the generators. The damage it had taken from bombings had darkened it, but Leon could still read it for the most part. It said there was a back-up generator underground in a tunnel. It had an arrow pointing to a spot on the ground as if there was a way to access the tunnel through the spot, but Leon saw nothing there. He got down onto his knees and began scraping away the rubble. Soon he uncovered a wooden staircase, buried under rocks. The wooden stairs looked unstable, but Leon would have to trust them for now. Leon would head down a few steps, and then move some more rubble out of the way. He was uncovering stairs for at least twenty minutes before he reached the bottom. Once he was at the bottom, the rocks leveled out and he was able to walk through the tunnel with ease.

After a few minutes of walking, he finally reached a metal box. It was about four feet tall with an antenna on it. Leon saw a big red button on the box, and he pressed it. He couldn't tell if anything happened—since he was underground—so he headed back up top to the surface. Luckily the generator worked. It would only be working for a couple of days, but that would be enough time for people to reactivate the defense grid on the moon. The defense grid fired a constant supply of lasers—lasers were banned for combat, not defense, a very fine line indeed—onto the alien ships and was able to push them back and allow for the few Earth ships that survived, to retreat safely.

Leon ran over to his ship, which managed to stay unscathed by stray fire while landing, and followed the pack of ships heading back to Earth in defeat. They completed one mission, but it was the wrong mission. If any side had a victory here, it was the aliens. It was the first victory of a long war.

CHAPTER FIVE

Willy was upset to see such a small group of ships returning from what should have been a simple get-in-get-out mission.

"What happened up there?" Willy looked out to a group of defeated faces. No one wanted to say how they had inferior weapons. No one wanted to say how they had inferior handling on their ships. No one wanted to, but Leon did.

"We got it handed to us up there, sir. Everything about their ships was simply superior to ours. I wanted to make sure the mission wasn't a total waste, so I backed out of the battle to activate a backup generator located under the city. A little bit of power has temporarily been restored, but it will only last another two or three days, if we're lucky."

"Never try to be a hero, soldier," said Willy.

"I'm sorry, captain."

"What's the status of the unidentified ships?"

"They're still unidentified," said one of the other pilots, "And still around the moon somewhere. The defense grid is holding them at bay for the time being."

"We'll need to scale-up the attack then. We can't let these guerilla rebels cause any more damage. I'll start recruiting more men for the attack. You men may head home; but be prepared to get called back here." Willy was silent for a moment before adding, "Failure is not an option."

Leon was starting to question if they had really just fought some rebels. How could rebels have such advanced technology and so much flight skill? Plus, there were too many just to be a rebel group. Leon was considering whether there might actually be another war on Earth, when Scott broke his concentration.

"How did the ship handle up there?"

"Not well enough," said Leon. "Better than what I had before, but still not good enough."

"I'll get working on a new ship then. I figure a better counter propulsion system, with a more balanced chassis, will do the trick."

"Do whatever you have to do."

Leon closed the hatch on his ship and locked it before leaving the hangar. The sun was starting to rise. The horizon was like a pull up bar and the sun was trying to get its chin over it. It clung on with all its strength, but it was a very slow pull towards the top. Nevertheless, it would eventually get there, just like it did every day. And if the sun was coming up, then the moon would disappear. It was strange knowing the target Leon had to defend was moving away from him.

Sudokus finally decided to get up from his chair. He walked out of the room and went onto a balcony. He saw a bustling city out in the distance. Voice boxes around the city would soon announce to them that they were winning the war. Of course, one battle didn't actually mean they were winning, but anything to boost morale is always good.

Sudokus knew he had the people by a string. It was almost metaphorical, thought Sudokus, how he stood on a balcony overlooking them, much like a puppeteer stands on a higher elevation, holding the strings to his marionette. He could make them say what he wanted them to say, and move where he wanted them to move. Yet his people knew nothing. They had all seen Sudokus before, but no one really knew who he was, what he did, or where he came from. Sudokus liked this. Knowledge is power, and his people had none. His soldiers, however, did. The soldiers knew everything about the operation, and were therefore powerful. On Earth, the soldiers didn't have as much knowledge, and therefore weren't as powerful. But Earth kept many secrets from all its members, not just its soldiers. Only a few select people knew all the secrets, and they would never give them up until it was necessary.

Now seemed necessary.

Earth had the technology it needed to wage a war with the aliens, and it was finally time to start revealing it. However, they would have to do it slowly.

The information would have to have a trickle effect, starting with the most powerful people and working its way down to the commoners. It just so happened, that previous events in World War four made Willy a candidate for finding out some of the secrets. However, there was one secret that was too precious to reveal. Leon did not know they were fighting against aliens, or that aliens existed for that matter, but they did.

No one exactly knew how there came to be such a small group of people who knew all the secrets, but it happened sometime after the reformations following World War Three. This group of people was the only group who ever actually held friendly relations with an extraterrestrial being. They conducted trade throughout the solar system and now they had alien technology. In fact, ogelan was originally alien technology no one planned to release, but the shortage of gasoline, and the failed release of the much-anticipated mass produced fusion reactors, forced them to introduce it to the public. They used some of this technology and their knowledge to gain power in government. Some took as much power as they could, while others tried to remain more low profile. One of the people who took as much power as he could was Winston. Winston is one of *them*, and until they decided to stop keeping their people in the dark, everyone would be doomed to fall victim to Sudokus.

CHAPTER SIX

Leon slept most of the day away. He was tired from the battle yesterday. Leon propped himself up in his hammock with his forearms. He let out a yawn and then rotated his body so his feet were hanging off the hammock. He looked at the clock on his paper-cluttered desk. It was four o'clock in the afternoon. Leon saw his communicator, which was also on his desk, was blinking. A red light was blinking on and off. Leon knew this was indicating that he had missed calls. Leon hopped out of the hammock and shuffled over to the desk. He picked up the phone and began listening to the three messages on the phone. The first was from Scott, who was updating him on the status of the next ship he'd be building. The next was from Ashley, asking if Leon could come in for another test flight. The third was from Willy, telling Leon the next battle would be at eight o'clock tonight. He informed Leon that people were forming an army as he was speaking. Leon didn't want to go back into the battle so soon, but he knew it wouldn't help to delay things.

Leon had four hours to kill, but he didn't feel like doing anything other than sleeping, yet he couldn't sleep. Leon decided to write in his journal. He rummaged through all the things on his desk until he found it. He opened it up and realized his last entry was from two months ago. Leon picked up a pen and began to write.

It's been two months since I've written in here. A lot has happened since then. First, I found a man in an alley. He was a very strange man and I tried to take him in my home to care for him because I thought he was injured. I left the house for a little while and when I returned, he was gone. I never did find out what happened to him. But, ever since then, I've felt like someone is watching me. Not just that, it feels like someone is looking for me, as if they want something from me. I try not to ponder these feelings too deeply, for they will only lead to me asking myself what the purpose of life is. Almost all the questions I ask myself lead to that in some way or another, and the only thing I can come up with is that religion is the reason for living. That never satisfies me, so I just try to do what is needed of me in the present, and what is needed of me right now is to fight in a battle, however strange this battle may be. Supposedly, we're just going against a group of marauders, but they seem to be very skilled. All I know is that we need to end this battle soon. If there's anything I've learned from the history textbooks, it's that long battles are never good. Well, they're good for whoever wins, but it's never good to assume victory.

Leon put the pen and journal back down on the desk and then looked at the time. It was four-thirty now. Leon wondered why he wrote. He had no aspirations of ever writing a book or anything. Besides, who would read what he wrote? Would the journal become lost and later found by some advanced civilization after humans are extinct? No, the journal would deteriorate beyond legibility before that happened. Leon knew some people wrote in journals because they had no one else to talk to, but Leon had plenty of people to talk to. Maybe it was just easier for him to have his thoughts on paper, rather than in his head.

Leon started flipping through the pages of his journal when a photograph fell out. He picked it up to examine it. It was a picture of his family. He was a baby in the picture, so he didn't remember when it was taken, but it must have been nearly twenty years ago by now. Leon looked at his mother who was a mix of many different races. Leon didn't even know where she was born. His father was born in Uganda, but he too was a mix of many different nationalities. Leon knew that a good percentage, maybe twenty percent, of his family was from the Uganda region, but just looking at him it was clear that he wasn't any one nationality. Leon was part of a growing population of people who had no true nationality. He was everything.

Leon knew his father was an army leader in Uganda who did some side-by-side work with Captain Willy. Leon heard him say that before, but it never occurred to him that it was the same Willy he was currently working with until after he saw the photograph.

Leon stuffed the picture into a drawer on his desk and then resumed flipping through the journal. He hadn't realized he'd written that much. Leon didn't feel like reading what he'd already written however, and he set the journal back down. It was time he start heading out anyway. It would still be a few hours before take-off, but at least he could talk with Willy. Assuming Willy wasn't busy with other things.

Leon headed off to the hangar where he was surprised to see Scott already there.

"What are you doing here, Scott?" asked Leon.

"New technological breakthroughs," said Scott without looking at Leon. Scott had bent himself down near the ship with some sort of tool in his hand.

"Really, what?

"Panoramic propulsion, that's what the rebels were using. Now you'll have just as much control as them."

"How did the rebels get a hold of this technology before we did?"

"I asked Willy that and he was really vague about it. I think he was trying to say the rebels stole the plans for it from some engineering company."

"That doesn't exactly explain it," said Leon. "If an engineering company had it, why didn't they just give it to us?"

"Well, what are you going to do about it? Some questions will just never be answered." Scott took off the welding glasses he'd been wearing in order to inspect his work. Finding it satisfactory, he put away his tools.

"What about these other ships, do they get the—what did you call it—panoramic propulsion?"

"Hey, if their engineers want to come in and do that for them, whatever, but I've done my job."

"Where's Willy?" asked Leon changing the subject.

"He's around here somewhere. He might be in his office."

Leon left the hangar and went into Willy's office. Willy was talking on the phone.

"With all due respect," said Willy, "I think they have a right to know. Yes, I know it could have negative implications, but…Well, yes, but…What if I just tell them that they're—" Willy stopped and looked up to see Leon. "We'll continue this later," said Willy hanging up. "Can I help you?"

"Who were you talking to?"

"Some old friends concerned about the battle we have ahead of us. We're not fighting marauders up there. I don't know exactly who they are, but they're organized: too organized to be any rebel group. We're going to go through extensive military training as soon as this battle is over. But, I'm getting ahead of myself. Did you come in here for anything particular?"

"Yes, actually there is something. I just wanted to talk some strategy. It appeared to me that last battle, we were very scattered, everyone just trying to see how many ships they could shoot down. We need to function as a team, and everyone has specific roles on a team. Some people need to be trying to shoot down the ships, and other ships need to be trying to force the enemy out of their normal positions. Some of us need to attack from behind and some of us needed to attack from head on. I think we need to diversify our attack."

"I think you're on to something there, but it's easier said than done. Our fleet isn't big enough to substantiate each role we would need to handle this enemy. But maybe, if we can just—"

"Don't underestimate us, sir. I think we have what it takes, we just need to communicate better."

Willy pondered all his options in silence for a few moments, then finally agreed to try Leon's plan.

Willy and Leon spent the next few hours drawing up different designs and mapping out the battlefield until they finally had a plan they felt could work. By the time Leon walked out of Willy's office, all the other pilots arrived and it was nearly time for takeoff.

Willy briefed them on the battle plan for about twenty minutes, and then the door to the hangar opened up. The pilots took off and went out into space, ready for a battle, and for victory.

Upon entering the battle, a scene similar to the first battle presented itself to the pilots. Neatly arranged ships surrounded the moon, just out of range of the defense grid, ready for battle.

Even though they recruited more pilots for this battle, they hadn't been able to replace all the lost soldiers from the first battle, so they were at a disadvantage. The pilots all began rushing to their position as the enemy began firing their lasers. It was clear to Leon which ships received the propulsion upgrade and which ships hadn't.

Leon's job was to stay just out of the main cluster of ships and just fire upon the enemy from a distance. Of course, his job depended on everyone else being able to do their jobs, but so did all the jobs.

At first, the battle was going according to plan. Everyone was doing their job, and the pilots actually looked like they had a chance for victory. The humans might have actually won, except for the fact that reinforcements showed up on the scene. Soon the newly arrived ships began firing on the humans and it wasn't long before it became obvious the humans would lose. Leon moved his ship in closer to try and see if he could do anything against the ships, but his bullets were just bouncing off like everybody else's. Leon used his new propulsion system to weave around the battle like a humming bird, but there was no point. The battle soon drew to a close the same way the first one had. The humans decided to retreat before they incurred too much damage.

When the pilots arrived back to the hangar, No one could find Willy. The only thing any of them saw was a note posted on the door pertaining to the date and time of a mandatory military training session. The note never used the word, but everyone had the feeling that this was the start of the next war.

CHAPTER SEVEN

Gako and Lada found themselves walking into Sudokus's office yet again. This would be the last time that Sudokus would personally give them a mission for a few months. There were only two ways to win a war in Sudokus's army. Kill all the soldiers, or kill all commanders. In Sudokus's experience, it was easier to kill all the commanders, because new soldiers could join the battle every day. Therefore, Sudokus's next mission for Gako and Lada was a simple one: the assassination of Winston, leader of the Northwestern quadrant of Earth. As leader, he had final say in all matters including military.

"Welcome," said Sudokus as Gako and Lada stepped in, "Please, come into my office."

Gako and Lada casually walked in, already having an idea of what Sudokus was about to say.

"Today is the day this war will officially start; if you can call it a war. Today is the day we begin the systematic assassination of our rivals. For now, it seems you'll just need to eliminate one person." Sudokus reached into a drawer attached to his desk and pulled out a picture of Winston. Gako and Lada carefully studied the picture, taking in every line and bump on his face until they had an image of him burned into their minds.

Under the picture was some text telling the coordinates of the capital building where Winston was located. "The informants are getting more efficient everyday it seems," said Lada. The informants in this case being the aliens cloaked as humans Sudokus sent out to gather information. "I don't think I need to give you any further instructions," said Sudokus ignoring Lada's last statement. "It's a pretty self-explanatory mission. And, since you've been so loyal to me throughout this, I'm giving you a big payout when you return with his head."

With that, Lada grabbed the picture and they headed out to the ship. Sudokus couldn't help but to think that they seemed like an odd pairing. Lada seemed to have all the assets one could need for her type of work—intelligence, accuracy with her weapon, a refined technique—but she still chose to work with Gako just for the brawn he brought. But why would you need strength for assassinating? Sudokus knew from all the knowledge he'd absorbed in his life, that the less intelligent one in a group like that always led to the downfall of the group, yet this group seemed different. Sudokus was distracted from his thoughts at the sound of one of his assistants entering his office offering to correct a grammatical error in the speech Sudokus would deliver later that week.

Gako and Lada had already taken off for Earth. They expected it to be the same routine as last time. They set the invisibility setting on the ship as they landed and cloaked themselves as humans. Lada made sure to land them within a reasonable distance of the target building. They got out of the ship and looked around at their surroundings. Lada was beginning to formulate a plan. Lada pulled out her sniper and began surveying the area around the building. She was safe in the cover of some bushes, and the long range on the scope meant she could stay a safe distance away for the moment. She looked at all the Ginyu guards patrolling around the building. She looked up at a window which was covered in a titanium grating and had at least three panes of glass. It was severely tinted and didn't allow Lada to see what was on the other side; but she knew something important must be behind it. Lada moved the sights around, looking for anything else that could help them. There was a covered manhole connected to a sewer near the building, but it wouldn't really help them.

"Hand me your shuka for a moment, Gako," said Lada. The shuka was the mechanism that operated the cloaking device; it controlled what image you appeared as to others. Lada adjusted a few settings on Gako's shuka, and then gave it back to him. When Gako put it back on, he transformed into one of the Ginyu guards. "Now you just need to sneak into the building and find the one they call Winston. When you find him, do not kill him. Use the communicator and tell me exactly where he is. I'll find a vantage point to shoot him." Gako left without saying a word.

Lada was truly a great sniper, but she needed to find a spot where she would have a clean shot. Lada was almost sure he'd be behind that window. She activated her thermal vision and began peering at the window. The thickness of the glass made it impossible to tell if there was a human behind the window, but there was definitely something there. Lada could faintly see the patches of reds, yellows, and oranges behind the glass. Lada crept out of the bushes towards a nearby tree. It was tall and the branches were thick to provide cover. She climbed up the tree the same way a python might, and then hung in the branches. She waited to make sure no one had seen her, and to her relief no one did. She was still a little ways off, but she would keep trying to work her way up closer to the building until she had a better angle. If the opportunity didn't present itself however, she would be willing to shoot from her current location.

Gako, surprisingly, was easily entering the building. Some guards seemed to look at him for a bit longer than they should have—indicating they were suspicious of him—but no one actually did anything to stop him. Gako's gun looked different from all the other guard's, so he did his best to conceal it between his arm and body.

No one really seemed to notice that Gako was having a hard time finding the front door, or how awkward he looked giving the appearance of being human. When Gako did find the door, he entered with ease and began navigating through hallways and going up and down stairs. Eventually Gako heard some people talking behind a closed door. Gako reached out and, after fumbling with the knob for a few moments, opened the door. There were other Ginyu guards already in the room, so Gako didn't look out of place.

"All I am saying," said one of the men in the room, "Is that if we don't at least give our soldiers access to some of this technology, defeat is imminent."

"I see your point," said another, "But if we give them this technology, assuming they can even handle it, we'll also have to explain how we suddenly invented all this new technology. And we can't tell them it was lost and we just discovered it, as some have proposed."

"We'll maybe we just tell them we have had contact with the extra-terrestrials. What's the worst that could really happen?"

Gako was looking around the room at everyone, not really paying attention to the conversation. He was more concerned with finding Winston, if he was in here. Soon he saw someone who looked like the Winston from the photograph. Another man in the room soon confirmed his thoughts.

"What are your thoughts on this, Lord Winston?"

Gako didn't really care to hear what Winston was saying, because now he was certain he had the right person. Gako lifted his arm to his mouth and let out what sounded like a cough. It looked and sounded normal, so no one paid attention, but he had actually given the signal to Lada that the target had been located. He then let out another cough-like-sound letting her know the coordinates.

Lada managed to work her way behind a stone column which was serving as part of a decorative gate. She took a risk getting to this spot, and she only had less than a minute to make the shot and get out before the patrol guard crossed through again.

It didn't matter how thick the glass on the window was, Lada was confident her specially designed bullets could puncture through it. Lada aimed towards the window. Since she couldn't discern anybody inside, she was relying on her thermal vision and the coordinates Gako gave her. If his coordinates were even off by a little bit, she could shoot the wrong person. Lada took a deep breath in and pulled the trigger. She didn't wait to see what happened to the bullet, she immediately began heading back toward the ship.

Moments before Lada let off her shot, Winston was giving his opinion on whether or not to approve an international army for this battle. Gako looked up just in time to see the bullet hurdling toward the window. He pulled out his gun milliseconds before the bullet shattered through the window, striking Winston in his medulla, and he began firing upon everyone else inside the room. He was able to clear the room in a matter of seconds, but he could hear footsteps coming down the hallway. Since this wasn't the first time he'd done something like this, he knew exactly what to do. He began running for the window, grabbing Winston's corpse just before he jumped out. Lada knew what to do as well, and she was flying the ship just beneath the window to catch Gako as he fell out of it.

Dozens of guards poured around and out of the building trying to figure out what happened, but the ship was invisible to them because of the cloaking device on it.

Gako threw the body into the back of the ship. It would serve as proof of their work for Sudokus. Lada never favored anyone to win a war before, but she did for the first time now. She knew if Sudokus won, then they would get even more jobs from him when he moved on to a different part of the galaxy. No one else knew that yet except her.

It wasn't long before the ship was landing back on Jupiter near Sudokus's capital building. Lada got out of the ship first and left Gako to carry Winston's body inside. Neither Sudokus, Gako nor Lada exchanged any words during their transaction. They simply handed the body to Sudokus, and Sudokus handed them their money.

Gako and Lada headed off for a private moon they had bought and turned into a personal vacation resort. This is where they would stay for several months. Now Sudokus could easily conquer Earth. It all seemed too simple for Sudokus. The amount of money he could make by exporting resources from this solar system to others was almost too much money for words to describe. Earth wasn't even putting up a good fight. During all the other planetary takeovers, the victim planet raised a fighting army within a day or two. Earth was merely sending out small groups of ill-equipped ships.

Sudokus looked out his window to see a fleet of ships just waiting to head over to Earth for the next phase of the takeover. There were huge ships, miles long, called command ships. They established control of a spot in space simply by shooting down all the smaller ships in the area; plus, they brought an intimidation factor similar to the elephants in ancient Indian armies. The command ships were indestructible from the outside. Moreover, while it was possible to disable it from the inside it's virtually impossible to get in.

There were thousands of fighter ships waiting too. They were faster than any ship on Earth and could destroy any ship on Earth in a few shots. Sudokus knew Earth would put up a fight, but the way things were looking, it'd be a short fight.

CHAPTER EIGHT

Leon was going to be a pilot for the army since he seemed to have a knack for flying; he still however, needed to be able to fight on the ground in case the situation called for it. So Leon entered into a military training program with a bunch of other recently recruited men. There would be one more battle to take the moon, but this would be a huge effort: failure was not an option. Most of the soldiers-in-training agreed that it was probably one of the other three world powers causing the trouble, most likely the communist Northeastern quadrant. This thought never occurred to Leon before, but it made more sense than the notion that they were fighting rebels.

The training program was intense and rigorous. Leon expected Willy might have been the drill sergeant for it, but it was a man Leon had never seen before. He was younger than Willy, but not quite as muscular. His name was Bennett. No one ever figured out his first name, because everyone had to call him Lieutenant Bennett even though no one knew whether he really was a lieutenant. Leon once made the mistake of calling him Mister Bennett and got stuck cleaning the dishes for the rest of the week.

The first day of training was basically just Lt. Bennett pacing back and forth in front of the line of men and telling them how terrible they were and how they didn't pay him enough to turn boys like these into men like himself. In addition, if Bennett suspected anyone of not paying attention to his speech, he grabbed them, pulled them out of the line, and told them he could kill a man in less than five seconds with his bare hands. Then he shoved them back into line. That was the first day.

The second day, and the rest of the week, consisted of the men jogging for eight or more consecutive hours. If you fell too far behind, you'd have to come back to the camp separate from everyone else and listen as Bennett accused you of being too unfit to keep up with the men and then he'd cut back your food rations. If you passed out, you got to take medical leave for the rest of the day, so you were better off passing out from dehydration than stopping to catch your breath.

In the second week of training, Lt. Bennett covered everything from hand-to-hand combat, to weaponry, and even survival under the harshest conditions.

At the end of the second week, Bennett lined everyone up again and told them they had gone from boys to adolescences, but they weren't men yet. Then he cursed the fact that the dire situation only allowed them for two weeks of training and told them if they managed somehow not to die up there, he'd finish the training when they returned. That was it for training.

Just before it was time for the pilots to depart, with some ground troops tagging along, they deployed a remote controlled scout ship to the moon. It was able to see the entire fleet. One of the command ships was there with smaller ships scuttling around it. It appeared that more of the smaller ships were arriving each minute. The scout ship was undetectable due to its size and distance from the enemy, but it was still close enough for the low ranking captain controlling it to see what the situation was through the ship's camera.

"There must be...two thousand ships around here by now," said the captain. "That one is huge too; it's got to be at least nine or ten miles from the nose to the engine. All the ships are black, which army has black ships? Is that some sort of space camouflage?"

"There is no ship on Earth ten miles long," said Willy, "Not even close. I don't think we're dealing with an Earthly power here."

The ship then turned its focus to the moon, where it observed aliens freely walking about, with no human opposition. The aliens even seemed to have spacecraft hangars to dock their ships. The camera could only capture a small section of the moon, but it was enough to realize that the aliens were indeed colonizing it. If there were humans left on the moon, they were not offering any resistance.

Willy knew that this would almost certainly be a suicide mission to send any troops into space combat with a fleet like that out there. Unfortunately, Willy didn't have much of a say, because he only commanded a relatively small group of men. There was a new system of command recently assigned based on service during WW IV (World War Four). Willy could only give the pilots instructions for now. He couldn't send them into war or take them out of war without having it approved. Plus, since this was a joint effort of pilots and soldiers, he only had half as much control as he would ordinarily have. Captain Drew was the man who controlled the ground soldiers.

But both Willy and Cpt. Drew had to send their troops wherever John told them too. John was the man who replaced Winston to become leader of the Northwestern quadrant, so as long as only the Northwest was a part of this war, it would be John calling all the shots. Right now John was ordering for a battle in space.

John was sure to continue what Winston started in not letting the general public know what was going on; at least not until *he* fully knew what was going on. Because even though John was one of the select few who knew about aliens and their technology already, he didn't know that Sudokus was behind all of this yet, and until he found out, he'd be sure to keep up the appearance that they were just fighting marauders. Although the soldiers, at this point, knew the battle wasn't as simple as first anticipated. No one dared say *war* yet. John knew as well as anyone that when the status officially changed from skirmish to war was just as important as the war itself, because everyone supports a war in the beginning. When they decided to call it a war, is when they'd get their support from the people. For now, they'd just send up more troops into the skirmish on the moon.

Willy had his orders from John to tell the pilots what they'd see up there, but not who they'd see. At this point, Willy knew they weren't fighting humans, but he was sworn to secrecy. Willy strongly disagreed with this and argued with the committee who helped make this decision, but in the end, he was outnumbered. So Willy waited until the pilots arrived into the hangar and then told his men what he legally could.

"Well, here we are in the hangar," said Willy. "We've been going through a condensed training program and now we have a more professional looking army. But that changes nothing. You will still have to work just as hard as before if not harder. True, we have more men than ever before, but we face a new challenge as well. Some of the soldiers have seen what I'm talking about, but most of you haven't. It seems the enemy has brought in a new type of ship. I don't want to alarm you, but I can think of no way to tell you the news without doing just that. This new ship which you will have to face is very large, some estimates range up to ten miles long, but it's hard to tell exactly how big it is with no reliable reference points nearby. Don't be alarmed by this ship when you see it. We have reason to believe that the ammunition we currently carry will be ineffective against it, so don't waste your bullets. Just try not to let it hit you.

"Defeat is not imminent. You can win this battle if you work together and battle within your limits. We don't need any heroes out there, we just need to get rid of enough ships so that the people on the moon don't have to cower in fear anymore, then we can come back and drive away the other ships later. And by the way, we'll be referring to the large ship as the command ship. Good luck to all of you up there."

Willy headed back into his office a bit disgusted by the speech he gave. He wanted to tell them more than that, but couldn't; at least not without risking his job. It was up to them to avoid dying up there now.

Leon and the other pilots began preparing for departure. Leon had a new ship for this battle, which Scott built while he was at boot camp. It was similar to the last ship, but now the ships were equipped with the recently unbanned lasers, although they'd prove to be less effective than the aliens'. Their effectiveness was less important than the fact that it was a step forward. The ship also had a new engine, designed by Scott. This wasn't standard grade yet. Another change was that all ships had to be a uniform color now, green with an orange stripe running along the side.

The space suits were the same color scheme as the ships. Leon slipped his suit on and then slid his helmet over his head. He looked through his black tinted visor. In the corner of the visor, there was a map where Leon could see any nearby ships, ally and enemy. He was too far away from any enemy ships to see them now, but all his ally ships in the hangar popped up.

Leon hopped into the cockpit and waited for the signal for him to blast off into space. The hangars' opening was big enough to dispatch fifty ships at a time. Leon slowly inched his ship forward until he was finally at the front of the line. The dispatcher gave the next fifty the signal to take-off and Leon took off with the ships to his left and right.

It only took a few moments to get into space and it took Leon the same amount of time to realize the aliens had a severe advantage. Leon was under fire as soon as he left the outer limits of Earth's atmosphere. The aliens had disabled the defense grid shortly after the last battle ended and Leon had to use all his evasive skills just to survive the first few seconds. Others weren't as lucky and died upon entering the battle.

Leon started firing at the alien ships, but they didn't seem to take much damage from his new laser. More damage than before, but not as much as he'd have liked. He locked onto one of the ships with his missile and fired. He watched it make contact, but all that happened was that the ship he hit lost control for a second. It soon gained control once more with no visible damage other than a dent. Leon came under heavy fire again as more enemy ships began to arrive into the battle. A ship snuck up behind Leon before he had time to see it in his map and it fired off a shot. The shot hit Leon and one of his two engines went out. This slowed him down, but he was eventually able to pull away and avoid any more damage from the ship behind him. Leon looked over to his left for a few seconds and saw the command ship firing off shots. Every time just one shot hit a ship, it destroyed the ship. Leon hoped to avoid that fate. Leon looked at his map and saw that the number of ally ships was beginning to diminish.

Then, from nowhere, a grappling hook, far more advanced than the centuries old Somalia pirate grappling hook it was based on, shot through the side of Leon's ship. Leon could feel the enemy ship dragging him towards it with the hook. The ship didn't fire at Leon; it merely pulled him in until their ships were touching. When Leon was close enough to see through the tinted glass of the enemy ship, he saw not a human pilot, but an alien. The alien stared at Leon with all four of its eyes for a moment, and then it began moving around inside of its ship until it disappeared from Leon's view. Leon looked over when he heard the noise of the alien carving a hole through his ship. The alien was trying to make a hole to get from its ship to Leon's. Leon pulled out his pistol and prepared for whatever was about to happen. He had no control over his ship since the alien had attached its ship to his for the moment. Plus, since one of his engines was out, his ship was weaker.

The alien finished cutting and kicked down the makeshift door it created. Leon began shooting right at its head as it tried to force its way into the small cockpit. The alien was getting closer to Leon, and Leon realized his pistol wasn't having an effect on the alien. The alien inched closer until Leon could see every bump on the alien's grey skin. It was practically on top of Leon when Leon remembered that he had a combat knife in his pocket. He pulled it out and stabbed it into the alien's throat.

Then he lunged at the alien knocking them both through the hole and into the alien's ship. The alien, who still wasn't dead, reached into his pocket and pulled out his own blade. It wasn't like any combat knife Leon had ever seen before, but he could tell it had a razor sharp edge. Leon still had his gun and he pulled it out again. He started shooting the alien with one hand while holding the alien's wrist—so it couldn't stab him—with the other. Green ooze started coming out of the alien where Leon was shooting it and he could tell it was losing strength. Leon finally placed a shot near the top of the alien's head and green ooze exploded out as the alien went limp. Training had paid off.

Leon crawled back into his ship from the alien's. He saw that he was now on a collision course with the side of the command ship. He worked quickly to cut the grappling hook with his knife, but stopped midway, realizing it would be too dangerous to try flying with a hole in the side of his ship. If he left the ships as they were, then the hole was covered. Leon got back into the alien ship and found what he assumed was the steering mechanism. Leon turned it back toward Earth and the ship complied. It wasn't a pretty landing, but the ships crashed back down onto the surface in an open field not too far away from the hangar. Leon was shaken up as the ships skidded across the ground kicking up a trail of dirt behind them, but he was lucky that the ships didn't flip over in all the commotion.

When he finally came to a stop, Leon got out of the ship and was able to get another generic ship and rejoin the battle. With the command ship in the sky controlling the battle though, Earth was quickly defeated. Once someone gave the order to retreat, no one hesitated to exit the battle.

When Leon returned, he saw that not many pilots had been as lucky as him. Only a fraction of the pilots who left the hangar returned.

Leon's other ship crash-landed in a deserted field not too far away from the hangar, so he decided to get Willy to look at it. He walked into Willy's office where he found him talking to a man he'd never seen before. The man let out a quiet cough, and then walked out of the office.

"Who was that?" asked Leon.

"No one important," said Willy. Then, changing the subject, he said, "If you came here to quit, there's a line forming somewhere outside."

"That's not actually why I came here. I actually wanted you to look at something I, uh, discovered."

Willy gave Leon a strange look, but decided to follow him anyway. He'd received stranger requests than that in the past.

Leon led Willy out to where his ship crashed. Willy saw the ship from a little ways off, but didn't say anything at first. He didn't want to jump to conclusions just yet.

"What the hell happened here?" asked Willy as he got up close to the scene.

"Before I tell you, come take a look inside; it will make explaining this a lot easier."

Willy walked over to the alien craft and peered in. It was a disgusting sight. Green ooze was everywhere. In the center of the ship was an alien body. The body was full of bullet holes and the knife was still stuck in its throat. It had a small trunk like that of an elephant where its nose should have been and just a slit where its mouth should have been. It was by far the most disgusting thing Willy had ever seen. He knew *who* they were fighting before, but now he knew *what* they were fighting.

"Start explaining," said Willy.

"One of my engines was blown out and this creature shot out what I determined to be a grappling hook—or some sort of claw. It implanted into my ship and started pulling me towards its ship. Once my ship was touching his ship, he started cutting a hole into my spacecraft. I pulled my pistol out and as soon as that…thing," said Leon ushering toward the alien "Came in, I started shooting it. I don't know how, but it just kept coming at me no matter how many bullets I pumped into it. Finally I grabbed out that knife," said Leon pointing to the one in the alien's neck. "I stabbed it in the throat, but it still wouldn't die. So I finally decided to just tackle it. I threw us both back into his ship and kept shooting at his head and at his chest; anywhere I thought would kill him. Finally he just…just exploded I guess. From the looks of it, only the top half of his head exploded. I had to crash land back down. I was lucky I guess."

"I'll send some people to look at this," said Willy. Then he added, "I suppose that means we aren't fighting anyone from Earth."

Willy took one last look at the alien, shuddering a little bit and then began walking away.

CHAPTER NINE

After that last loss, the whole command system for the military was shaken up. Leon wouldn't even begin to understand how the chain of command was decided until much later in the war. The way things worked out though, Willy suddenly became one of the high-ranking commanders. He still only had control of the pilots, but now he had total control of them and was under very loose constrictions.

Leon thought this would be a good thing, because Willy seemed very commonsensical. Leon was right in his assumptions. Willy decided to do something unprecedented immediately after moving up in the rankings. He began reaching out to high-ranking officials in the other four quadrants of the globe for an alliance. The leaders Willy talked to wanted concessions from the northwest, mainly capital and resources, but Willy figured that after this war, none of the deals he made would matter anyway. The people he'd made the deals with would either be dead, or the Earth would be in too much of a shambles to worry about something as trivial as a deal made before the war. In some ways, he was right, but in other ways, he was very wrong. Willy just wanted to tell the pilots that they were in over their heads and pull out of this war until his men got the proper technology they deserved. Unfortunately, the only two things he couldn't do were give out secrets concerning alien affairs, and put his army on strike.

Willy ordered workers to bring the alien ship Leon recovered into a special room to preserve the alien inside, and scientists came out to observe it the next day. Their hope was to figure out how to create a ship like the one the alien had, so Earth could use them. Not even these scientists knew that this technology already existed out there somewhere. There were very few people who knew and they wouldn't (or in Willy's case, couldn't) tell anyone, not even for the benefit of the planet.

The scientists also looked at the alien to try to figure out a weak point on it. They hoped to identify some sort of vital organ which, when destroyed, would be an instant kill. If it took everyone as long as it took Leon to kill one, then they would never win in a ground war.

The scientists invited Scott to work with them and the engineers to design a craft like the one Leon brought back. They eventually came out with a ship very similar to the one they were hoping to match. It looked like a mix between the style of ship Earth used in the last battle, and the alien ship. The ship had thicker but lighter armor, and overall, it was much better than the archaic, ineffective ships they'd been using previously.

It took a week, but now that the new ships were complete and standardized, and the newest pilots had arrived, it was time for yet another battle for the moon. People were growing increasingly paranoid at the fact that the moon was cycling through phases. Constantly waxing and waning.

Willy was somewhat nervous about this upcoming battle, but then again, he wasn't the one actually risking his life. Willy watched as Leon and some other pilots he didn't recognize walked past him into the hangar. This hangar was different than the one they'd departed from last time. This one was much bigger. It had to be in order to accommodate the extra ships that joined their fight because of the alliances Willy made.

Leon entered his ship wearing the same space suit and helmet as he had worn the last time, but he was hoping for a completely different result. One-hundred ships could take off at once from this particular hangar, and Leon was in the second row. Leon took off shortly after the first one-hundred and within seconds he was back in space.

Leon started firing as soon as he could see a ship. He wanted to shoot first this time rather than be shot at. The lasers still worked, just not as well as the alien's. However, they seemed to work well enough, because for the first time, Leon saw an alien space craft go down at his hands. He destroyed an alien ship. It was a remarkable sight too, to see the ships which were beginning to seem indestructible, come apart with an explosion. It made him realize that, although he hadn't been a casualty, he had also not helped in this chain of battles at all until just now. He did bring back an alien ship, which served as a template for the current ships, but that was a fluke. Now they were in a battle, and not just a one-sided affair.

The command ship was the thing standing most in the way of victory now. It could take down a ship with one shot and it rarely missed. Leon found he had enough skill to avoid all the shots directed at him by the command ship, and by the smaller fighter ships as well, but he couldn't say the same about the other pilots.

Leon had to make a sharp turn to avoid a laser beam headed toward him and ended up cruising in the direction of the moon, which allowed him to see an alien hangar with ships coming out of it. He knew this meant that the aliens were planning to set up a base on the moon. That would be like a moving platform they could survey the Earth from, but Leon wasn't prepared to let them have that so easily. Leon locked a missile onto the hangar, fired, and watched as part of the roof subsequently caved in. Leon saw another person follow his lead and fire another missile at the hangar. That hangar was destroyed and useless now.

Leon continued flying over the moon until he saw what appeared to be a factory. Attached to the factory were two pillars with blue smoke coming out of them. Leon fired another one of his missiles at this building. More ships were joining in

Leon's effort, firing their missiles at anything they thought worthy of destruction. Leon had his sights set on another alien hangar, but had to do a barrel roll to avoid a laser.

Leon decided to give up on shooting down the alien buildings for a moment to rejoin in the fighting for a while. That was what they came up here for anyway. He was able to bring down three more alien ships before he decided to fly in for a closer look at the command ship. He had to avoid constant laser fire from the command ship, which had several dozen turrets mounted on it to shoot down any ships that got close to it such as Leon was doing right now. Leon fired a few missiles at the ship but he might as well have been trying to kill an elephant by flicking water droplets at it. The ship just looked too big to defeat.

Leon couldn't help but think that it would be impossible to take back the moon with the command ship looming. It was indestructible for the moment, and who knew how many alien soldiers and pilots were inside of it. Leon decided to talk to Willy about this while in the midst of the battle.

"Hey Willy," said Leon.

"What is it?"

"How soon could we build a giant ship? We're going to need one to use against the alien's."

"Leon, it's not a question of *how soon*, it's a question of *if*. I don't think we could actually do that."

"We need something more powerful to take this one down, and if we don't, then we can't land on the moon. It's going to destroy all our ships."

"I'm not a miracle worker, Leon," said Willy. "If we tried to build a ship that big, and it failed, do you realize how much capital and valuable time we would've wasted? It would be nearly impossible to carry on with this war then."

"I'm just saying," said Leon, "We might not have a choice. You can't always be conservative; sometimes you need to make an all or nothing move," Leon paused for a moment, to see if Willy would say anything else, but when he didn't Leon added, "Over and out, sir."

Leon put his communicator away. He came across another factory with pillars of blue smoke coming out of it and wondered what they could burn that would create blue smoke. He shot a missile at the factory knocking down one of the pillars. Then he returned to the fighting once more, taking down another two ships. The laser turret on his ship was much more effective than the turret that fired metal shells.

Then, Leon took a hit from the enemy. The ship held up, but barely. He was losing control and the ship began to shake and sway. He didn't have a chance to steer back toward Earth so he settled for a rough landing on the moon.

Leon couldn't get the ship to start up again so he had to get out. Never stay in one place for too long. Now that Leon had seen the laser turret work in battle, he figured that all the guns should use lasers and he wished the sidearm he had in his pocket could shoot lasers.

Leon ran to the nearest building and crouched near it. He had to minimize his chances of a ship shooting him from above. Leon crept along the building with his back pressed to the wall. He had plenty of oxygen stored up in the tanks on his back for now, so that wasn't a concern. Leon decided to pull out his pistol in case anything came around the corner of the building toward him.

Leon finally made it around the side of the building and saw a glass door. Inside were aliens who looked similar to the one that attacked him only that these aliens had wings. They seemed to be at a restaurant of some sort. They were looking at something and all eating. Leon couldn't tell what they were eating but he realized that they were looking at a quad-dimensional television. The television was rooted into the ground, and projecting out holograms of ships buzzing around, except it was as if the ships were real. They filled the entire room and buzzed right around the heads of the aliens. What Leon eventually realized however, was that the television was showing the war going on above. Leon wondered why the aliens would be filming the war and showing it on television. They seemed to cheer though, when one of the Earth ships was destroyed, like it was some sporting event. Then a thought occurred to Leon. If they're watching the war, did they see him crash land and get out alive? Leon continued to watch the television. He saw a ship crash. He saw himself get out. Leon realized that there was about a five-minute delay. Would they see Leon sneaking around to where they were? No. The camera apparently lost interest in Leon and focused in on another Earth ship, which took a hit and exploded. There was a loud cheer.

Leon continued to walk around, wondering how the aliens managed to erect a restaurant in the few weeks they'd been occupying the moon. He also found it a bit strange that the aliens viewed war as a sport. Were the humans making it that easy for them?

Leon continued walking around, looking for any sight of something which could either fix his ship or take him back to Earth. Suddenly, an ally ship landed down next to him. A man Leon had never seen before poked his head out and told Leon to get in. There wasn't a lot of room, but for the time it didn't matter.

"My name is Alexander," said the pilot in the ship.

"I'm Leon. How did you find me?"

"Just luck that I saw you. They say pilots develop better vision than most. You realize it's not safe to be out here alone, comrade."

Leon could tell from the fact that he said "comrade", that he was from the Northeast, an entirely communist section. For some reason, people from that quadrant had a weird habit of sticking, "comrade" into the majority of their sentences.

"I know it's dangerous," said Leon, "But my ship took a hit and I had to land to avoid becoming a sitting duck."

"I don't know about you, comrade," said Alexander, "But this seems like a suicide mission. How can we possibly destroy that gigantic ship? It has destroyed at least one-thousand other comrades."

"We need one of our own."

"I don't see why we can't get one, comrade."

Alexander turned out to be a good pilot. He was almost as skilled as Leon. He took out five more ships before returning to Earth for more fuel.

"Well comrade, for now our paths diverge; but I hope they cross again one day—hopefully on better terms."

Leon watched him take off and then returned to the hangar to see if there were any more ships available. There were, but for now he stopped in the canteen to join a group of people on break from battle, eating. You could take lunch breaks every now and then, but the chefs would start yelling at you if you stayed there for more than fifteen minutes; and they were just as mean as Lieutenant Bennett.

After Leon filled his stomach, he got into a ship and reentered the battle. Amazingly, there were still a decent number of people fighting off the aliens. Everyone was constantly launching missiles and firing lasers. Some people focused on the enemy ships, and some people were destroying alien buildings on the moon. Leon hoped Earth ships had already hit those aliens who were watching on quad-dimensional television. Then he realized something: Earth was winning. Just barely, but slowly and surly, Earth was gaining an edge.

Leon turned back to head toward the moon and saw a group of ships had already landed there. Leon decided to join them to see if he could assist them in whatever they were doing.

Leon saw the men enter into a recently bombed out building and he followed them inside.

"Is this our foothold?" Leon asked one of the men. He knew one of their objectives was to set-up a foothold, but this seemed like a bad spot.

"For now it is," replied the man.

Nothing was in here. It would serve as a hideout, but strategically, it wasn't anything special. If it was going to be a foothold, they'd need to bring in some supplies to sustain themselves inside there for a protracted amount of time.

"If we bring shovels," said one of the men, "We can expand this place and turn it into our hangar. Then we can collapse the roof so the ships can get out of here." Everyone agreed with him. Part one of the mission was complete.

It wasn't long before troops began arriving with supplies to build a hangar. The work went fast, but the pilots wanted to work even faster, knowing that the command ship was still looming just outside.

Leon borrowed the ship of someone who stopped to rest at the foothold they set up, and used it to take down another alien ship. Leon could tell that the aliens' numbers were beginning to decrease. At this rate, the only ship left would be the command ship.

Eventually, something strange happened. The command ship's engine silently clicked on and the ship began to turn around. Once it turned a full one-hundred eighty degrees, the command ship sped up to a blur and then it was gone. The rest of the surviving alien ships followed in short order. The battle was over and the humans had won—one victory for Earth.

But even though they won one battle, there was still a lot of work left. They still had to finish turning the foothold into a hangar for a start. Earth was a long, long way from winning the war. For all anyone knew, the command ship could be back tomorrow and bring more ships with it. Earth couldn't afford to lose the moon again. A hangar was finished in two days and mechanics installed a missile defense grid on the moon to shoot down the alien spacecraft if they returned.

Leon was a pilot and he couldn't stay on the moon. He headed back to Earth where he belonged to figure out what the next move would be. In all likelihood, they would send Ginyu guards to the moon to do what they did best: guard. By now, all the soldiers knew who they were fighting.

CHAPTER TEN

The command ship never came back. It instead landed back on the clouds of Jupiter where Sudokus was. The soldiers aboard the command ship were about to partake in a post-defeat ritual. Sudokus was waiting just outside the ship when the soldier came out to talk.

"Earth is more powerful than first thought," said the soldier.

"Or maybe you are weaker than first thought," said Sudokus.

"They use good strategy, sir. They bombed out all the buildings on the moon so we could not continue to get the materials we needed to keep our ships in the sky and ready to fight. We pulled back before we lost any more ships. We could still return there and take back what was once ours; we just need a few days to recoup."

"Why should I send you back there when you have already failed once? Do you think I have unlimited resources at my disposal and can just afford to throw away fleet after fleet of perfectly good ships?"

"Sir, I realize that we need to be economically conservative during any war, but you and I both know this will be an easy victory should we ever decide to send a full force out."

"What makes you think I want to send a full force out? I want to force those meat sacks to surrender using as few of my soldiers as possible."

"Easier said than done, sir. But I assure you, if we were to have one more chance, they would not stop us."

"What makes you think I will give you a second chance? I've decided to feed you to Jum-Jum. She's hungry anyway."

The soldier knew he messed up. If defeat was inevitable for a squadron of aliens, they'd return to Sudokus. Then one of them would attempt to convince Sudokus as to why they should get a second chance. Only one was ever able to make a strong enough case and he died in the next battle. Purely a case of irony. This leads one to question why they'd return to Sudokus if that meant they'd probably die anyway. The answer is surprisingly simple; Thousands of years' worth of artificial selection has led to an almost robotic creature. The thought of just running away never even crosses an alien's mind.

As to the question of what Jum-Jum is; she is the extraterrestrial equivalent of an animal. She was also Sudokus's pet whose diet consisted of defeated soldiers and the occasional prisoners of war. She was huge, and always hungry. She had four legs with five claws on each foot. A shell protected her back and stomach. She had a head with two eyes that were on stalks, and she had a bird-like beak. Her tail was as long as her body and covered with spikes. Sudokus kept her in the basement of the spherical building that he spent most of his time in.

Sudokus inspected the command ship as a small group of aliens came out of his spherical building to lead the defeated army into Jum-Jum's lair. The ship had a few scratches and a dent, from the few stray bullets that penetrated the force field, so the mechanics would need to scrap it. There could only be perfection in Sudokus's army. Perfection triggered his satisfaction receptors.

Inside the building, Jum-Jum could hear the footsteps of the soldiers approaching. She had been sleeping, but now began to stir. The soldiers stood on a trap door in the center of the room. When most of the aliens had crammed their way into the room that the guards had pushed them into, one of the guards pushed a button on a wall, which caused the floor to start shimmering. The floor shimmered faster and faster until it disappeared and everyone fell through. Then the guard pressed the button again and the floor shimmered back into existence. The next group of aliens who hadn't been able to fit into the room the first time quickly squeezed their way into the room and the same thing happened.

The lighting in the lair was dim but bright enough so that you could see Jum-Jum just before she ate you. Some soldiers looked for something to hide behind. There were pieces of rotting wood all around but it only made it more exhilarating for Jum-Jum. Jum-Jum crawled out of the crevice she was sleeping in and began on her meal. She knew it might be a while before her next one so she savored it.

Although Sudokus wasn't giving those exact soldiers a second chance, he was willing to try to take the fight to Earth again. Not in space however, on the ground. He needed to change tactics in a situation like this.

CHAPTER ELEVEN

Some human pilots stayed on the moon, just in case, but most headed back down to Earth to wait. None of this mattered to the aliens though, as they sped right past them and into earth's atmosphere to engage in another battle. No one on Earth knew what exactly was going to happen next. Different people of importance discussed what the next move should be, if there should even be another move. In the end, however, it would be the aliens who came to them.

Leon was back in boot camp with the other soldiers when the announcement telling all troops to mobilize for battle came. One of the remote operated ships orbiting the planet spotted a command ship approaching.

Everyone was scrambling to wherever they needed to go. Ground soldiers went one way, and pilots went the other way to the hangar. Everyone thought it would be another space battle, but the announcement didn't give any specifics, so Leon waited along with the other pilots, ready for whatever their next instructions would be. The soldiers waited just outside the hangar, in case they have to board a transport ship to a different location.

The men watched a monitor which was showing the view of one of the scout ships. They could see the command ship approaching the outer limits of Earth's atmosphere, except there were no other ships around it like there usually were. Then, the bottom of the ship opened up and a ship about a third of the size of the command ship lowered out and continued descending downward until it penetrated the highest clouds on Earth. The soldiers were the first to see this ship first hand as it descended only a few hundred yards away from them. The pilots waited inside the hangar having no idea what was going on.

This secondary ship landed and a door opened up granting view of an army of alien soldiers. The soldiers all looked the same: five to six feet tall with wings like a housefly, except bigger, on their back. They all wore armor that was the same muddy brown color as Sudokus. They marched out in columns towards where the human soldiers were waiting.

The soldiers had good training and knew they'd have to wait until the ground troop commander, Cpt. Drew, gave them the signal to fire the first shot. If they never heard from him, the rule was to shoot only after fired upon. That was apparently the alien's rule of thumb too, because Cpt. Drew never gave the signal, and the aliens marched past the human soldiers.

This left a few puzzled faces among the soldiers, but it wasn't long before they realized the aliens were heading toward a major city not too far away. Drew must've realized this too, because it was only a minute or two after the aliens passed that he gave the signal and the human soldiers shot first.

The soldiers for both sides began dispersing among the long abandoned buildings of the ghost town they were in. Ghost towns were always good for any kind of military affairs, because no civilians ever visited a deserted town.

Both the humans and aliens had very similar levels of skill, but the aliens had a huge advantage in the form of their wings. It was nearly impossible to hit them once they were flying. Plus, the aliens had more innovative ammunition. Maybe at one point in history the aliens used the simple hard-metal bullets, but now they used bullets that would penetrate into the body cavity, and then expand—when they weren't using lasers anyway. It wasn't gruesome to watch, because no one ever "blew up", but the pain was excruciating as the bullet would grow just large enough to destroy almost all of the major organs. Yet, this was just a small part of the alien's arsenal, and they had even better guns they could switch to if necessary.

In a battle like this, Willy would only call in the air unit if necessary, and it was necessary at this point. Cpt. Drew contacted Willy, who in turn gave the signal for the pilots to engage in the battle.

Leon was once again in a ship designed by Scott after he wrecked his last one. The planes took off within a minute of receiving the signal and joined in the fighting. At first, Leon couldn't see the enemy because he was looking on the ground. Then, something made him look straight ahead. To his surprise, he saw the aliens, all flying with their insect-like wings. Leon quickly regained his composure, and began shooting with the lasers on the plane, which worked as well as the ones they used in space. Leon was able to take down a few of the aliens but not nearly enough. He ended up colliding with one of the aliens and it splattered on his windshield—just like an insect. Leon couldn't help but think that this looked like a locust invasion, such as the ones the ancient African Ibo villagers looked forward to because they could collect locust by the hundreds and feast on them for days.

The more Leon looked at the splattered soldier, the more he thought these aliens were just like overgrown houseflies. The collision killed the insect but also prevented Leon from being able to see. Leon pulled up to avoid hitting any of his own ships. Leon looked for a button to activate a windshield wiper and found it after a few seconds of looking. After clearing his window, he turned his ship around and started back into the fight shooting down as many aliens as he could.

But for as much help as the pilots provided, the ground soldiers were useless and they eventually had to retreat. The pilots had to pull out once the ground soldiers retreated, because standard procedure required it. They went in with them, and they went out with them.

So everyone had to watch as the alien army marched closer to a major city. No one was angrier by this lack of action than Leon, but he was just as powerless as the person next to him was. Even Willy couldn't send out his pilots unauthorized because this was a, "New type of threat which required the utmost caution." At least that's what the higher ups said.

For the next week, the alien troops kept marching on, shooting anyone who opposed them. Earth's army chased them down to try to steer them clear of the public. Their chief concern was keeping anyone from seeing this alien army so they could continue to label this as a skirmish and not a war.

Eventually the human army was pushed back to a bombed out city along the Pacific coastline. The scientists for the army were trying unsuccessfully to create a weapon that could kill the aliens instead of just deterring them. It seemed that even the occasional bullet that hit its mark didn't kill.

The army had divided throughout the helter-skelter fighting and the battalion Leon was loyal to was reduced to staying in a small building that barely had enough space for everyone to have a sleeping spot. For a hangar, they just had a flat field outside. They knew that the aliens would come across them eventually, but they would just have to push them either north or south—anywhere but a populated city.

It was getting late in the night and Leon sat up in his bunk which was underneath another soldier's. Leon had thoughts rushing through his head, and he decided this would be a good time to write down his thoughts so he could have them organized. Leon pulled out a pen and the journal he'd been carrying around in a small sack.

I don't know if anyone will ever read this, but if someone is reading this, know that life does exist past Earth, and, from my experience, the aliens are warmongers. And why shouldn't they be, we're warmongers too. If creatures of the same species can't get along, why would an intelligent creature of a different species give a damn about us? And all the stuff you hear about aliens having advanced technology is true. Is it possible that this is because people have already made contact with aliens and are speaking from firsthand experience? I don't know, and probably never will. You have to be really important to even begin to be able to answer that question, and the only way to be important seems to be born into it. And it always appears the most important people are the politicians. Come to think of it, I don't even know how government positions are decided. They always just pick an important person who was supposedly next in line for a job when someone leaves.

I don't even understand the chain of command for anything. I know that the quadrant leader, John, is the most important person, but I don't know who's just below him. And it's the same with our military; it's like we just got an army as an afterthought and never got around to making a clear chain of command. I know it's made harder by the fact that we have soldiers from other quadrants with us, but if we had an effective system, we could just force them to assimilate. But we don't have an effective system, so they just end up making things more confusing.

The other thing I don't get is why we only seem to improve upon technology after we need it. But we produce it quickly as if we already had the blueprints for it and were just too lazy to make it. I won't speculate as to why it is. All I know is that if there is some all-powerful force out in the universe, I need him to produce a miracle now to save us.

CHAPTER TWELVE

A miracle did come: a very small miracle. Leon was still up even though it was late at night when everyone else was asleep. He was still thinking of a way to stop the aliens. Then something hit him on the head. He looked up and only saw the ceiling staring back at him. He looked down to see if what hit him was on the ground. All he saw was a tiny, round piece of metal. He picked it up and laid it in the palm of his hand. Suddenly three tiny, metal legs popped out from the bottom of the object, lifting the piece of metal a few centimeters off Leon's hand. A door opened up and a rope ladder fell down from the door. Three tiny creatures climbed down the ladder and onto Leon's palm. Leon looked to see if anyone else was seeing what was happening but they were all asleep.

The three creatures were all green, yet looked humanoid, and they were small. Incredibly tiny. Leon examined them more closely and realized that they had no ears, no nose, no hair and no pupils. Their skin was a dark green, and their eyes were completely white.

"We come in peace," said one of the creatures as if it was a generic welcoming by foreign diplomats.

Leon jumped back, startled at what he heard.

"Identify yourselves," whispered Leon so as not to wake anyone.

"We come from Mars and we have been traveling the galaxy for twelve years. We were forced to evacuate when Sudokus's troops over took our city of Trexal. We have been looking for a place Sudokus doesn't have control over and now we have stumbled upon your world. You have the last free planet in this solar system and we would like to assist you in keeping it that way." They were only telling a part of the truth for now; it would've been too much for Leon to hear that this was part of his destiny.

"Why would you want to help us, you're one of them," said Leon wondering if they could even understand him. Then, suddenly, his mind was flooded with answers. First, he saw as these aliens boarded their tiny ships. Then, Sudokus's command ships cruised over Mars, firing laser beams down upon the surface and causing untold amounts of damage to the infrastructure. Next, he got the image of the tiny ship flying through space inspecting different planets until it finally went to Earth. Then the ship cruised around, undetected due to its size and cloaking device, until it came upon Leon's-now-abandoned home. It then left the home and went to the location where Leon currently was. The image of Sudokus's red eye overwhelmed Leon suddenly, and the vision ended.

Just from that, Leon now understood why these aliens wanted to help, and he knew that they could somehow communicate mentally. Some sort of telepathy. He also knew who the true enemy was, and its name was Sudokus. Leon wanted to know more about the robot with a name, but it seemed the aliens were eager to continue with their own mission. One of the aliens climbed back into the ship and pulled out a tiny gun.

"This is one of our gas guns. It was very effective against Sudokus's soldiers in the regular sized version the Martians carried, but ours are too small and they couldn't hold enough gas to defend against the soldiers. However, our ships detected larger amounts of this same exact gas on this planet, and if we could make these guns in their larger size, then they would be useful to us.

Leon set the aliens and their ship down onto the nightstand next to his bed. Then he proceeded to take the tiny gun from the aliens. Leon looked at it more closely. It looked just like any other gun made on Earth, just smaller. Leon handed it back to the alien. He noticed that one of the aliens had some sort of a hand held device in its grasp. The alien started pointing it around in different directions and then walking to different places where he pointed the device. He eventually jumped onto Leon's bed and then started shimmying up the ladder leading to the upper bunk bed. He crawled into the pocket of the man on the upper bunk and pulled out a small bottle of Insect repellent. Leon couldn't help but notice that the bottle of insect repellent was the same size as the alien, yet he was easily able to pull it out of the man's pocket. He jumped back down to the nightstand with the bottle.

"This is the substance we load our guns with," said one of the aliens.

"Insect repellent?" asked Leon, puzzled.

"This is not insect repellent; this is one of the most lethal poisons known. The species on this planet just happen to be immune to it. Gather up as much of this stuff as you can and then we can make larger guns for you to use, this substance will easily kill all of Sudokus's soldiers."

Leon was skeptical, but he figured it was worth a try. With all the strange events that had been going on lately, Leon wouldn't be surprised if these aliens actually did know what they were doing.

"You guys will have to stay in this drawer," said Leon pulling open a drawer on his nightstand, "Until I can figure out what to do with you." After that, Leon attempted to go to sleep, but it was hours before he could calm down enough to do so.

The next morning Leon approached Willy in his office. He wasn't sure how he could explain to Willy what the aliens told him without showing him, so he decided to bring the aliens with him.

Willy was startled to see the tiny aliens in Leon's palm and asked, "What the hell are those?"

"They're aliens, but good ones."

"Why would you think they're good?"

"Because of what they showed me. They can somehow communicate with my mind, and they showed me how some sort of robot tried to kill them by sending those big ships to their planet."

"Well what are they doing here, in your palm?"

"I don't know why they came to me, but they said they want to help us and they told me that generic insect repellent is the most lethal poison known to aliens. If we could just get some of that, we could turn this battle around."

"That's great news and all, but don't you find it strange that in the midst of an alien invasion, even more aliens come to us? Don't you find that just a little bit strange? Plus, it's nearly impossible to get any sort of good insect repellent anymore. Unless you get it from the streets or something, but it isn't necessarily an item your average vendor would be carrying. We need to focus our energies on proven tactics."

"I think this is our best option," said Leon.

Willy turned his back and looked out of a window overlooking the ocean. It pained Willy to know so much, but not be able to tell anyone. He knew who Sudokus was, and he knew there were both good aliens and bad aliens, but he couldn't even hint to Leon that he knew any of this. Even more, he wished he knew why he couldn't tell him. It's not like they wouldn't find out on their own eventually. Willy finally decided to forget about the silly rules made-up by some people who supposedly knew what they were doing for the sake of accomplishing something worthwhile. Willy turned back around to tell Leon what he knew, but Leon was gone, and Willy didn't want to chase after him. He could only hope Leon was right about those aliens.

Leon left the room and started walking through the streets of the bombed out city with his mind under the complete control of the aliens. He did not know where he was going, but with the little aliens guiding him, he did not need to know.

He eventually came to a stop in front of a partially collapsed building. Judging from the smoke stacks on top, it was a factory. Leon reached out for the rusted door handle, but it broke off when he tried to turn it. He ended up having to force the door open with his shoulder. The inside of the building was dusty, and barren.

Leon, suddenly able to break free of the aliens mind control, looked around. He didn't know where he was, and he wasn't quite sure how he got here. He started walking deeper into the building and noticed a rusty staircase leading up a countless number of floors.

"There's no way I'm going up all those stairs," said Leon. He was talking just as much to himself as he was to the aliens.

The aliens took back control of Leon's mind and Leon looked over toward a hatch on the ground. Leon walked over to it and pulled on a handle on the hatch.

When the hatch opened, Leon couldn't see anything. There was just a dark abyss below him. If Leon had been in control of his own mind he would have never gone down there, but the aliens wanted to go down. Motion sensing lights began turning on with every step Leon took. The stairs went downward for sixty feet. The further down Leon went, the cleaner and less rusty the walls around him got. When Leon finally reached the bottom, he was in a pure white room.

Leon now became aware of a soft beeping noise as the aliens once more released their mind control over him. Leon looked down at one of the aliens who was pointing some sort of a sensor that beeped at various speeds depending on which direction he aimed it. He pointed the sensor toward some boxes a couple of feet away from Leon, who then walked over to them. Leon began opening up one of the boxes; it was a small green can labeled, "G. I. Insect Repellent: 25% more effective."

"How did you guys know this would be here?" asked Leon looking down toward the little aliens. The answer came to him in the form of more telepathy when one of them told him that the small beeping device was actually a substance detector that could be set to sense a substance such as insect repellent. Leon grabbed as many boxes as he could and started hauling them back up the stairs, hoping the insect repellent would do what the aliens said it would do, but he was cautious about aimlessly listening to them. But he figured it couldn't hurt just to try what they suggested. The soldiers couldn't perform any worse than they already were.

CHAPTER THIRTEEN

Leon returned to base with eight boxes, each with forty cans of insect repellent inside. Willy looked up from the paper work he was doing when he saw Leon enter his office.

"I got the insect repellent," said Leon, "I think this might really work."

"It better, because we're officially out of options," said Willy. "The aliens are almost here according to outside sources, and morale among the troops is at an all-time low. I don't remember a single time when we were fighting in the plains of Uganda that my men and I didn't think we could kill every single person who opposed us. But you should see the amount of people who come to me every day saying they want to leave. And do you know what? I have to tell them they can't leave because I got a memo from the higher-ups that no man, woman or child can leave their military position for at least one year." Willy stopped talking, realizing that he had gone on a tangent and lost the original point of why Leon entered. "I'm sorry about that, Leon. It's just that there is a lot of stress and a lot of unknowns right now, and it seems impractical for me to concern myself with insect repellent."

"Hey, you said yourself that we're out of options," said Leon. "So this is all we have the way I see it. I brought back as much as I could, and there's more not too far from here if we run out. We can't use it while it's in these canisters though; we need to modify our guns so that we can load them with insect repellent as ammunition."

"We have people who can do that," said Willy.

"Scott might even be able to do that; I'll go find him now. I'll take care of everything concerning this next battle, if it's alright with you, sir."

"You can do what you want, just don't tell anyone that I said anything you're going to do was O.K. with me. Just pretend I don't know about your extraterrestrial friends, and pretend I don't know about the repellent." Willy wanted Leon to pretend, because he was going to have to pretend too. He didn't want anyone else with any authority to know about this, or they might interfere and just make things worse. Leon left to go find Scott then, and Willy decided that when the time was right, he'd tell Leon everything he knew. Assuming he didn't die before then.

Leon walked around the base, looking for Scott. He couldn't find any sign of him above ground, so he went into the basement where he found Scott sleeping. Leon nudged his elbow into Scott's side to wake him up.

"Ugh," said Scott groggily, "This better be something important, Leon."

"Scott, I need you to start modifying all the firearms we have so that we can load them with insect repellent," said Leon.

"Have you lost your mind," yelled Scott.

"No. Just trust me; this is the only way we won't die."

"I might not be able to do this, I only specialize in aerospace engineering, so don't expect any miracles."

"It wouldn't be a miracle if I expected it, now would it?"

"It's just an expression, Leon. Now let me get to work. I hear the enemy is nearly upon us, and I'll never finish unless I start now. Oh, and one more thing, I'm not going to tamper with all the guns, unless you know for sure this will work."

"I don't know for sure, but the guns we have now are obsolete anyway, so there's nothing to lose, either way."

Scott got some of his colleagues and they worked all through the night fixing up all the guns and modifying them to shoot out gas rather than metal. If the engineers had worked any slower, all hope for humanity might have ended at that little outpost by the ocean. But they worked with haste, and were able to distribute a decent number of guns by the next day when the army of aliens crossed their paths once again.

CHAPTER FOURTEEN

The three hundred men who had been fortunate enough to receive the modified guns stood with their new technology just outside of the base. They stood in plain view, since there was nowhere to hide, and they faced away from the ocean, waiting for an army of aliens to come in and kill them. Most of them thought death would be their fate. They already lost a couple of battles with the aliens, and that was when they actually had bullets in their guns. Now they waited for a well-trained army to come toward them so that they could spray them with insect repellent. It was no wonder morale was low.

It was a while before anything actually happened; some people began thinking that the aliens weren't going to attack for another day. The soldiers listened to the constant ebb and flow of the waves as they lapped against the beachfront. Then, the rhythm began to change, and it became irregular.

No one wanted to look behind themselves at first, in fear of what they might find, but eventually the tension got to them. Everyone turned and was horrified to see two large, grey ships approaching their location. The ships had to be at least three hundred yards long, maybe even four hundred. They had large cannons mounted on top of them. Hundreds of soldiers were waiting on the deck of the ship and ten times as many were below them, out of view. The humans had good enough training to stay calm, but no amount of training could prevent the instinctual shaking everyone got in their knees. If Lieutenant Bennett was here, his knees might even be shaking.

Willy stood alongside of the ground troop commander, Cpt. Drew, and stared out at the ship through a pair of binoculars. It was obvious that there were aliens on the ship. Willy knew Cpt. Drew's soldiers would be useless until the ship made landfall, but that would never happen if his pilots could do anything about it.

Willy ran into his office, grabbed the microphone and said, "All pilots report to the hangar." The message blared out over the speakers located throughout the base.

Leon and the other pilots who had survived the previous battles began running toward the hangar. Willy didn't have to give them instructions or a pre-battle speech, he simply pointed at the ship, told them to take care of it, and they all took off as soon as they could, flying toward the ship.

As they got closer, they realized there were two ships; one was slightly smaller and hidden behind the other. They still both looked menacing as they began firing their laser cannons at the planes. Most of the pilots were able to avoid the fire, but some weren't so fortunate. It was easy enough for Leon to avoid the blasts coming toward him. He seemed to have a knack for evasive maneuvers. The pilots communicated to each other while in the air and eventually decided that some of them should try to infiltrate the boat while the others cleared the top deck.

Leon volunteered himself to be one of the men to infiltrate. He and the other ships all touched down hard onto the two boats. About fifty people landed on the ship Leon landed on. Aliens were swarming around on the upper deck yelling out in a language Leon could never begin to comprehend. Leon began shooting out the insect repellent. It came out hard and shot out about fifty yards before the air diluted it too much for it to be effective. As soon as a stream of gas hit one of the aliens, they doubled over in pain. Most of them fell to their knees and started coughing up this green substance, and then their heads eventually exploded with the ooze. It didn't take long before the pilots who landed with Leon killed all the aliens on the upper deck with the help of the planes above.

Leon ran over to what he thought was the hatch leading down into the lower part of the ship. He pulled it open and he could see countless aliens standing about ninety feet below, just close enough for him to shoot. He started to shoot downward into the ship, but no sooner did he do that than did the aliens see him and begin to return fire. There was a lot of confusion and Leon slammed the hatch closed before an alien could hit him with an expanding bullet.

It didn't take Leon long to realize they'd need to strategize and work as a team if they hoped to take down this ship. He just hoped the people on the other ship were able to come through on their mission.

"How are we going to kill the aliens down there without getting ourselves shot?" asked Leon.

"We need to find a way to stick the nozzles of our guns into there without exposing ourselves," said one of the men.

"Yeah, that way we can suffocate them with the gas," said another man.

"But how will we do that?" asked Leon.

Everybody started yelling at each other and nobody really had an answer until a small silver disk came hurtling toward Leon. It was those little aliens; they had flown over in their ship to meet up with Leon. Leon explained the problem to the little aliens and they instantly had a solution. All the other men with Leon were too distracted talking amongst themselves to notice the little aliens as they extended a tiny drill from their ship and began drilling holes through the floor just big enough for the pilots to stick the barrels of their guns through.

The sight from below must have been terrifying for the aliens on the ship. They're aware that there are people just above them, and they're just trying to make it to the shoreline so that they can attack what they believe is the final base that the humans occupy. Then from above they see the barrels of guns point down toward them and a gas starts leaking into the ship.

Since the gas has nowhere to diffuse, the air starts getting more and more concentrated with the spray. All of the aliens start to choke and cough up the thick green liquid. The boat turned into a death trap and they had no chance to escape.

After a few minutes, they had all died and Leon opened up the hatch. A strong smell of dead flesh came through as soon as he opened the door. Leon looked down and saw the heaps of dead bodies. To Leon, they all seemed identical, especially now that they were dead. Just heaps of brown bodies sprawled out all over the floor. Leon closed the hatch back up and turned his attention toward the other ship that was coming in toward the base. The pilots on the ship killed all the aliens on the upper deck, but they hadn't been able to penetrate to the lower level.

Leon was about to hop back into his plane and fly over to help the men on the other ship, but before he was able to do that, his mind was taken over again. Suddenly, he found himself climbing down into the main part of the ship. Normally he wouldn't have just been stepping all over dead bodies, but he was not in control currently. Yet, in his mind, he was still disgusted by the sensation of stepping on the fleshy bodies and hearing their blood ooze out of them. Leon opened up a door leading to a room that had a lot of buttons and controls. He walked up to a half sphere embedded into a metal panel. He put his hand on top of it and started spinning it to the right. The ship started turning the direction he spun. Leon could see what was happening, but he couldn't control it. It was like watching a movie, except you're strapped into your seat so that you can't move at all. Right now, Leon's movie was showing his ship about to crash into the other ship; and that's exactly what happened. Apparently, the little aliens knew exactly what they were doing, because with just one hit, they capsized the other ship while they remained afloat. Furthermore, they left the ship sailing in the opposite direction of the shore.

Leon got control of his mind back after that and he realized that although all the aliens would probably drown, so would the humans on the ship. Leon ran out of the room, but stopped when he saw all the dead bodies lying on the floor. He took in a deep breath to calm himself, and then sprinted across the bodies to get back up top where he hopped into his plane. Everyone else already decided to abandon ship. He didn't see anybody remaining as he took off.

Leon flew over to see the ship slowly sinking in the depths of the ocean. Leon knew he'd sunk it just in time. If it had gotten any closer, it would have been able to open up fire on the base. Leon flew his ship down lower to look for survivors. He didn't see any aliens, but he saw many humans wading in the water, waiting for help to arrive. He slowed his plane down as much as he could and went down as close to the water as he could. He was able to slow down enough to open up a side door on his plane. He reached out and grabbed a hold of a man floating in the water. He pulled him into the cockpit and flew back to the shore where he dropped him off. He rescued a few more people in this same manner.

It was late at night when everyone arrived back at base. No one talked, because they were busy eating, but everyone knew that they now had a chance to beat the aliens, or at least not die any time soon. The next day Willy addressed the group about some important matters.

"I would like to congratulate all of you who helped to defeat the aliens at the battle yesterday. We now have an opportunity to defeat the aliens and I think we have what it takes. But if we're going to do it, we can't stay here. I have been able to make radio contact with a group of ally troops who said we could join up with them. It won't be easy to get to them, because they're over in Northern Russia. It is very cold in Russia as you all know, and ships don't always handle well in that climate. But the benefits outweigh the risks because they have even more troops than we have. So we have to leave today, because the aliens will most likely be back to attack us soon. The higher-ups say that was just them toying with us, and if they send in their ground troops again, they wouldn't hesitate to get rid of us just as anyone of you might clear away an anthill outside. All pilots will take their ships and head out as soon as possible. All non-pilots—ground soldiers in this case—will have to start walking until we find the nearest operating air base. The aliens haven't destroyed too much of the area yet, so it shouldn't be too hard to find one nearby. Believe me, I wish we could take a transport, but they all were damaged or destroyed during the fighting this past week. Our original mission was to keep the aliens from making contact with the public, and the higher ups feel we have all done that job valiantly. But now they think it is more important to confront these creatures with whatever is necessary to push them back where they came from. Gentlemen, today we have officially entered a war."

Leon, and everyone else, was surprised to hear that last bit of news. The word "war" had a growing taboo on it ever since the "skirmish" started, but now one simple sentence lifted that taboo.

The pilots headed over to the hangar. Leon made sure that he brought the tiny aliens with him. He shoved them into his knap sack. After filling up their ships with the ogelan fuel, and plugging in the coordinates of their destination, they started up their engines and were gone. They left wondering if the rest of the men would ever join them.

PART II

CHAPTER FIFTEEN

The flight to Russia was a long one. Leon and the other pilots decided to fly in a 'V' pattern, like migrating geese. They didn't have to worry about fuel because the ogelan was almost four times as efficient as gasoline. The only thing they had to worry about were all the blinking lights in the sky. There was no doubt in anyone's mind that those lights were coming from alien ships floating out in Earth's orbit. Either they didn't see the ships flying below them, or the aliens just didn't care about them, because they didn't attack the humans on their journey.

It was a full day of flying before they finally landed at their destination. It was cold, just as Willy had said it would be. Colder than anything Leon had ever experienced. Luckily, the pilots wore heated suits. Some soldiers, who had been at the base for a while, ushered the newly landed pilots into the building, which several fathoms of snow layered over the Earth had submerged underground. The doorway on the outside was just barely above the snow, but a short staircase on the inside, just beyond the door, carried down a couple of feet, making the top floor a few inches below ground level, and the bottom floor of this multi-floored building a little over a mile down. It was like an skyscraper, but it went down instead of up. Inside, Leon saw well over three-hundred thousand soldiers all eating and drinking in some kind of cafeteria; one thing Leon was beginning to notice was that even in crisis, people would still be sure to meet their metabolic needs; it was an invariable constant. It was a very large cafeteria, and only a fraction of the people in the building were currently eating. Leon walked down the short flight of stairs to join them. Everyone seemed to be having a good time; they seemed unaware of the war at hand. Leon scanned the faces, trying to see if he knew anyone here. Amazingly, he did. Alexander—the person who had helped Leon to get off the moon when he had crash-landed during the battle in space—was here.

"Alexander," said Leon.

Alexander looked over at Leon, but didn't recognize him. "Do I know you, comrade?"

"I'm Leon, the one you rescued from off the moon during that space battle."

"Ah, yes. Hello, comrade, take a seat. Make yourself comfortable." Alexander patted the seat right next to him, a signal for Leon to sit there. "How has the world been to you, comrade?"

"Not too bad, I'm still alive, aren't I?" Leon and Alexander both let out a laugh. Then a woman wearing a light blue shirt, with a white apron, came over to Leon with a plate of hot food. Leon suddenly realized that he hadn't eaten since he began his flight to Russia. Leon began eating his food and soon, a server brought a glass of water to him. Leon ate his food quickly and then just sat there resting and digesting.

Leon looked over at the door that he came in from. There was a steady stream of people filing in. They were all soldiers, ready to fight if need be.

"How long have you been here, Alexander?"

"I landed back here after that last battle in space and I've been here ever since then. I thought they were supposed to keep us pilots together until someone solved this "crisis," but the damn fools split us up. Is that what they called it for you, a crisis?"

"No," said Leon, "They've been calling it a skirmish up until yesterday. Now it's a war."

"Well if it's war for you, it's a war for me too, I guess. Corrupted system is what it is, comrade," said Alexander taking a sip from a hot beverage. "Ever notice how new technology only seems to come around in a crisis? Oil crisis lead to Ogelan, and Space crisis led to better lasers. You know, comrade, I found an old Soviet history book which said lasers have been used in warfare here on Earth since the early twenty first century. How could we have not perfected lasers in all that time?"

"You believe those old history books? They said people back then had little regulation on what they published."

"Let me ask you this, comrade, who are they?"

"What?"

"You said, '*They* said people back then had little regulation'. Well, who are *they*, and why do they get to tell you what people back then were like? I'll tell you right now that people don't change, just the environment around them does. People are still animals and an animal only tries to do two things in life: Not die, and pass on his genes. Those are the only reasons we're here, comrade."

"Don't get philosophical on me now, Alexander. Let's just get back to discussing this war."

"Ah yes, comrade. Where was I? Oh, yes, that's right, the fools split us up. Some pilots were on the moon, some came here, and some went to other places. We were lucky not to be attacked by any alien soldiers, but that could change sooner than you might think."

"Why is that?" asked Leon.

"Ever since we sent out the message for anyone fighting against them to come here, comrades from all the sectors have been arriving. I am sure the enemy will follow some of them. You can't have a migration of caribous that big without the snow leopard following them to snap up a tasty straggler."

Leon nodded in agreement with Alexander. Alexander stood up and left with a group of people then, as if he was never talking to Leon. Leon did not know where they were going, but he wasn't interested in finding out either. He was more concerned with sleeping.

Suddenly, a thought struck Leon, if everyone was gathering into this one base, then one huge bomb could kill everyone and end the entire resistance. Leon didn't bother to tell anyone this thought, he wouldn't know who to tell anyway.

Then the same woman who gave Leon his food came to Leon with a small piece of paper. Leon read it. All it said was, "Room number: 34,566". Leon flipped it around, but nothing was on the back. Leon saw a group of people walking toward a door off in the distance. He decided to follow them; he figured that they must be going somewhere quieter than this cafeteria. He needed quiet to sleep.

The door led to a maze of hallways, stairways, and more doors. All the doors had numbers on them. The one Leon read said, "One". Leon looked back at his card: 34,566. Leon started walking down the stairs. When he got to the next floor down, he read the number on the door, "One-thousand". Leon figured that each floor must have one-thousand doors—it was a very large building. Leon was about to start walking down the next flight of stairs, when he heard a bell ring in the distance. He looked over and saw an elevator open and some people get off. Leon caught part of their conversation as they walked by.

"Do you think they'll attack tomorrow?"

"I don't think, I know! If you look into the sky at night, you can see some of their smaller ships buzzing around, they're scouting us out."

"Possibly, but—." The two men stopped their conversation as they walked past Leon. Leon wasn't sure why they stopped, but right now, he was more concerned with getting onto the elevator. He was able to make it on before the door closed and then he plugged in his floor number, thirty-four. It was amazing to Leon that they could make a building this far underground. When Leon got to his room, he found there was already someone in it.

"Are you my bunk-mate?" asked the man in the room.

"I guess I am," said Leon double-checking the number on his card.

"Well don't just stand out there, come in, make yourself comfortable. Well, as comfortable as you can get anyway. The room isn't quite big enough to hold two people, and we might have one more person coming. It depends. If we're lucky, it will only be the two of us."

Leon sat down on the side of the bed and took his boots off. He didn't know whether to go to sleep yet. The man was just walking around the room, almost as if he was trying to keep himself awake. Leon had a chilling thought that the man, for some reason, wanted him to fall asleep first.

"Aren't you tired," asked Leon.

"I can't get to sleep. I'm almost positive that we'll go to battle tomorrow."

"Why is that?" asked Leon.

"There are rumors going around that the Ginyu Guards, the ones that were supposed to be holding our base at the moon, are losing control. They've been under attack ever since they went there. So, now, all the pilots might have to go up there; and if they can't get the situation under control..." his voice trailed off.

"Has anyone actually confirmed these rumors?" asked Leon.

"Not as of yet, but I'm sure they will soon. After a pause he added, "You're a pilot, aren't you."

"Yes I am," said Leon.

"I could tell by your suit. You might get sent up there soon, so I suggest you rest up now." Leon took his advice and went to sleep, wondering if he would have to go to battle. Just before he drifted into sub-consciousness, he reflected on a thought he'd had earlier, and he decided that if a bomb were dropped onto this base and killed every human able to fight, the resistance wouldn't die because the resistance was a thought, not a group of people. He would never know that those were the last words of Harem before he died back in Leon's home.

CHAPTER SIXTEEN

Leon woke up early the next morning when he heard noises. The noises were everyone walking out in the hallways toward the cafeteria, talking and laughing. Leon noticed his bunkmate was gone. Leon realized that he must have left to eat breakfast and decided to get some as well.

He put his boots back on and headed for the elevator. He had to jam into the elevator with a bunch of people who were mostly soldiers from the looks of it. Leon made it to the top floor and sat down in the same seat he ate at last night.

As soon as he sat down a lady brought out Leon's breakfast which consisted of eggs, sausage, and a biscuit, plus water to drink. Leon just finished his biscuit when Alexander sat down next to him.

"Looks like we'll have to do a little check-up on the moon, huh comrade?"

"That's what I've been hearing," said Leon.

Leon took a sip of his water. A lady brought out Alexander's plate of food; its contents were identical to Leon's.

"When do you think they'll send us out?" asked Leon.

"As soon as breakfast is over," said Alexander. Then, almost as an afterthought, he added, "So eat slowly, comrade."

Leon finished his food and looked up to see that some people were still eating. He then headed back down the elevator to his room. Once there, Leon took the aliens out of his sack and began talking with them.

"Do you guys know what has happened to the others we left behind?" asked Leon.

"Yes, we do," said one of the aliens telepathically. "They walked for a little while before stumbling upon an airport that was making one last flight out before it shut down for good. All the air bases are shutting down as they hear about the invasion. Their plane landed a few hundred miles west of here and currently they are on another plane headed to this location."

"And what of the invading aliens?"

"They have stopped marching and returned to space. We think Sudokus wants them to lay low now that our troops are growing in strength in numbers. He probably feels that a battle now would be too indecisive. He'll probably want to learn more about how we fight before engaging us in an all-out war. So the aliens have all headed back to the command ship to wait until they receive further instructions. Hopefully they won't return any time soon."

"And who exactly is Sudokus?"

"You are not aware yet? Some people around you know. Even your Captain, William, knows. Surely William has told you."

"Willy? No, he doesn't know any more than I do. No one on our planet knows anything about what's going on."

"No, people do know, but only a few people we suppose. This makes things more complicated than we originally predicted. We should start from the beginning of the story.

"Sudokus is not an alien. He is instead a robot made by some life form that lived and died long ago. Unfortunately, whoever this life form was had technology beyond his times. Some would theorize time travel was involved in the creation of Sudokus, others are not so sure. But this is beside the point. The technology in question is not a solid, a liquid or gas, but it is instead energy. Energy is not the right word, but that is the only way to describe it so it makes any sense for you. It was not really energy, but assume it is for a moment. This energy went into Sudokus's programming and became his mind and Sudokus learned how to learn. Now Sudokus is an immortal being with his library of knowledge constantly expanding. But something went wrong, and suddenly Sudokus decided that he needed to conquer lands. You could view it as imperialism, which we believe was a practice here on Earth only a few centuries ago. Sudokus took our planet, he took all of the other planets in this system, and his army is constantly growing. Now he wants this planet—but we cannot allow that to happen."

Leon would have liked to continue the conversation with the tiny aliens, but an alarm sounded, and a loud voice commanded all pilots to the hangar. The aliens hopped back into their ship and Leon shoved them into his sack. Leon rushed to the elevator before a huge crowd arrived. Once he was at the top floor, Leon ran over to the hangar. The hangar was huge, bigger than any he'd ever seen before. There were a lot of planes as well, and Leon wasn't sure which one was his because aviation mechanics serving as valets had brought all the planes into the hanger. Then Leon felt someone tap him on the shoulder from behind. He turned around to see Scott standing behind him.

"I know where your ship is, Leon," he said with urgency. "Follow me."

Leon followed Scott through crowds of people who were all looking for their ships. Scott opened the door to one of the ships and climbed in, cramming himself into the back. Leon followed him in, started up the engine, and took off.

"When did you get to Russia?" Leon asked Scott.

"I flew in with all of the other troops just a few minutes ago. I found you because I wanted to make sure you had someone to help you out in case you got in trouble. I heard that you've been having problems with crash landing lately."

"You could say that," replied Leon with a smirk.

It looked like it was going to be another space battle when Leon broke through the clouds and got into space. He slowed down enough to see what was going on. There were hundreds of little ships buzzing around and firing lasers toward the moon. The Ginyu guards who were there were helpless because they were only trained in crime enforcement. They could break up a riot, even apprehend the occasional run away spacecraft, but this was a bit overwhelming.

Leon and the other pilots were receiving instructions, "To hold fire" through the radios on their ships. So Leon waited patiently in the cockpit.

"If things work out," said Scott, "You won't have to fly in this ship anymore. I'm working on a prototype for a new ship, one that would be faster than this one and have more effective artillery. Maybe even something better than the—," Scott was suddenly cut off when an announcement came through the radio for all the pilots to, "Fire at will".

Leon didn't have to be hear that twice. He accelerated his ship and started firing upon all the ships buzzing around. He saw all the other ally ships doing the same. The enemy ships gradually turned their attention from the moon, to their attackers.

The battle was a draw for a long time, even though the humans greatly outnumbered the aliens. Leon was doing his best to avoid enemy fire, but lasers were flying everywhere.

"Get out of this spot," said Scott, "There are too many stray shots flying around. I think I see a better spot just a bit lower down."

"We all have a role to play and I'm just doing what I have to. Besides, I can avoid getting hit, just don't distract me."

Leon felt the ship shake as a shot glanced off it. He locked onto an alien ship when he regained control, and shot it down. Another shot glanced off Leon's ship and he was finding it increasingly harder to steer now.

"What's going on Scott? I'm having trouble steering."

"We got hit on the wing; the ships unbalanced. You'll have to make an emergency landing." Leon turned his ship back toward Earth. "No, don't head back to Earth, you'll never make it. Land on the moon and I'll fix the problem."

Leon was lucky nothing hit him as he headed toward the moon. He got out of his ship and immediately some Ginyu Guards ushered him into a bunker. Scott stayed behind to work on the ship. Leon noticed other pilots were also waiting in the bunker while mechanics repaired their ships.

Normally, Leon didn't like Ginyu Guards. But the Ginyu Guards seemed to have a respect for Leon now, and Leon in turn respected them for that. Leon wondered if they viewed him differently because he was a soldier now.

"How goes the battle, soldier?" asked one of the Ginyu Guards.

"It seems like it's at a standstill," responded Leon, "But considering that we outnumber them, it is as if they are winning."

"Point taken, sir. Is there anything my men could do to assist this battle?"

"It takes a lot of fire power to take down those ships. Do you have anything?"

"Our engineers are working on turret guns that would be able to take care of these ships, but they aren't finished as of yet. It's more of a remodeling of the defense grid we had, except this one would be more powerful."

"I know a very talented engineer named Scott. He could probably work on them. Scott has proved to be the best engineer and mechanic that I've ever seen. In fact, he's working on repairing my ship as we speak."

"Is that so? Well maybe we will have him help us out after this battle is over."

"I think Scott will be a very busy man after this battle is over," said Leon. After a pause he continued, "Everyone is going to want his help, but I don't know if he'll have time to do any extra work."

The conversation ended when the bunker trembled slightly. Leon stumbled and fought to keep from losing his balance. The Ginyu Guard next to him seemed more stable on his feet and hardly stumbled at all as the shaking stopped and started irregularly.

Scott came running into the bunker toward Leon. Leon noticed he had his arm above his head to protect himself, but it was just instinct, Scott's arm would do nothing if the roof collapsed.

"The ship wasn't in too bad of shape, I got it back working again," said Scott.

"Great, let's go then." With that, Leon and Scott went running toward the ship. Laser beams were pounding the ground around them, but nothing scathed them as they got into the ship.

Leon got right into the battle, although now it seemed that the humans were at a slight disadvantage. However, Leon was determined to change that. He began shooting at all the enemy ships that he could see, and he was taking down a lot more than he expected.

For a moment, Leon thought he had single handedly changed the tide of the battle because now the ally ships outnumbered the enemy ships once again on his radar. Then Leon realized what was really happening. The aliens were slowly retreating, just like last time.

Neither Leon, nor any other human, knew why the aliens were retreating. They would never even know the real reason why the aliens started this particular battle. It was actually very simple why the aliens did what they did; it was to keep Sudokus safe. At the very beginning of the battle, three rather large ships flew just outside of the spray of laser beams. Each one was carrying a ruler from a different part of the solar system. They were rulers appointed by Sudokus to do his bidding, similar to what ancient Assyrians had done all those millennium ago. The battle was an orchestrated distraction so no one noticed those three ships as they travelled to their destination. Now they were out of harm's way and, having completed their mission, the aliens retreated back to where they came from.

CHAPTER SEVENTEEN

Sudokus waited until all his appointed provincial leaders arrived at his home on Jupiter, and then briefed them about his new plans for the solar system. He gave them a quick run-down on what they could expect him to say in the speech he was about to deliver. He had the leaders join him out on the balcony for effect. He noticed his people seemed to like it when he was with other powerful people, although the provincial leaders really had no power.

Gathered below him were hundreds of thousands of people, all eagerly anticipating his speech. He clutched the guardrail with his crab claw-like hands. He could have cut through it like a hot knife through warm butter; but Sudokus had enough dexterity not to do so. He just gently held onto it as he leaned over to get a view at his people below. They all cheered at the sight of Sudokus as their training told them to do. His muddy brown metal was extra shiny for this event. His red eye stared at everyone at the same time.

"My people," began Sudokus. "You have been in this conquest for the past one-hundred years—since the bombing of Neptune, all the way to the massacres at Venus. But now your patience has paid off. We only need one more planet under our rule to have dominion over this solar system. This solar system we call home." Sudokus paused for a moment. This served as the transition into the next part of his speech.

"As you know, we are setting our sights on Earthlings now. This task does not appear to be a difficult one, but now is not the time to let-up. Now is the time to give our best effort and for you to give your strongest support. You have been supporting this war since day one, and you've had every reason to. No battle has ever been lost." Sudokus knew that was a lie, and maybe some of the people who cheered below knew it was a lie too, but they had to accept whatever he said, or risk being hunted down by secret police. Everyone, at least subconsciously, feared the day when a group of heavily armed and armored alien police would barge into their house in the middle of the night and take them away forever.

"We know all about humans' tendencies and all of their weaknesses after observing them for thousands of years. We can, and will, crush them. Most of you have even been watching your monitors to see as our powerful troops tear apart battalions as if they were wet paper. You have cheered as you see our war hardened troops return home after each conquest, and you have mourned when you know one of the troops is missing in action. However, you also know there is no reason to mourn, for our troops are expendable. When's the last time we used a naturally born troop to fight? Never since I've been around. Gene splicing and cloning are terms familiar to all of you, and most of you might even have children created like that, but these creatures are not like us. We *make* soldiers and when their metabolic actions cease, they are still soldiers. That's why when all this fighting is over, there will be a time of peace the likes of which no one has ever seen.

"Peace is only one word, my friends, but it carries so much weight. Because when we have peace, there will be no more uncertainty. No uncertainty means everyone from the slaves to your provincial leaders will know their proper place in society." From birth, society told the aliens, like the ones below Sudokus now, that the slaves were somehow less alive than they were, and the slaves' lives had no meaning, so they didn't care how the slaves were treated. Sudokus continued, "It will be a golden age. There will be political stability, a flourishing economy, and peace. Our slaves will be able to double their output during this golden age, and this is good news for everyone. The quality of life will double, while the cost-of-living will be cut in half. Then, when this solar system has established itself as the most dominant in the galaxy, we will move on to the next solar system. Then we'll control that one and move on to the next, and the next and so on. When we have taken control of all the solar systems in this galaxy, we will have accomplished something no one else has done. We will have a monopoly on an entire galaxy, on the Milky Way galaxy. Monopolies mean money, and that's all anybody really wants. Not because they want something with monetary value, but because money equals power. All you who stand below me now love money, do you not? So why not be happy now, for when we take control of Earth, we will be the ultimate power in the galaxy. Of course there will be armies who oppose us, but no one can stop us. No one will stop us, because we are leading the way in a new style of warfare. Look around your towns and what do you see? E-posters (electronic posters) of the new soldier. A soldier even more disciplined than our current warriors—a soldier whose very skin is bulletproof and whose heart is an energy consuming engine. A living creature has its limits at some point, but a machine can do anything. I see the future, and in it, are machines tending to your every need, and protecting you from those people who do not yet understand. Imagine when machines raise children, and all information pumps into your mind by machine. Will that not be a glorious time?"

Every one cheered in agreement and Sudokus had to wait almost a full minute before it died back down. Sudokus knew not everyone agreed with his vision for the future, but those individuals had a way of disappearing from society. Then, only the ones who shared his ideals would raise children. They of course would teach their children their same ideals, which were ultimately Sudokus's. In this way, artificial selection occurred, and only the ones most like Sudokus survived—and no one could really complain about the system. The people who complained and called it corrupt surreptitiously died, and there were less of those people with every passing generation. Yet, even Sudokus thought the system was corrupted, but greed and corruption stimulated his satisfaction receptors, so doing it made him want to do it more. The people meant nothing to the society; they were just the ones who held money in their bank accounts until Sudokus needed it, and that's what this speech was really for: money.

"But nothing is free, however. As I look down at the generous people below me, I feel that I must once more ask you to reach into your pockets to fund this war. Every day, new weapons are imported, and every day, you people help pay for them. Now, you will get a return on your investments. As soon we take over Earth, money will flow back to the people.

"I leave you with this last thought; our brave soldiers are fighting as we speak, to keep you all safe. So if you don't want to support these wars for me, support these wars for your soldiers and support these wars for all the generations which come after you."

With that, Sudokus unclenched the guardrail and walked back into the building with the rest of the provincial leaders. He could hear the people chanting and cheering as he walked away and couldn't help but think of how stupid they were. They were stupid for believing whatever he said, and they were stupid for becoming brainwashed into worshipping him. They were even less important than the slaves were; they just didn't have to do as much grueling labor.

Sudokus flipped on a monitor. It was a simple monitor, but it was efficient to use, and efficiency satisfied Sudokus. He observed the monitor with all the provincial leaders in the room and they observed the slaves of Neptune as they worked in their fields. They harvested materials in front of a factory that had two pillars billowing out blue smoke.

"Now for the real reason I called you over here," said Sudokus to the men in the room. The slaves will never revolt, correct?" Everyone nodded and agreed. "But do you know why?" Sudokus paused and there was silence as they tried to figure out what Sudokus was getting at. "It is said that you can have power over a person until you take everything away from that person. I make sure to leave them with something. They have each other. If they misbehaved, they *think* slave owners and plantation workers would separate them from their friends and families and send them to another galaxy. It is easy enough to export a slave. But that's why they don't revolt, because they fear separation. If you actually separate them though, they have no reason to work. So why am I hearing reports that some of you are allowing the separation of slaves on your home planets? I could have each one of you killed at any time if I wanted to, don't think you're important or have any power. I gave you specific instructions not to separate any slaves. So the next time I hear one of you is going against something I said—well Jum-Jum is never too far away. Now get out of my sight, all of you. And I hope you paid attention to my speech, it wasn't *all* lies."

It was true that the slaves didn't really know they had horrible lives. Each farm had a slave guard and, although it wasn't Sudokus's idea, when they got bored they told stories of people whose lives were worse than the slaves' were. Of course, these stories were not true, but the slaves believed the stories. This further convinced the slaves that they weren't in that bad of a situation. Some slaves even considered themselves lucky—they were confused fools.

By some accounts, they were lucky though. They were the result of an experiment gone terribly wrong. One of the aliens visited Earth and brought back a single mosquito during the exploration days. Scientists then cloned that mosquito several times. Then the scientists experimented on those mosquitoes until they determined that it would be beneficial to splice the genes of the mosquitoes, with the genes of a race of alien on the planet Saturn. The first experiment went horribly wrong. The aliens came out as the hideous, flightless creatures, now known as the slaves. The next experiment was perfect however. When the door to the gene-splicing chamber opened, perfectly built specimens came out. Those now served as the soldiers in Sudokus's army. Their only downfall was that insect repellent could kill them; but Sudokus was unaware of that.

Sudokus walked to the back of the building and looked out of a window. He saw the slaves working in the field. He thought about how ugly they looked. They were a dark brown color. They had three legs, with no arms. They had wings, yet they couldn't fly more than ten feet at a time. It was more of a long jump than a fly, anyway. They had three eyes, attached to stalks, and the pupils were all different colors. They had a ring of pink fur where their legs met their stocky, dome shaped bodies. They had pink fur around their ankles too. The claws on their feet were yellow—a repulsive shade of yellow that suggested some sort of fungus. Sudokus knew that he was right in making them slaves. They were too hideous for the public to see.

Sudokus sat back down to think about how exactly to handle the turmoil that would soon come. Unlike what he'd said in his speech, he didn't think that he could easily crush Earth. In fact, Sudokus prepared himself for the worst. Nevertheless, he already knew exactly how this conquest would end. There would be a fight to the death with someone. He was not sure whom he would need to fight with, but something was telling him that he would have to fight someone in the near future. He could see it happening in his eye. However, Sudokus was confident that he would win the fight. No human could challenge him. It would take no effort at all for him to snap the neck of any human who tried to duel with him. Sudokus stopped thinking about the fight then, he knew it wouldn't happen any time soon.

CHAPTER EIGHTEEN

Back on Earth, Cpt. John was trying his best to create confusion surrounding the war. He worked with the other three leaders of the world to convince every country (the plan was too complex simply to work with quadrants, they had to revert to archaic references of countries) that they were fighting against another country. He told the Americans that they were fighting the Chinese. He told the Chinese they were fighting with the Brazilians. He told the Brazilians they were fighting with the Russians, and did the same for as many countries around the world as he could. Surprisingly, this plan worked and though people were a bit confused by the fact that there was still a war after "The final war," it was better than telling them whom they were actually fighting.

The second thing John did was to deny the existence of extraterrestrials. The government and the different world leaders had always been doing this, but never while in the middle of a war with them. Belief in aliens was steadily rising however, in spite of John's best efforts. However, due to John's assertiveness during these turbulent times, he was beginning to gain power internationally, for better or for worse.

John also knew he had to make certain that the soldiers were isolated from the general population, or it would become known who they were fighting. So their return after their staged battle—in which the provincial leaders slipped past them—was under heavy surveillance. However, the soldiers didn't know they were being isolated yet, and there were subdued celebrations as people talked about their victory-by-default. However, Leon was too tired to do anything but rest.

Willy was also not celebrating. Willy, in fact, was ill tempered when the pilots arrived back to Earth. It didn't take long before someone filled him in on what happened during the battle. He decided to address all of his men at the same time. Willy ordered all the pilots who fought in that battle into the cafeteria, and then talked to them.

"I am not satisfied. In fact, I am just short of being disappointed. We had more men than they had, yet we only won because they retreated. Why?" He paused, but no one spoke. "We should have killed all of them. Now, we will have to fight them again. It may be tomorrow, next week, or next month, but we will have to fight them again, you can count on that. If that's the best you can do, it may not be a long war. Now I suggest you all start taking more pride in your performance and stop letting these animals step all over you. You've grown up your whole life hearing that you are the dominant species and top of the food chain; now start acting like it, because right now, there's another species trying to outdo us. They have some advanced technology, but they don't have anything that we shouldn't be able to handle. If we have more people than them, and everyone takes down one ship, we'll win. Especially if there's no command ship like there wasn't in that last battle. Now, the reason we all came to this Russian base is not because we enjoy the frigid temperature; the reason is because it's isolated and won't draw any attention from the aliens. With that said, if you want to keep dragging this war out, we'll have to move even further north, into the tundra. So I suggest you all get your acts together," exclaimed Willy gazing over everyone in the group, "And stop treating this like boot camp. Boot camp was easy: this is real life. You're all dismissed to your rooms until further announcements."

Everyone went to their rooms to sleep except Scott. Then again, Scott wasn't a pilot, so he didn't have to listen to Willy. Scott stayed up, wanting to make a better aircraft for battle.

He worked through the night, piecing together parts until he had a prototype ready. He didn't finish until just after the sun had risen the next morning, but when he stepped back and looked at it, he knew it was done. He was about to look for Leon, when Leon came into the room.

"Leon," said Scott, "I was just about to look for you."

"That's funny," replied Leon, "I was looking for you too. Well, what did you want to say to me?"

"Mine can wait, what did you want to tell me?"

"I just wanted to ask you if you're still my personal engineer, you know, since this got changed from a skirmish to a war."

"Why wouldn't I be? I'll keep working for you unless they say something about it."

"That's good. I was telling this Ginyu guard that you might be able to help him with their new defense grid, but then I told him you were going to be busy."

"You're right I'm busy, I just finished a prototype for another new ship."

"You work fast. How do you build all these ships so quickly?" asked Leon.

"I'll show you. Follow me."

Scott ushered Leon to a big door in the back of the room. For the first time, Leon saw what a professional engineer's workshop looked like. There were gizmos, gadgets, and tools everywhere. Leon recognized some of the equipment just from working around aircraft so much.

There was one thing that Leon didn't recognize, however. It was a big machine, right at the center of the room. It was twice as tall as Leon and ten feet wide. It was in the shape of a cylinder. Leon walked around to the other side of it. There was what looked like a handgun—something like a pistol—

mounted and welded onto this side. It pointed down onto a slightly elevated platform protruding from the object.

"This is how I'm able to make these ships so quickly," said Scott.

"But, what is it?" asked Leon.

"I bought this a few years ago; I can't remember what it's called, but it can make parts. Here's how it works; you draw a picture of what you want it to make on a piece of this special paper," Scott pulled out a stack of papers. They looked like ordinary sheets of graph paper, except that they were shinier. Scott drew a simple cube on the paper and then showed it to Leon.

"Now, you stick the paper into this slot, and the machine will convert any energy around it into that shape. But don't worry; it only takes the energy of the non-living and inorganic material." There was a revving up noise, and then the room got cold.

"Did it just take out all of the heat energy from the room," asked Leon.

"Not all of it. It also took some sound and light energy. But here's the best part."

Scott pointed toward the thing that looked like a pistol as it lit up, turning a bright white, and then it shot out a beam of energy, too bright for Leon to look at. The whole room lit up for a second, and then it went back to normal, except it was still a bit cold. The heating system kicked on a few moments later and the room soon warmed up again.

"Voila," said Scott. He picked up the cube and tossed it to Leon. Leon caught it and began examining it. It felt metallic; it was definitely solid anyway. "Then all I need to do is make all the other parts that I want, and then I can connect them to build the ship."

"What if you need a big part?" asked Leon.

"You can program a scale on the machine. If I were to put that same drawing into the machine and set it on a double size scale, it would be twice as big. But enough of this, I still have to show you the ship."

Leon followed Scott as they headed back into the other room and inspected the ship. It was similar to the other ships he'd flown, at least on the outside. It was the standard green with orange strip. It was sleek and stealthy looking. The window was tinted grey.

Scott opened up the door to the ship and showed Leon the inside. This was the first ship Leon had seen that had two seats. Although the ship wasn't really any bigger than any other ship, and the second seat seemed more like an afterthought as it was wedged in behind the front seat. The control panel was easy enough to read, it looked just like any other that Leon had seen. Leon noticed that there was a display panel for a map on this ship. Most ships he'd used only had one in the helmet. He thought that could be useful—or it might become a distraction. He heard there was a reason ships switched the maps into the visor of the helmet.

"So, what's so good about this one?" asked Leon.

"Everything. Faster speeds, more damaging lasers, harder to be detected by enemy radar, and my favorite feature, the buddy seat. You know I'm not letting you fly alone anymore since you had to crash land last battle. How many times is that now?"

"Three, but it will never happen again."

Leon closed the door to the ship and inspected the outside one more time, nodding his head in approval. It was time for dinner, and Leon learned from boot camp that bad things happen to those who are late for dinner, so he figured he could test the ship in flight at some other time.

So Leon headed to the cafeteria where he met up with Alexander. The same older woman who always brought out his food arrived with some meat that Leon didn't recognize.

"That's Bear, meat," said Alexander noticing Leon staring at it. "They say it's good for you. But you can never believe what they tell you, comrade. It doesn't matter; I think that it tastes good, that's enough for me."

Leon took a bite, he couldn't agree with Alexander that it tasted good, but maybe his culture made his taste buds more spoiled than Alexander's were.

"Why do you think those aliens retreated yesterday?" asked Leon.

"They were probably frightened. For good cause too, comrade, I was ready to shoot down one, then it flew away, like a tiny insect just before you try to squash it. Although I have to say, Captain Willy was right. I know we outnumbered those things, so if we all just shot down one, we'd win. It seems some of our fellow pilots didn't learn much in the pilot camp, eh comrade?"

"I didn't actually get any training, and neither did any of the pilots who've been with me," said Leon in between bites of food. "We got training in ground war, but the training was cut short due to 'skirmishes'."

"Well that's the problem. How can they send out a comrade without training him? A team is only as strong as its weakest player. We'd almost be better off leaving the less capable ones behind, comrade."

Leon nodded his head and finished the rest of his meal in silence. He enjoyed talking to Alexander, but at this point, he'd rather let the aliens win than hear "comrade" one more time.

When Leon finished his meal, he headed off to the elevator alone. When he got to the door of his room, he saw a note that read, "Due to battle injuries, you will be without a bunk mate for a few days."

Leon pondered what "battle injuries" meant. His bunkmate could be dead for all he knew. He opened up the door and walked in. He took his boots off and slipped out of his flying suit for the first time since he arrived in Russia. He slipped into a pair of pajamas that were hanging on a hook on the closet door. They weren't really pajamas, more like casual wear, but they served the same purpose.

Leon was tired, but he couldn't go to sleep. He was nervous about the next battle. How often could he keep having lasers glance off his ship before one eventually destroyed him? He decided to go look for Willy just so he could talk to him and clear his mind.

Leon left his room and went back into the now deserted cafeteria. He was hoping Willy might've still been eating in there. Leon was about to head back to his room when he heard a voice.

"Can I help you?" Leon spun around to see a janitor standing behind him holding a mop. He was an older man, who seemed not only worn down from the stresses the war seemed to be placing on everyone, but from life in general as well.

"Possibly," said Leon. "Do you know where Captain Willy is? He was the one who called all the pilots into the cafeteria earlier."

"Sorry, I'm just the janitor." He started walking away, but then he suddenly stopped, turned back around and said, "I can only suggest that you look in room number one-hundred."

Leon went over to the elevator. He hit the button to the first floor. The door opened up and Leon made the long walk to room number one-hundred.

Leon heard voices in the room talking, but he couldn't understand what they were saying, nor did he care. Leon knocked on the door and the talking instantly stopped, as if they didn't want anyone hearing it. At first, no one came to the door, so Leon knocked again. Then he heard footsteps and finally the doorknob turned and a man opened it up slightly to look out at Leon.

"What do you want," snarled the man at the door.

"Is Willy in there?" asked Leon trying to see past the man into the room.

The man looked back over his shoulder. Then he looked back at Leon and said, "He's in here, what do you need him for?"

"I need to talk to him, privately."

"He will be out shortly," said the man. Then the man closed the door and the talking started back up. Leon patiently waited for a few minutes. Willy didn't come out. He waited a few more minutes; Willy still didn't come out. Then, after forty minutes of waiting, the doorknob turned and Willy stepped out.

"What do you want, Leon?"

"What took you so long? I've been out here forty minutes."

"Sorry, but you caught me at a bad time," said Willy, "Now what do you want?"

"I think we need training for all the pilots?"

"That's what you wanted to tell me? Training would just be a simulated version of what you already do."

"I know, but I figure that if some of our men can't even take out one ship, then further training is required."

"I can't help you with that. We don't have time to train during a war. But as long as I'm out here, there's some stuff I've neglected to tell you."

"Like what?"

"It's a long story, why don't you come with me to the lounge."

"There's a lounge in here?"

"This floor has everything, just follow me."

Leon followed Willy to a door that read, "Private lounge". Willy pulled out a key card and opened the door.

"Take a seat, Leon," said Willy as he sat down on one of the couches. "I meant to tell you something a while ago, back when you showed me those three tiny aliens. I wanted to tell you everything I knew, but I couldn't, and I still can't. But I don't care what happens to me, I have to tell you now." Willy stood up and made sure the door was locked. Satisfied that it was, he sat back down. "Like all stories, this one starts a while ago. It started when I was about thirteen years old, many years before you were even born. I was one of the foot soldiers in World War Four. The greatest war of all time," he added with a look of nostalgia. "The war that divided the world into four. I should probably fill you in on this war, seeing as they pretty well erased it from the record books—at least all the good information anyway.

"There was a lot of tension after World War three. The Russians were upset that all of their nuclear arms stored away in Somalia had been taken away by the Americans. They didn't believe the American's claim that they had destroyed all the weapons. They feared the Americans were just building up their own arsenal. So the Russians announced that they had a new type of weapon even more powerful than any ever used before. They said they had a tower somewhere that could shoot out bolts of lightning. They never gave an exact range for how far it could shoot, or its exact coordinates, but they claimed that if there were any foreign satellites flying over their country, they could shoot them down.

"Of course, no one ever knew if this weapon was real or not, but it frightened many people. So there was a war. It should have only been between the United States and Russia, but then their allies became involved, and to make it even worse, the Russians went on to say they didn't even station this tower in their country, but rather in the heart of Africa. That's how I got involved. The United States ruthlessly invaded many African countries until we finally declared war on them and in doing so, declared war on their allies. We never really knew who we'd battle with from day to day, but there was always a battle waiting for us. We even had to fight the Russians at some point.

"My officers awarded me many medals for my efforts. I don't have them anymore; they took them away a few years ago in their efforts to erase this war from the record books. My most prestigious medal came from when I was a prisoner of war. I was able to escape by stabbing one of the guards in the neck with a stick I found and sharpened. I took his gun and shot everyone without mercy. I survived for a week off of the different berry bushes around the camp. Eventually, a battalion from the North American alliance—NAA as they called them back then—found me and took me back to an army base in America. There, I started to get recognition for my different actions beyond simple medals. I moved my way up the ranks until I headed my own battalion of foot soldiers. We won many battles; we were one of the most successful in the entire war. Although, thinking back on it, I don't know who I was fighting for then. I started fighting for Uganda, and I ended up fighting for NAA.

"After the war, they called me down to a meeting with a bunch of other army commanders. The man running the meeting had been the African leader who helped to end the war. He handed us all badges that said what branch of the army we would control if another war ever arose. We were the best and most successful; therefore, we would lead once again if the situation called for it. We knew we would never fight against each other again, but if a rebellion ever sprung up, we would've used a huge army, just a little bit smaller than the one we have right now, to smother it. The name of the army was, strangely enough, WAR. It stood for World Army Reserves. They should've changed the name since it wasn't just the army; it was also the navy and air force. That's what my badge says, "Primary air force commander of WAR". We never imagined that we would use our badges to determine what branch of the army we would control against an alien army."

"But, how did the war end?" asked Leon.

"There were overt threats to detonate anti-matter bombs. I'm sure you know that anti-matter will destroy all matter that it comes in contact with; it makes a violent explosion too. It didn't take long before people realized this war had to be resolved before that happened. The leader from the Democratic Republic of the Congo, the one I mentioned earlier, had come up with a treaty. Since Africa is in almost every quadrant of the Earth, he decided not to pick sides when creating the terms.

"The treaty he made was risky at the time. He proposed that we should divide all the resources of the world equally among the quadrants of the Earth. Normally, no one would have accepted this treaty, but with the threat of an anti-matter bomb looming, we all quickly signed the treaty. A council of people at the conference then appointed leaders to each quadrant. This officially established the four super powers that we have today. Other than the unexpected death of Winston, everything is the same as it was when the war ended thirty years ago."

"If all the resources of the world were divided up equally, why are resources so scarce?"

"That brings me to the next bit of information. I can't accurately speak on everything, seeing as I myself am not part of the group who knows exactly what's going on, but I know enough to teach you a few things.

"The year was 2662. That was the first year that a human being carried on a conversation with a being from another planet. I'm sure someone had made contact beforehand, but this was the first time an actual conversation took place. The communication lasted many months, as both sides had to find a way to overcome the language barrier, and it was an arduous challenge for both parties. However, we were able to use visuals to associate with words—almost like a primitive form of sign language—and from there deciphered a basic understanding of the language. Since I was in the World Army Reserves, I got to hear that conversation. It started like any normal conversation, with the two greeting each other and introducing themselves, and then they began talking about other things. They talked about what they looked like—because this conversation was purely audio—they talked about what they ate, and they talked about the populations of their planets. Then they talked about trading, and over the next few weeks, we imported things from his planet, and exported from ours. I was never able to see the transactions take place, but I heard there were big ships that would drop down in the most unpopulated places, and some aliens would walk out and then the exchanges would occur.

"Then the alien talked about a robot named Sudokus. But I'm sure you've heard about him by now."

"Yeah, those little aliens told me about him."

"And that's what this war is really about. *They*— whoever it is who knows all of this stuff—knew the aliens would attack us. Unfortunately, I've been out of the loop for some time now, I don't know what's really going on anymore. All I know is that somewhere out there, there are some friendly life forms left. You might know the only three for all I know. So make sure you keep those guys with you at all times. Those are direct orders from the Captain."

"I have one more question, Willy."

"Make it quick, because I have to get back to my meeting before they come looking for me."

"You said you were an air force commander for the World Army Reserves, but how did they get an army of ground soldiers to do the fighting?" asked Leon.

"Each commander had the responsibility of getting his own troops any way possible with as little help as possible," said Willy. "I got my pilots the same way I got you. I probably should have done my recruiting sooner, and that way I could've trained you. I guess that's how I could've answered your first question. I can't train you guys, because I waited until a war was imminent to recruit you."

"Well I guess that was just a really long answer then."

"I have to get going now; head back to your room immediately."

"Actually, I think this couch is more comfortable than my bed. I'm going to sleep here tonight."

"They're going to kick you out if they catch you, but go ahead." Willy headed toward the door but didn't open it. "There is one more thing I should tell you, Leon," said Willy. "There is still a lot of corruption in the air. I would be very careful if I were you." Then, Willy left.

Leon considered following him to ask who he thought was corrupt, but something told him Willy didn't even know exactly what he meant. It was just one of those feelings.

Leon found a television chip sitting on the table and slipped it over his eye. Far from the quad-dimensional television, this was just a small chip that slid over your eye about an inch away from the cornea and projected images to you. It projected a show called the final frontier on some sort of science channel. It was about different theories on the universe. This particular episode was about parallel dimensions. Leon turned the volume up by simply willing it with his mind.

"We have determined, many years ago, that this universe is expanding," the show began. "If it's expanding, that must mean that it has outer limits. If something is infinite, it can't increase. Only finite things can increase. So what would happen if we left those outer limits?

"Scientists are revising the old theories that other universes lie outside of our own. They now say these universes are touching ours, but don't overlap. If they ever did overlap, some astronomers predict that both universes would destroy each other. They feel this way, because energy can neither be created nor destroyed, all the energy that we have right now, has always existed. If the universes overlapped, energy would transfer with untold consequences.

"The great physicist Edgar Roeth, born in 2601, came up with the equation to figure out the result of the addition or subtraction of any amount of energy from the universe for any amount of time. He determined it would equal instant destruction. If energy were added, the temperature throughout the universe would heat up drastically, burning everything living and non-living. Even the planet Earth would turn into a ball of magma. If you take away energy, the temperature would drop to a point where even a star like our sun would stop carrying out nuclear fusion and in essence, freeze. It's possible that some creature, adapted to far different circumstances than our own could survive a very small drop in the total level of energy; but the chances of that are very slim. The equation suggests that if energy levels were to increase or decrease by even a fraction of a joule, everything living would die, and everything non-living would combust, or freeze.

"Some scientists have theorized that a hole could be opened that would feed energy into another universe. Scientists continue to explore the notion that black holes could do this, and they even feel as if a wormhole under the right circumstances could this. So what if that happened? Most likely nothing, as the latest theories suggest that every black hole that sucks energy and matter in, spews it out on the other side in the form of a white hole. Since there are white holes in this universe, all the energy is transferred in equal amounts, preserving equilibrium. But if equilibrium was ever lost, everything would crumble and fall apart, organisms and planets for both universes. It would be quite a sight if anything could live long enough to see it. This is why some scientists believe inter dimensional travel is impossible. The energy inside of the travelling capsule would be added to that universe's energy, thus destroying it."

Leon's eyes were getting heavy. He knew he wouldn't manage to stay awake much longer although he found the program interesting.

"Of course these are only theories for now, but they are strongly supported theories. But if our universe is expanding, and touching other universes, how do they not overlap? The only explanation is that the other universes are shrinking. Then the universes touching the shrinking universes are expanding. When a shrinking universe reaches the size of the string inside of an atom—the smallest thing humans know of—it will have a big bang and begin rapidly expanding for a short amount of time, and then slowing down until it reaches its maximum size before shrinking again. Scientists believe the shrinking process would look like the growing process, except in reverse, so the universe would slowly start to shrink, but the smaller it got, the faster it would shrink. Anything inside would eventually be destroyed simply because there wouldn't be enough room.

"So what does the edge of the universe look like? Many believe it is just a layer of energy from the original big bang pushing outwards. There is far too much energy for anything to diffuse through, and on the other side is retreating energy from another universe. When two universes' energies are touching, we say this universe is parallel to our own. All other universes are just alternate dimensions.

"So what does this energy look like? Well, much like a fire, energy can change colors as it changes intensities. What the color of energy on the edge of the universe would look like is anyone's guess. Edgar Roeth offered one explanation before he passed away, he hypothesized that its color would be blue. He said—" Leon's eyelids closed at that point and the feeling of sleep overwhelmed him.

Leon woke up to someone shoving him. At first he couldn't see who it was, but then he saw a man shaking his shoulder. Leon didn't recognize the man, but he knew he was trying to wake him up. Leon got up to see that he had left the television on, as apparent by the fact that the only thing he could see in his right eye was an environmental commercial about the plans to re-attempt the release of a mass-produced nuclear fusion reactor. He pulled off the television chip and saw a clock that read six a.m.

"You can't be up here. Head back to your bunk," said the man.

Leon rubbed the dirt out of his eyes, and then left the room hoping that the man was no one of importance. When Leon got down to his room, he saw that the note concerning his bunkmate was still on his door. He ripped it down, still wondering what exactly they meant by battle injuries. Then he thought back to what Willy said. There is corruptness in the air.

Leon jumped into his bed and considered asking the tiny aliens that were in the sack what they knew about parallel universes; but he was too tired and fell asleep.

CHAPTER NINETEEN

At eight o'clock, Leon woke up from two hours of sleep and headed to the cafeteria for breakfast. It was a normal breakfast of eggs, bacon, and toast: no bear meat. He didn't see Alexander today as he normally did. Leon didn't care. He was still thinking about parallel universes.

Leon was stuffing the last piece of toast on his plate into his mouth when he saw Willy walking toward him.

"Leon," said Willy when he was within arm's length, "There's going to be a huge battle tomorrow. We've decided that we need to bring the battle to the aliens. It wasn't my choice, but we still have to go along with it. Plus, the foot soldiers haven't seen any action since we expanded, and the ground troop commander, Captain Drew, feels like his men are ready to make a difference. As I always say, expect the best but prepare for the worst. It's the only thing that got me through the last war. One more thing, that insect repellent we used last time won't be available to us this time. No one has been able to detect any of the stuff anywhere near here, so it's back to the old bullets. But that doesn't concern you much, unless you're planning on getting out of your ship to fight. But whatever happens, good luck to you out there, soldier." Willy patted Leon on the back and left.

Leon knew he had to find Scott to test that ship. As soon as he was done with breakfast, Leon ran down into the workshop. He saw Scott tightening a few screws on an electric powered hand saw.

"Hey, Scott," said Leon.

"What's up?"

"I need to test out that ship. I heard there's going to be a huge battle coming up and I don't want to use a ship I'm uncomfortable with."

"O.K. Just let me tighten this last bolt." Scott tightened a bolt and then walked over to the ship and opened the door for Leon. Then Scott used a remote to open up a big garage door that led outside.

Scott quickly jumped into the plane and took the seat in the back. Leon of course took the pilot seat. He slowly accelerated outside the garage. Once outside, he sped up on the icy runway and took flight. It was just a casual flight once they were in space, although Leon was always on the lookout for an alien ship wandering through. Leon knew he could get in trouble for flying about alone (or with Scott in this case) but he felt he had special privileges since Willy knew him and liked him. Well, "like" might've been a strong word, because Captains generally don't like the people they lead, but he at least wouldn't care as much when Leon did something like this.

"So Scott," inquired Leon, "How did you manage to get sole access to the workshop?"

"I know a guy."

"A guy? That's vague. There has to be more to it than that. I mean, what if everyone answered questions that vaguely. You don't have to hide anything from me, if there's—"

"Fine," said Scott cutting Leon off. He had a hint of irritation in his voice. "It's not because I know a guy. Why can't you just accept simple answers? If you really must know, it's because of my dad. He was an engineer, and he was an even better one than I am. I learned everything I know from him. He was the aerospace engineer for the North American Alliance during World War Four. He was so good, that everyone assumed I'd be just like him. So when he told them that he was retiring from the world army reserves, everyone assumed I'd take his place. So the guys at this base decided to let me use the workshop and in turn, I just have to help make all their mechanical stuff. To be more precise, I don't have sole possession of the workshop. Other people can come and go as they please, but they usually don't come because they think I'll make them look bad or something. I hate people thinking that of me. I didn't really even want to be an engineer; he pretty much forced me to. If I could really be anything I wanted, well I don't know what I'd be. I can't do anything but this. Life hardly ever works out like a fairy tale, so it's not like somebody is going to come along and let me live the life I always wanted to. I'll come to work every day, get my paycheck, and then spend it on whatever I need to live, and that's going to be all my life is until I die or retire. So, what's your story?"

"What do you mean?"

"I just told you a story about me; tell me a story about you. Nobody just exists, everybody had to come from something, and do something to end up where they are now. What did you do?"

"The Ginyu guards took my parents away from me when I was young and I never saw them again," said Leon. "I know they're dead because I would have heard from them if they were still alive. I had to take up a job on an assembly line when I was in my early teens. I was putting the wheels on the legs of planes. That's how I afforded to live. I never bought a house and for the longest time, I didn't even own a car. When I was sixteen years old, one of the elder pilots let me fly in his plane. He never told me why he was letting me fly with him. I personally think he was losing his mind a little bit. But he told me how to fly the plane, and then one day let me actually fly it. The plane looked nothing like this one; it was about twice as big with more controls. He let me fly the plane every day that he didn't have to work. Eventually I learned how to fly all on my own. One day, he stopped showing up to work, but his plane was still there. So during my lunch break, I took the plane out for a joy ride."

"Didn't anyone try to stop you?"

"The other pilots weren't mad at me, in fact, they applauded my flight skills. They let me keep the plane and join them. However, that didn't last long. I never heard why, but the company I worked for broke apart soon after I became a pilot. I became a mercenary of sorts, getting work wherever I could. Eventually I moved to sector 14427—formerly New Mexico—and some government organization hired me as a test pilot. Then you found me. Which leads me to my next question, what exactly did you do before you found me?"

"I worked as an aerospace engineer for European Space Organization. I was planning to bring you back there with me before this war started. Did you know they planned to build the first ever hotel in wide-open space? Then they realized that they would never make enough profit to pay for the darn thing, so they just stuck to building hotels on the moon. Which, in case you haven't noticed, the moon's been full for a while now, so that's a good thing."

"Yeah, I guess it is a good thing," said Leon looking at the moon, which wasn't very far away now.

Satisfied with all the testing he'd done while conversing with Scott, Leon headed back to the workshop and parked the plane like a professional.

As Leon was about to head back down, Scott stopped him and said, "Leon, don't be surprised if next time you go to a battle, you see a friendly command ship. Me and a bunch of other guys have been working on our own ship to combat the aliens. Personally, I think we could've done a better job, but it definitely brings that intimidation factor."

"I was never worried about that. *They* always find a way to make new technology in times of crisis."

"One more thing, take the schematics for this ship. I think a pilot should know the inside of his ship just as well as the engineer."

"Thanks, I'll be sure to hold on to these," said Leon placing them in the desk drawer next to his bed.

CHAPTER TWENTY

Leon headed over to the elevator having had completed the test flight of his latest ship. He was about to hit thirty-four, so that he could go to his room, but then he hit one, so he could go to the private lounge. He knew he needed a key to get in, but he could find Willy and use his key if he really needed to.

He found the private lounge easily enough and he tried turning the doorknob. To his surprise, someone had left the door opened and he was able to get inside. He found the television chip sitting on the table and slipped it over his eye. It was on a different channel than the one he was watching last night. It was some sort of historical show.

"WAR isn't just a term to describe a series of battles," the show began, "It is the acronym for the World Army Reserves. For years, questions have surrounded its formation, and for years, they said that it was in case there was a rebellion here on Earth. But why would such a large and elite army be necessary to squash a rebellion? How organized could one rebellion be? The thought that it was an army to battle aliens began to arise. You can go back over two-thousand years and see stories, videos and pictures of aliens. There are countless eyewitness accounts and even physical proof of objects found nowhere else on Earth. Yet, all of the four world leaders deny the existence of life beyond Earth, even though scientists say that there is a high probability that somewhere among the billions upon billions of planets, life exists.

"Psychologists have suggested that here could be a perfectly good explanation for this. Imagine what would happen if the existence of aliens was confirmed. There would be mass panic, people would fear abductions, and people would be connecting anything out of the ordinary to aliens. So, did they really establish WAR to fight an alien army? We asked—"

Leon changed the channel to see what else was on, as he had long ago stopped watching shows that debated the existence of aliens. Although he still found it surprising that your average civilian didn't know that they were in the middle of a war with aliens. Leon continued flipping through channels until something caught his attention.

"Trips to the moon are more affordable than ever now, and with so many hotels, don't you deserve to know which ones give you the best deals? Hotel Comparison Incorporated strives to give the best hotel offer. If the hotel we suggest isn't the best out there, you'll get a full refund and we'll give you a free three night stay in the hotel of your choice." It was just a commercial and Leon continued flipping through the channels. He stumbled upon a few things. There was a court battle on who was liable for damages to the propulsion system of a hover car. There was an interview with Northwest ruler John on what his plans were to improve what Winston had left him. There was also a new report on how investing in ogelan companies was even more profitable than investing in gold.

Leon turned off the television and removed the chip. He wasn't sure what he hoped to see when he turned it on, but definitely not anything that was showing.

Leon thought back to the first show that was on and decided it wasn't just coincidence that it was on. It probably came on to make people believe that the existence of life beyond Earth was only possible and not definite. The average person would think that if aliens were real the show wouldn't have to debate it anymore, but if they saw no show, their mind could think what it wanted to. A wandering mind could be dangerous. At least with this approach, nothing would change, because people for centuries have known that aliens may or may not exist.

Leon decided that's what the problem was with people; they could never make up their minds as a whole. It's true or it's not, aliens exist or they don't, my religion is right or yours is. It was always the same thing and Leon couldn't stand it. That's why Earth was in this war, they couldn't agree on anything. How can you have unity if you can't agree on anything? Some things are facts and some things are not, and there isn't always a grey area. Can everyone pray to a different God and be right? Everyone is just looking for someone to follow, and the people who are willing to lead are unwilling to speak the truth. Because the truth hurts, and people don't like it when you hurt them.

Leon headed down to his room. He found a pen and notepad on a desk next to the bed. Written on the first notepad sheet was, "Courtesy of room service". Leon ripped off that piece of paper and threw it into the trash. Leon wanted to write something down. The pen trembled in his hand as he strained his brain to write down something that would capture the emotion he was feeling. After a minute of just staring at the blank piece of paper, he stabbed the pen down into it, leaving a smudged, black dot. Then Leon went to sleep.

CHAPTER TWENTY-ONE

Leon awoke the next morning to the sound of an alarm. It was the alarm signifying that it was time for battle. Leon quickly threw on his flying gear and was about to run to the elevator, when he remembered what Willy had said, "Expect the best, but prepare for the worst."

First, Leon grabbed the little aliens who had been staying in his room. They seemed happy to finally be able to go out again. Then Leon went up the elevator and to the cafeteria. No one was in there, not even the janitors. There was food in the kitchen however, so Leon grabbed an impromptu breakfast. The chefs must have abandoned the food in the middle of cooking breakfast, because it was still semi hot. Then Leon ran out to his ship where Scott was waiting for him.

"What took you so long?" asked Scott.

"Just grabbing some breakfast," replied Leon.

Leon enjoyed the neat and convenient arrangement of the ships in the hangar just before they had to leave for battle. Although Leon never really got used to the agonizing wait before take-off. But he just kept telling himself that even the best musicians in the world could get nervous before a performance.

But there was something else different about this battle. In all of the battles before this, he was just responding to alien ships threatening to cause damage. Now, if everything went right, Earth would be on the offense. Leon didn't know why this made him nervous, maybe it was the fact that they had no idea what they would be doing when they met up with them. Then a thought occurred to Leon; if they were the aggressors, what separated them from their enemy? Was it the fact they were acting in defense to the initial attack? Was it because humans somehow had morals no other creature possessed? Then again, weren't morals something humans just applied to other humans; so who isn't to say the aliens didn't think they were being moral? Deep inside, Leon thought he knew the answers to these questions, but he didn't want to think about it before a battle. Like Alexander said, humans are just animals, and animals only live not to die and to pass on their genes. Self-preservation: that was all the reason he, or anybody else, needed to go to war.

When Leon got into space, he saw the command ship Scott had told him about. It looked like it might fall apart if someone loosened two or three screws, but in terms of size, it was at least big enough to make the enemy think twice about getting near it. The aliens command ship was still a lot better though. But the most noticeable difference was the coloration. On the sides of the ship was a flag painted with WAR colors.

"Leon," started Scott, "That's the flag of the world army reserves. Green and white vertical stripes, with a red and blue horizontal stripe in the middle. A lot of people don't even know that's our flag. And if it were up to me, it wouldn't be our flag because it looks stupid."

Leon heard Willy's voice coming through the radio on his ship and told Scott to quiet down so he could hear. "All pilots are to set coordinates for sector 1.5, 160 degrees.

"Scott, that's really far from here," said Leon.

"Just put it in hyper sleep and enjoy the ride like everybody else."

Leon set the coordinates, put it in hyper sleep, and the ship sped up until everything was a blur. Then the ship filled with a fast acting sleeping gas. Just before Leon fell asleep, he saw other ships, including the command ship, doing the same thing, and zoom away to their far off destination.

None of them realized that they would be gone for longer than they expected. John and the other world leaders didn't want them coming back and telling stories of alien fights. There would be untold consequences if that happened. So the orders came that no soldier was to come back until they won the war, or until they all died. The world rulers all thought they'd never see those soldiers again, and that was fine with them.

CHAPTER TWENTY-TWO

Leon and the other men awoke to see Jupiter looming, only about sixty miles away. But Jupiter wasn't their destination; their destination was Ganymede, one of Jupiter's moons. The espionage team for the military managed to gather information that Sudokus would be there. What the humans didn't know was that their spies had gathered bad information. The informants they talked to were actually aliens working for Sudokus. They were simply leading the humans into an ambush.

"Be ready for anything, men; the aliens may be aware of our presence." The voice went through the radio transmission to every man who was in a ship. The voice was that of a simulated voice program, which had the uncanny ability to mimic a human voice. It sounded like the voice of a female, which really seemed to calm the men down just before a battle. Yet, in your subconscious, you knew the voice wasn't a human voice. It still had the ever so slight echo that is characteristic of a machine-produced voice.

That radio transmission was the first thing Leon heard since going to sleep. Leon woke out of his sleep, but he wasn't groggy at all. When the hyper-sleep woke you up, you felt awake and energized.

Leon stared down on Ganymede. It was very intimidating to think that a force far greater than your own was looming so nearby. It was the same sensation you get on Earth when you're swimming in the ocean and see a shark nearby. Then the radio chimed back in, "All pilots are to hold their positions. The command ship will head down to the surface to unload the ground soldiers. Your orders are to provide cover fire for the soldiers. This isn't going to be easy, and a quick retreat may become necessary."

Leon watched the command ship lower down to Ganymede. After the ship landed, the radio chimed in one last time, reminding all the pilots to be ready to provide backup.

It must have been a strange sight for hidden alien soldiers, to see the battalion of foot soldiers—all one-hundred of them—all walking with their guns pointed at anything that moved. Poor scouting meant they attempted to camouflage in their grey space suits. A mission like this required too much dexterity, so rather than oxygen tanks, the soldiers inserted a small cube into their mouths. The cube would convert the carbon dioxide within each man into breathable oxygen.

Leon waited in his ship above the moon. He couldn't see what was going on below, so he had to wait for the radio to tell him what to do next. Leon waited a long time, wondering what was going on under him.

Below, the soldiers walked hesitantly. They didn't know exactly what they were looking for. Some had seen the aliens more up-close than others, but no one had an exact description of the aliens. To make matters worse, alien vegetation had grown all over the planet, making it impossible to see more than a few feet in front of yourself. Plus, the alien wildlife ran around, rustling the bushes. Even the most disciplined soldiers struggled not to waste ammunition when something darted out of a bush and brushed past their leg.

The aliens had exceptional camouflage, and they didn't travel together. They all crept through the jungle as individuals to avoid detection. The aliens slowly converged together until they were in position for attack.

There was an eerie calm as the humans continued walking. They could tell something was nearby, but they didn't know what or where it was. Then, the attack started.

Bullets were spraying like mad from both sides when the aliens burst out from the brush, but the humans were taking the worst of it because the aliens were able to shoot from high up on the trees. The humans had nowhere to hide, and had to shoot up towards them. Insect repellent would've been of great help, but only bullets were available at the time.

The humans darted through the jungle trying to avoid death. There wasn't much they could do against their enemy. The aliens knew the terrain better and used stealth to navigate. When the humans arrived, their goal was to search for Sudokus's headquarters, but it soon became apparent that even if it was nearby, Sudokus's soldiers had it too well defended. They didn't even call in for the planes for air support because it wouldn't have helped. They wouldn't be able to tell friend from foe in the dense jungle.

Few of the humans even saw the enemy in all the commotion. There was panic on the part of the humans. They lost their objective, and now their basic survival instinct was kicking in as they retreated from the slaughter field.

The soldiers were running back to the command ship, when they realized the aliens had managed to surround it. It was a battle just to get into the ship, and once they did get in, they had to push out the aliens that were trying to force their way in through the hatch. Once all the humans were in, and all the aliens were out, the ship took off. It was another disappointing defeat. It seemed that the alien's abilities and technology were so far ahead of humans, that the humans couldn't even compete. But the real reason the humans couldn't compete was because humans had stopped evolving long ago when they created ways for even the weakest of individuals to survive. All while the aliens were artificially selecting individuals, cloning, and gene splicing. Their way may not have been as good for each individual, but the results were clear on the battlefield.

CHAPTER TWENTY-THREE

Leon never got to hear what Cpt. Drew said to his men after that loss, but he imagined it would have been something along the lines of what Willy told them after their near loss. All that mattered to Leon now was the new coordinates he was given. As he waited in his ship, the simulated lady's voice told him some numbers, and he was able to use his map to figure out they were heading to another one of Jupiter's moons. This time, Europa was their destination—not to find Sudokus or anything, just to lay low. Plus, by this point, everyone with more importance than a common soldier knew Earth didn't want them back until this war was over.

The flight to Europa was a short one, and the ship landed there in an hour. The Earthlings thought the planet would be empty, but instead strange looking aliens nothing like the ones they'd just been fighting surrounded them. They were the slave aliens, and they all stood around the ship as it landed. The sight of the aliens caught Cpt. Drew off guard as he looked out the window of the ship to see them. He didn't know whether to get out of the ship and risk another battle, or just fly to a different moon. Willy saw them out of the command ship's window as well, but he didn't want to tell anyone that he knew these aliens weren't hostile. He knew many things from being able to listen in on the discussions the humans had with the aliens, but his superiors required secrecy of him on all of it. Nevertheless, he would break his promise every now and then, like in Leon's case. Willy pondered what the best thing to say at this moment would be, but then Cpt. Drew began speaking.

"Any volunteers to clear out the area?" No one wanted to get out of the ship at first, for fear of what these strange aliens might do. Then one of the soldiers decided to go out there. He already had injuries from the previous battle and he figured he wouldn't make it back to Earth anyway. One of the things they told you in boot camp was that, "The army is always more important than the individual".

Cpt. Drew opened the hatch and the soldier ran out with one hand one his gun and the other hand limp, the muscles inside of it destroyed by a stray bullet in the last battle. He didn't shoot; he only pointed his gun at the aliens. The aliens backed away whenever he pointed the gun at one of them. It soon became apparent that the aliens were defenseless. The soldier fired off a few shots into the air and the aliens scattered away into the brush. Once there were no more aliens nearby, soldiers started coming out of the ship to set up a camp. Willy called in the pilots to help.

Leon got out of his ship and began helping out with setting up tents and building structures that would serve as hospitals and canteens. While working, the little aliens informed Leon that they were on a slave farm, except the slave owners had left to head to the main planet of Jupiter a few hours ago. So now the slaves were just sort of wandering around, looking for someone to lead them until the owners returned. Sort of like what people do, except none of the slaves were capable of stepping into that leadership role.

After working for several consecutive hours, all the soldiers set up tents for the night. Everyone took shifts standing watch, just in case those aliens got too close. There was rustling through the brush all night long, but no alien dared to get too close. The aliens also made strange sounds as they communicated with each other. It sounded like a combination of a snake hissing, and an elephant trumpeting. The sound went on all night long, but Leon didn't notice it in his tent. The three tiny aliens were preoccupying him more. Their ship had a satellite sticking out from the top that Leon had never seen before. They had used the satellite in the past, but when not in use, it could fold into the ship. The satellite spun around as it searched for some sort of signal. After a few minutes, the satellite went back down into the ship. Then the ship opened and the aliens walked out.

"We've received a message from the resistance," said one of the aliens telepathically.

"I thought we were the resistance," said Leon.

"You are, but this is a message from the natives of Mars. Someone named Harem sent it a while ago, but now he is dead."

Leon thought the name sounded familiar, and then he remembered that Harem was the alien he saw disguised as a human back on Earth before the war started. Then Leon realized that wasn't his memory, but rather information the aliens had fed into his mind.

"Relax your mind, Leon, and we'll send you the message." Leon closed his eyes and tried to relax, but thoughts buzzed around everywhere. The aliens kept urging Leon to relax, and after many minutes, Leon began to reduce the number of thoughts he had buzzing around, and soon, an image became visible to him. As he continued to relax, the vision began turning into a scene, and there were many images, moving and flashing through his mind until he began to decipher a story. Yet, it was as if this event was unfolding right in front of his face. The scene was a chaotic one as aliens were running everywhere. Ships hovered just above the surface firing laser beams down onto the planet. Then one alien ran in the foreground, taking up the entire field of view. Eventually Leon recognized the alien as Harem. Harem started shouting out different things which Leon couldn't understand, then had to escape to a tiny ship that blasted away and out of sight. Leon realized this was the same event the aliens showed him before, except from someone else's perspective. Now Leon saw actual troops marching through the cities, killing anyone who dared show their face during the invasion. Then the vision ended and Leon opened his eyes.

"That was a call for help from Harem. He says that there is an army hiding deep under the surface of Mars. Or at least, there was when this video was shot."

"So let's go find them," said Leon.

"It won't be that easy. Those command ships that you saw in that video are stationed around every planet—except Earth, that is."

"I see how that might be a problem, but given the circumstances at hand, don't you think it's worth it to try to look for them anyway?"

"Think about all of your options first, young one. No reason to drown trying to save someone if there's a boat nearby."

"Let's see, I know that all we really have to do is head back to Earth and just stop any incoming invasion, but that's easier said than done. I can't think of anything else we could do off the top of my head."

"Concentrate, young one. You know of other things that could help you, just think."

"I…uh…I don't know, O.K? I just don't know what you want from me right now. You just showed me that message, but now you're saying I have to think of another way of beating Sudokus other than finding the rebel army. How do you expect one person to be able to make a difference anyway?"

"History always gives credit to one person making a difference."

"But it never is just one person. I remember learning that in school. No one person has ever single handedly made a world changing difference, he always has people behind him, supporting him. They just don't get mentioned."

"You're off to a good start, little one. Teamwork is definitely going to be a factor here. Now what do you know about the enemy: think."

"Let's see, they can be killed by insect repellent, I know that, but we have none. Even if I got some, it only works when fighting on the ground, so it would be of little use to me."

"Are there any other options, little one?"

Leon paused to think, but left without any more ideas, he decided to vent his frustration towards the aliens. "Why do you keep calling me little one, when you three together can fit into my palm?"

"We may be small physically, but our minds are bigger than any other life form's. Unless you can count Sudokus as having a mind, that is. And, as you are demonstrating now, your mind is small, and has much expanding to do. We can sense indecisiveness in you, and, although you seem to be aware of everything going on around, you seem to interpret it too late. That is why you are the little one. Now, let's get back to the task at hand, shall we? We can tell your mind has already begun to expand just from this short conversation, so we'll answer your questions, and then allow you to rest. You will have to take one or two people you know particularly well, and head off to find this base. We'll be able to go with you and help navigate around the command ships. But there will be some unexpected things along the way, and you may need to stop other places. So it's up to you to decide on the specifics of all of this, should you choose to go through with any of this. Do you accept?"

"I'll do it. I'll head to Mars with Willy, Scott, and you guys, and we'll find those rebels, and somehow, we'll join them. That plan may need some work, but either way, I'm going." So Leon left to go look for Scott and Willy and somehow convince them to go.

Leon went walking through the camp, and just happened to stumble upon Scott. Scott was sitting nearby his tent. It was nighttime, but Jupiter reflected just enough light, and had enough moons, that it never really got dark.

"Hey, Scott," said Leon as he approached him. "You said you were my personal engineer, so now you have to go with me to a different place, just for a little bit."

"What are you talking about?"

"I intercepted this message from rebels on a different planet. They're alien rebels though, so they might be able to help us."

"Don't even waste your time; any rebels have probably been killed by now. Plus, it's too dangerous for just two guys to trek the solar system during a time like this."

"That's why I'm going to try to convince Captain Willy to come with us."

"You really have lost your mind, Leon. The Captain is far too busy to go with you on a suicide mission."

"If I could convince him to go, you'd come too?"

"I would. But you're not going to convince him, so none of us will be going. Why don't you get some sleep now? Once you're rested, you'll realize how stupid all of these ideas really are, and you'll forget them."

Leon took Scott's advice and went to sleep, but he knew that he wasn't going to change his mind about this. He couldn't even get to sleep at first, because he was getting more excited about the idea the more he thought about it. Eventually though, Leon did get to sleep.

When he awoke the next morning, he immediately began looking for Willy. He found him, but knew he needed to wait for a time when Willy would be alone.

It was nearly halfway through the day, and Leon thought he'd never get a chance to speak to Willy privately. Then, as he was walking out of his tent for about the third time that day to see what Willy was doing, he saw all the soldiers running around. Some soldiers were running into the brush, and some soldiers were running out. Leon grabbed the side arm he had and began navigating his way toward the brush around camp to see what was going on.

As Leon got closer, he saw the slave aliens running around wildly, as soldiers—who didn't really know what they were shooting at—fired recklessly into the fray.

Leon was about to turn back to look for Willy to tell him that they were wasting bullets, when he felt a hand grab his shoulder and he was thrust back.

"Leon," said Willy, "Leave this type of work to the soldiers."

"Actually, Willy, I was about to look for you. I wanted to tell you that we need to stop wasting our bullets on these aliens, they're harmless." Leon wondered if Willy already knew this, because it was no sooner than Leon spoke, then Willy whipped out his communicator and told Cpt. Drew to order his soldiers to stop firing unless the aliens made an advance. Normal procedures would have required that Willy first question why Leon felt this fray was unnecessary, and then discuss with Cpt. Drew whether the reason provided by Leon was valid. But Willy did none of that, and Cpt. Drew surprisingly didn't argue with Willy. Then again, not many people did argue with Willy.

After the scrum, Leon followed Willy back to his tent. They stepped inside to talk and Leon then proceeded to tell Willy everything he had told Scott, and Willy had a slightly different reaction.

"How do you know this isn't a set up? You're tiny alien friends could be working for them." Willy wanted to trust the small aliens the first time Leon showed them to him, but after they walked into that trap on Ganymede, he was reluctant to believe anyone about issues concerning the war.

"Sir, I assure you, these guys have never steered me wrong before. They definitely are on our side."

"I'll assume that's true for a second, but how do you propose that we get from Europa to Mars?"

"Well, we do have my ship, and we do have the command ship, but I think neither of those are ideal. I think I can convince the aerospace engineer, Scott, to build something just for this mission."

"Well, I do agree we'll lose this war if we don't do something, but it will also look bad if I leave my pilots in the middle of a war. Oh, what do I care about how I look? I'd rather look like a deserter than dead from a bullet wound by the enemy. When do you plan to leave?"

"It depends," said Leon surprised things were going this smoothly. "If Scott can build a ship we can use by tomorrow, I'd leave then."

"Go talk to Scott then. Just remember, this is a stealth mission, so we can only tell a few select people where we're going. I'll worry about who I let know about my absence, and you should refrain from telling anybody but Scott."

Willy left the tent then. He was about to tell Cpt. Drew, but then he decided that he should wait until the night before they left to do it. If he told him now, there would be too much time for Drew to think about the situation and do something stupid, like ask to come along.

Leon told Scott that Willy agreed, and although Scott couldn't believe it, he agreed that he'd build a ship just for this mission. He told Leon he could build one in by the end of the week, so Leon passed this information onto Willy. Then everybody waited at camp for a week to pass. No aliens attacked, and no humans attacked. Everyone just waited.

CHAPTER TWENTY-FOUR

A week passed, and now it was a matter of hours before departure. Willy didn't know how to spend these last few hours; he was just pacing around, checking up on the progress of the ship. Scott was doing a surprisingly good job of scavenging spare parts from the command ship and the sun was just beginning to set when he finished. Willy decided it was time to tell Drew. Willy walked over to Cpt. Drew's tent and walked in to the partially opened flap.

"I won't be seeing you for a while," said Willy. "I'm going on a mission to Mars with one of our pilots. I'll need someone to take charge of the other pilots while I'm gone."

"Slow down there," started Drew, "Why would you need to go to Mars?"

"We've intercepted a radio transmission giving word that there is a rebel base on Mars. We'll be leaving early tomorrow."

"What do you plan to do with the pilots?"

"I assume you can appoint someone to temporarily take my place."

"You've given me short notice, but I'll find someone." And with that, Willy headed back to the tent. Willy was a man of few words.

Back in the tent, Willy walked in on Leon and Scott arguing. "We should head to Earth first, just in case the army is short on materials," said Scott.

"We might not make it to Earth without that army accompanying us," said Leon.

"You're assuming they have ships to accompany us with."

"What are you two babbling about?" Willy stepped into the tent with the intent to settle this dispute quickly.

"Scott thinks we should go to Earth to pick up his parts making machine, but we have to go to Mars first to join up with the rebel base."

"A machine that makes parts? That sounds like it could be helpful; and if this is sabotage, we'll need all the help we can get. So let's head to Earth first."

"Looks like you're out voted," said Scott, directing his gaze toward Leon.

"Fine," said Leon with a hint of disgust, "We'll head back to Earth first, but don't think we're going to get a hero's welcome. They're going to be on high alert for any approaching ships and our ship won't register as an ally ship." Leon was right about that. The ship was not expertly constructed; it barely even qualified as space worthy. It was basically a rectangular prism with a tail pipe. If the aliens didn't shoot it down, some trigger-happy defense grid worker might. And on top of that, Willy knew they weren't really supposed to go back to Earth anyway, but the exact orders only prohibited the army as a whole from returning, it didn't specifically say that an individual couldn't return.

Back on Earth, things were starting to get out of control as political debates and negotiations were breaking down. John was campaigning for surrender to the aliens, so a peaceful change of power could take place. All the other powerful politicians wanted to force the aliens to retreat out of Earth's outer reaches, but they argued over how to do it. It seemed politicians were ignoring John's solo campaign in all the debating, but soon

Ginyu guards started giving campaign donations to politicians to encourage them to negotiate a surrender. The Ginyu guards were anti-war after all, since a war might mean they would have to fight.. With the new incentive of money, politicians started converting over to John's campaign. It would be simple to surrender to the aliens with no army around to object.

The people, however, no longer supported this war, and it was getting more and more complicated trying to explain to them who they were fighting against. People were especially mad because they thought there would be no more wars. So the prisons became flooded with rioters, and the Ginyu guards resorted to shooting anyone who seemed to be causing trouble seeing as there was nowhere to put them.

Even more burdensome than the rioters were the angry parents, who complained that they couldn't contact their sons and daughters while they were off fighting. They argued they should have the right to, but their cries went largely unheard or ignored.

The Northwest quadrant was in the most trouble however, because Willy had promised to trade capital for human resources, and now the other quadrants wanted their capital, but the Northwest had none to give during the war, so the threat of civil war loomed. The treaty signed after World War Four was the only thing making an all-out war difficult to start.

Nevertheless, Earth still looked like Earth for the most part when you got past all the politics. Someone just walking around would still see the tall glass buildings and the hover cars zooming. They'd still see those people who sat in their house, drinking the fake alcohol and smoking the fake cigarettes; either too lazy to care, or oblivious of what was actually going on. The keen observer would notice more than just everything that was happening on Earth, and the truly keen observer would see that what was happening on Earth wasn't all that different than what was happening anywhere else in the solar system. The only difference was Sudokus didn't rule Earth.

CHAPTER TWENTY-FIVE

Leon, Scott and Willy were cruising through the solar system on their way to Earth. The three tiny aliens also accompanied them in this special ship, but they stayed in Leon's bag and out of the way for the most part. The aliens were there to provide a route for Leon to take to avoid conflict with the enemy. For now they were safe, because they were going to Earth, but they'd need to be more careful when they headed to Mars.

As the strange ship began to descend near the Russian base, Ginyu guards began gathering below to see what was going on. By now, even the Ginyu guards knew who they were fighting (The only people who didn't know were the civilians).

The Ginyu guards stayed a safe distance away as the doors opened up. They were either going to have to shoot, or talk. The first person to step out was Willy, so the Ginyu guards lowered their guns and saluted him. Then they saw Scott and Leon walk out and took their fingers away from their foreheads. There were three Ginyu guards, but the one at the front seemed to have the highest rank, and would be doing all of the talking.

"Is this what's left of the army, sir?"

"No," said Willy trying to determine if he was joking, "We just needed to stop back to pick up some stuff."

"We can't let you stay here, sir," said the Guard. "Cpt. John said that no man currently in service may return here; Northeastern president Mdedev approved that action. If you don't leave now, you'll have to be dishonorably discharged."

"This is important. We're going to lose a lot of progress if we don't get what we need. This isn't our last stop either and we're on a tight schedule. Just let us get one thing from here and we'll be gone."

"Captain Willy, you know that I can't let you stay. I can't go against my superiors. So either you leave, or I'll have to take the three of you into custody until they do something with you."

"With all due respect, I am in the military, and therefore, I am your superior. Now let us inside of the base or we'll have to force our way in."

"All right, men," said the Guard. "Take these civilians to a holding cell for the night. We'll need to impound their ship and report this incident."

The guards once again raised their guns and began moving toward the men when, suddenly, the three little aliens came out of the parked ship. Leon looked back to see them. He wanted to tell them to get back into the ship, or grab them before anyone saw them, but it was too late.

One of the Ginyu guards raised his gun to shoot, but stopped. Leon looked toward the other guard, who had also stopped moving.

"What just happened?" asked Leon.

"I don't know," said Willy. "They just stopped moving."

"What should we do?" asked Scott.

No one answered Scott's question. It was rhetorical anyway. However, Leon's question was answered. It was the little aliens—they had somehow frozen the guards. They could control their minds in the same way they could telepathically communicate all of their information to Leon. Leon wished these little aliens told him about this skill sooner, but he was just glad that they chose a good time to use it. Leon told Willy and

Scott to get the machine while he started up the ship. He wasn't
sure how long the aliens could keep the guards frozen.

The inside of the Russian base was empty for the most
part. There were no chefs, and no janitors; just some rats eating
crumbs left behind from the last dinner.

Scott ran straight to the workshop, which was on the
ground floor. Willy followed close behind and it took the two of
them to lift the machine and carry it back to the ship. Once they
made it back outside, they loaded it into the back and Leon took
off for Mars following the three little alien's instructions.

The Ginyu guards soon regained their ability to move,
but they couldn't remember anything that happened, so they just
went on guarding the base as if no one had ever tried to get in.
The Ginyu guards were as robotic as one could get while still
being considered human. Some people even thought they were
robots since they never showed their faces. But they were simply
the result of constant physical abuse and mental programming of
a normal human being.

The flight to Mars was without incident, thanks to the
navigation of the three aliens, but hostile ships surrounded the
planet, dispersed throughout the outer limits of the atmosphere.

Leon stayed a safe distance from the ships so everyone
aboard the ship could strategize. They had the exact coordinates
of where the rebel base was, but it was dangerously close to a
command ship.

"Why can't you just control the minds of the people
aboard the command ships?" Leon asked the three aliens.

"Because, we can only control weak, less advanced
minds; like the mind of a human. An alien's mind is far more
complex—although only a few are advanced enough to control
minds. Even Sudokus can't do more than just influence an alien.
The only way to penetrate down to the surface will be to create a
distraction."

"It would take a big distraction though," said Leon.

"Yes, but sometimes big things come in small packages,"
replied the aliens.

With that, the three aliens went out with their disc-shaped ship to be the distraction. Leon watched as they darted around the command ships. At first, it seemed like they were going unnoticed, but then one of the command ships fired its laser. A whole chain reaction was set off and all three ships within firing range began shooting. The tiny saucer darted around doing barrel rolls and loop-de-loops. Their evasive maneuvers mesmerized Leon and he nearly forgot to take advantage of the distraction. Willy had to yell at him to get him to snap back to reality and start flying again. Leon bolted forward and found some room to sneak in behind one of the ships. They were able to touchdown on the surface without detection. It didn't take long to reach the coordinates of the base, but there was nothing there.

"I told you this was sabotage," said Willy, "Our troops are probably getting destroyed without us there."

Leon stared ahead into the empty space, double-checking that they were at the correct coordinates. They were at the right coordinates, so the base had to be somewhere nearby. Then Leon realized something. If your enemy is above you, then you're two options are to go even higher than your enemy, or to hide under something. The only thing here to hide under was the ground. Leon began digging. He used his hands to scrape the loose dust off the surface until he uncovered a slab of silver. He continued digging until he found a handle attached to that slab. He pulled the handle, and a door opened up. The door opened slowly and it took considerable effort on Leon's part. Dust bounced into the air and tumbled to the ground as Leon pushed the door above his head to its fully ajar position. A dark tunnel waited below the trio of men. At the end of the tunnel was a light. Trusting the three tiny aliens would eventually catch up, they began their descent downward.

CHAPTER TWENTY-SIX

Sudokus could sense the group as they attempted to join up with the rebels. He had been checking up on Leon ever since he had first encountered Harem. Whenever he saw Leon in his big red eye, his dissatisfaction receptors tingled. Sudokus realized it was time to call Gako and Lada into his office.

The two greatest assassins in the solar system were enjoying the pay they'd received from their last mission, but now it was time for work. Sudokus waited in his office until they walked in, fully equipped and ready to kill or capture anything Sudokus wanted them to.

"I have a job for you two," began Sudokus. "I know it seems a bit trivial, but that makes it no less important." Sudokus had no inflection in his metallic voice and no facial expressions. It's strange looking at someone and having no idea what they're thinking, and when it's a machine you're talking to, and not a living being, that sense of strangeness seems to turn into one of intimidation. "This won't be an easy assignment," he continued, "But the greater the risk, the greater the reward." Sudokus pulled out a photograph of Leon, and then handed them a piece of paper stating his current location. "I need Leon Dudley eliminated. It may be hard to find him, because he gives off a relatively low amount of mental frequencies, but he is growing in strength and cunning. What's worse is that he seems to be trying to take matters into his own hands. He has too much determination to ignore. Call me over-cautious if you want, but I'm still paying you for this, so take it seriously. And if you see the humans who travel with him," Sudokus paused, "Feel free to do with them what you want. On second thought, the one engineer could be of use to me. Try to bring that one back alive. And as long as you're at it, bring the machine that he clings so closely to as well. He'll need it. Just be careful, as there are rebels in the area."

Gako and Lada headed out to their ship. Gako didn't have significant thoughts very often, but he unexpectedly had one. Once Earth was officially conquered, what would happen? Would there be any more wars? Would there be anyone to assassinate? Would all this money Sudokus was paying them even be worth anything? If all the planets were unified under a single ruler, many things would change, wouldn't they? Gako pushed the thoughts out of his mind. He hoped that Lada hadn't been reading into his mind while he was thinking that.

Sudokus watched out of a window as he saw Gako and Lada zoom off toward Mars. If Sudokus's creator programmed Sudokus with the ability to fear, he might even be worried about what Leon might do to him if they ever met again. However, he was sure that Gako and Lada would kill Leon now.

Sudokus began thinking of other things, and his satisfaction sensors buzzed when he thought of Scott. He knew Scott could help build his long dreamed of fantasy: war mechs.

Sudokus's vision of mechs was the vision of an army of robots that were unstoppable, and unbeatable. They'd be robots with some of his qualities, but geared towards war. These wouldn't just be any robots either; anyone could design a fighting robot. These would be special. He simply needed the right person to design them—someone with the foresight and skill to make a robot with a reputation known throughout galaxies light years away. Sudokus needed someone to design the mech.

However, Sudokus also knew that taking Scott would weaken Earth's army. Leon relied on Scott's ships, and Leon was one of the better pilots in the army. He hadn't shown it much yet, but Sudokus could see it in him. The way Leon managed to get hit, but always safely land, and even when the alien docked his ship, he survived. And now Leon's discipline was increasing, and it would be even harder for any of Sudokus's men to defeat him, so Sudokus would end him now by sending in Gako and Lada. If you weaken the pillars in the foundation, even the most well built structures will fall. It was by this thinking that Sudokus determined killing Leon would lead to the end of Earth's army. Plus, killing Leon now would mean the alien rebels could never join the humans, and Sudokus could crush both rebel groups if they remained separate.

But inside, Sudokus knew that wouldn't be what happened. Somehow, his assassins would fail to kill Leon. Sudokus called in one of his advisors to establish a backup plan, for when this one failed.

"From now on," said Sudokus, "Leon is public enemy number one. I want images of him placed all around. Also, make sure everyone knows his crimes. Make up crimes if necessary. I want him to be the most hated man in this solar system."

"A wise move, sir. In times of war, there must always be a common enemy. May I just suggest you have a second common enemy to replace him if he dies? You know, so that you can keep everyone focused on something."

"He won't die. Get this straight, I'm not doing this as a political move, I'm doing this out of actual dissatisfaction. I really want everyone to hate Leon." The advisor stared at Sudokus for a moment in disbelief. "You have your orders," snapped Sudokus, "Now make sure somebody carries them out."

CHAPTER TWENTY-SEVEN

Leon, Willy, and Scott made their way through the tunnel and into the rebel camp. Leon hoped that the tiny aliens would be able to join them, but they were still somewhere outside for now.

Underneath the surface, it was like a completely different world. There were freshly paved sidewalks, fountains, and aliens walking around for the sake of walking. It was as if they had made their own society, away from Sudokus's grasp. It was almost too perfect. Leon decided that either the command ships waiting outside must not know about this rebel base, or they had a reason for not destroying it.

The base was deep underground, but it had an elaborate lighting system that made Leon feel like he was strolling through the park on a sunny day. But strolling through a park was a fuzzy memory buried in the back of Leon's mind. Ever since the-now-dead Winston had become leader, parks and playgrounds had become things of the past. Maybe it was even before that. He couldn't remember.

An alien snapped Leon out of his daydreaming. The alien was just as tall as Leon and dressed in a dark, yet elaborate, outfit. He had an oblong shaped head with big black eyes.

"I already know why you've come here," said the alien, "Your help is greatly appreciated, but futile. The command ships are simply waiting us out. Our food supplies are already beginning to dwindle and we don't have nearly enough ships to launch an assault. As for your little alien friends, they'll soon be coming in through a different entrance to this place. And what is this place, you ask? It's my little Utopia, if you will. You can have a perfect world, as long as you don't intend for it to stay around for too long. The longer you stay, the more problems you'll encounter, and the more compromises you have to make. It gets messy after a while."

"I'm sorry", said Leon, "But who are you."

"That is not important. What is important is that we don't have enough time to make all the ships that would be necessary to escape here, and we don't have enough skilled pilots. But there is one thing I can do. We won't all get out of here, but I'll make sure you do, and maybe you might even surprise me and help us out. I'm going to need to strengthen your mind right away. Yes, I'm sure that's the only way."

The alien motioned for Leon to follow him and Leon did, though he wasn't sure why. This alien didn't even bother to tell him his name, and he claimed that not everyone would live, yet Leon trusted him. Leon wanted to ask questions, but the alien seemed to be controlling his mind, forcing him to stay quiet and walk.

They went into a relatively small house near the center of the town. The alien sat down, but did not offer Leon a seat. Leon realized this was because there were no other seats.

Leon looked around the room. It was a pure and glowing white, and gave the impression of being bigger than it actually was.

"I have no time for formal introductions now, but just know that your mind is weak right now. Sudokus could easily force you to drink arsenic if you got within fifty yards of him. Any alien with an advanced mind could. My goal is to fix that. First, I'll start with mind reading. There are several ways to prevent someone from reading your mind. Due to the urgency of our current situation, I will only teach you two of them. The first way is to calm your mind completely. Try it now; try thinking of nothing."

Leon tried to calm himself, but with all that had been happening lately and the suddenness of this whole situation, all his thoughts were scattered.

Soon, Leon became aware of a very slight disturbance. It felt like an octopus was reaching all of its tentacles into his mind and feeling all his memories. The arms took whatever they wanted from the rush of thoughts flowing in Leon's head, and there was no way to get rid of them despite Leon's struggle. Eventually, the arms retreated, making sure everything looked the same as when they had entered.

"You'll have to try much harder than that," said the alien, "A technique I sometimes use is to think of the air, and nothing else. Then simply forget about the air as well. Try again."

Leon started thinking about air. The air is invisible and silent. His thought patterns didn't change much when he stopped thinking of the air. He could feel the tentacles again, but this time they seemed limp and lifeless. They were more like vines on a plant that grab onto something for support. Only there was nothing to grab onto and the tentacles pulled out. Leon thought he had passed when a sudden pain hit him. His concentration broke and all of his thoughts scattered. It was as if someone had fired a gun inside his brain. The tentacles quickly rushed back in to feel around.

Leon opened his eyes, not realizing he had ever closed them. The alien was sitting very calmly in his seat.

"You must not get frustrated. Just work harder. Before we continue with that exercise, I want to teach you a new technique. Hopefully this one will be easier for you to learn. This method involves trying to read your opponent's mind. You have to try to predict what he is going to do. If you're in a fight, use this technique. It's based on knowledge of your opponent, and probability."

Leon spent the next several hours working on these techniques. He couldn't hope to become a true master, but as long as the aliens couldn't read his mind at will, he'd have a chance.

Meanwhile, Scott was working with the parts making machine in the garage. It wasn't the ideal workshop for him, but it would do. He had sketches of the different parts for all the ships he planned to create for the rebels and he was running them through the machine and watched as pieces of metal came out. The room cooled every time Scott used the machine, but an advanced heating system allowed the room to maintain a decent temperature. Scott already had designs for ships, so it didn't take long before he had all the parts for a diverse fleet. Now he just needed help assembling them. Luckily, willing and eager volunteers were already pouring in. There were aliens of different shapes and sizes, all able and willing to assemble the ships.

The rebels definitely needed a lot of help to fight back. No one in there was a trained soldier or pilot, and they had very few vehicles—so a mass exodus would have been impossible without outside help. Now that help had arrived however, it would just take a bit of luck for an escape.

Luck was something the base didn't get much of however, and now was no exception. Gako and Lada were closing in on the planet now. They could see it off in the distance, surrounded by ally ships. Then again, a mercenary could never really have any allies, just non-enemies. Gako and Lada both had their guns loaded and were ready for anything that could jump out at them once they landed. This wasn't going to be a stealth mission. It was the type of mission requiring strategy on their part, and confusion of the enemy.

Back on the surface, Leon was getting a grasp on his newly acquired skill, but there was still one more part to it. He needed to be able to share his information with the beings whom he chose to, while keeping it a secret from people he didn't want knowing. The three aliens entered the room as if on cue.

"Your last task will be your hardest," said the alien in the dark outfit, "You must prevent me from finding out what number your thinking of, while allowing your friends over here to find out." He gestured toward the aliens who hovered.

Leon began the task by thinking of a number. Then he quickly shifted his thinking to air, and then nothingness. In doing that, he lost his number. He thought of the number again and it appeared as a colorful mass in an empty space. He saw the tentacles coming toward the number. Thinking quickly, Leon envisioned a wall surrounding the number. The tentacles reached forward, but hit the wall.

Then a new presence entered the space. It was like a dark blob, trying to engulf anything it came across: including the number. This blob represented the three little aliens; however, the wall blocked them as well as the tentacles. Leon envisioned a hole in the wall, hoping the blob could go through it, but it backfired and the tentacles started trying to squeeze into it. Leon quickly sealed the hole back up. Then he realized what he had to do. He simply imagined the number into the blob and then cleared his mind. He opened his eyes and saw all the aliens nodding in approval. The number just happened to be thirty-six, but that didn't matter. It was the fact that he was able to give this information to one being, while concealing it from another.

Outside there was a loud boom, which cut short Leon's moment of victory. Leon heard the noise first, and then saw its impact. People started scattering around and running through the streets to find a sturdy building to hide in. Everyone knew the day would come when the lasers would start pummeling down onto the underground town.

But this wasn't really an attack, it was an intentional distraction organized by Gako and Lada. It worked perfectly too, because they were able to force their way through crowds of people without really being noticed. They looked through the chaos hoping to find Leon or Scott. Fortunately, Leon had just completed his mind strengthening, but Scott didn't have that luxury. Lada was able to pick-up on Scott's mental frequencies and track him down.

Gako did all the dirty work of busting into the garage and shooting down everyone in the room except for Scott. Then Gako grabbed Scott who was trying to crouch behind a crate to hide. He injected a sleeping serum into Scott's arm to stop him from squirming. Gako was waiting for Lada to pick-up on Leon's mental frequencies, but she couldn't. They wanted to stay and search for him, but the lasers were still raining down and severely limiting the time they had to search. They knew the roof could collapse at any moment. Lada gave the signal to leave and Gako followed carrying Scott. They dumped Scott into the back of their ship and Gako quickly ran back to grab the parts machine before they took off for Sudokus's location. They only completed half their mission, and it would cost them dearly later on.

CHAPTER TWENTY-EIGHT

Leon gathered in the center of the town with the rest of the surviving aliens. The lasers had finally let up and there was time to regroup. It didn't take long before Leon realized Scott was missing. However, no one could confirm what exactly had happened to him. He could have somehow ran away during the commotion, or a piece of the roof could have caved in on him. There were chunks of debris everywhere, so searching for him would be a lengthy process.

Soon the three little aliens flew over by Leon and told him what had happened. They said that two beings of great power had entered into the room during the chaos and taken Scott away. However, the three aliens didn't know where any of them were now, because their mental frequencies were too far away for detection. They then proceeded to tell Leon that they suspected the assassins Gako and Lada of being the kidnappers. Leon didn't know who Gako and Lada were, but he took the aliens word for it.

Leon joined up with Willy then, and they were able to work together to regain control of the situation. They knew it was no longer safe in this place, and an immediate evacuation would be necessary. Fortunately, some of the ships Scott was working on were ready for use. There weren't any trained pilots, but Leon figured he could just give everyone a brief overview on how to use the ships before takeoff.

Everyone gathered into the hangar and anyone who was willing to fly entered into one of the ships. Leon briefed them on some of the most basic controls, such as acceleration, braking, steering, and firing the lasers. The alien who had been working with Leon earlier served as the translator and it didn't take long before everyone was ready to head out.

To escape, they'd first need to get rid of the command ship directly above them. Once that was out of the way, the majority of the aliens could rejoin with the humans on Europa. Leon hoped there would be some way to get the rest of the aliens as well, but for the moment, there was not. The only possible way would be to get a command ship. Leon looked up to the command ship in the sky, but quickly shook the idea out of his head. Yet he couldn't fully shake it, and he kept thinking that if there was some way that he could bring the command ship down in one piece, then he could use it. But before he could do any of that, he'd have to take off from the hangar.

The door leading from the hangar to the outside opened up, clearing a big hole on the surface. Ships began pouring out of the hole and headed up to the sky and toward the command ship. Leon led the charge with Willy in the clunky, three-man ship. Willy told Leon to take one of the new ships, but Leon had a feeling he should use this ship. Or was it the little aliens telling him to do that? Either why, he was taking it with Willy inside.

Leon didn't exactly know how to go about destroying a command ship, but he figured everything must have some weak spot. Leon flew near the command ship, analyzing it, trying to solve it. Some sort of metal alloy unheard of on Earth made up the outer casing of the ship, and it was impervious to lasers. There was a black tinted window on the front of the ship, but it wasn't ordinary glass; Leon wasn't even sure if it was glass. Either way, it was impenetrable. Other than that, the only things on the ship were the cannon barrels that protruded out from the sides and top of the ship, and the tailpipe connecting to the engine. If there was some way to disable the guns, it would help, but the only way to do that was to go inside the ship.

Leon knew what he had to do then. The single tailpipe on the ship was just large enough for him to fit his ship through. He'd be able to fly right through and into what he assumed would be the fuel tanks. The engine remained off while the command ship wasn't in motion, so once Leon was inside the tail pipe, he wouldn't be in any danger.

Leon camped out in a safe spot, hugging close to the planet, away from any stray fire. He watched as the command ship blasted beam after beam of its deadly energy, and tried to find some rhythm. Once he figured it out, he'd be able to time his acceleration just right to minimize the chance of a laser hitting him on his way there.

"What are you doing, Leon?"

"We're going into the tail pipe, Captain. It's the only way to get these rebels out of here safely. I'm not going to destroy the command ship; I'm going to take it down to the surface, so everyone can use it."

"What makes you think you can do that?"

"A ship as big as that has to have multiple engines. So if we go through the tailpipe and end up destroying one of the engines, there's got to be at least another engine to fly it. Then we can find the controls and…" Leon drifted off, not knowing how to finish that thought. There was no time to think right now.

"How do you know you'll be able to—"

"Hold that thought," said Leon as he accelerated towards the ship. He found the rhythm to the ship's constant laser fire, and knew it was the right time. Willy gripped onto his seat cushion tightly, as the ship sped towards the opening.

Leon was within a few yards of the opening, when he began to question if it really was big enough. If he was in his normal ship, he would easily fit, but this one seemed a bit too clunky now that he was up close.

The tips of the wings scraped hard against the metal as the ship squeezed through and made it into the ogelan-filled fuel tank. The ship was still speeding as it entered this reservoir, and crashed through the side, spilling countless gallons of ogelan into the lobby of the ship.

Soon all the fuel poured out carrying the ship with it. It flooded into a larger section of the command ship, drowning anyone who was within sixty feet of the fuel tank. The wave of ogelan carried the ship until it finally crashed down into some sort of storage room.

"Are you hurt?" asked Leon.

"No, I'm fine," said Willy. "You?"

"Never been better. Let's just get out of here and take a look around."

After Leon and Willy managed to pull themselves out of their wreck of a ship, Leon asked, "Hey, Willy, don't you think it's strange this alien vessel would use the same fuel as we use?"

"To be honest, kid, it's not strange at all. Who do you think we got the fuel from in the first place? I told you we've been trading with aliens for a while."

Willy pulled out the gun he'd brought with him and headed towards a door on the command ship, stepping through puddles of the fuel. Leon followed, but stayed behind Willy. They were careful as they navigated their way through the twists and turns of the corridors, taking each step through the thick, dark blue, jelly-like ogelan. The ship seemed even bigger on the inside than it looked on the outside.

Eventually Leon and Willy came to a closed door. They could hear voices on the other side, although they were in a foreign language. Willy moved in close to the door and pushed it open just enough for him to see inside. He saw the room was full of aliens with guns, talking to each other as they paced back and forth. Willy closed the door again to think for a second before he charged into the door shoulder first. He followed his charge by quickly rolling behind the corner of a control panel that rose a few feet off the ground. Willy then got up to a crouch just high enough so he could shoot over the top of the structure. Willy still used what Leon would've considered an old-fashioned gun, although it was the same style of gun used when he fought in World War Four. Yet, the gun seemed more effective than any gun Leon had seen before, and with a little bit of strategizing, Willy was eventually able to clear the room. Leon stepped into the room expecting to have to help Willy, but he found himself simply standing back and watching.

"So how exactly is that antique so effective at mowing down these aliens," asked Leon.

"It's not an antique, Leon. I used this style gun in World War Four when I was a soldier. And this is the same style of ammunition. They made a rare and super dense metal in the twenty-seventh century, but when they realized that same metal was perfect for building on the moon, they took it all to use for constructing hotels and factories there. Some apparently stayed on Earth and found its way to the black market where shady peddlers sold it. This gun isn't even government issued; I actually own it. These bullets cost me a pretty penny, but as you can see, they're worth it."

"That's nice, Willy, but we still have to find the controls to this ship so we can bring it back down."

"Leon, this is the control room. Look around you—that's the first rule of war: always know your surroundings. There's a control panel, maps, and everything you could possibly need to control a ship."

Leon finally looked around him and saw that what Willy said was correct. Leon ran up to the control panel to see it looked similar to the one he'd seen on the boat. It worked the same way as well.

Leon had to be fast in steering the ship down and loading everyone onto it. It wouldn't be long before one of the other nearby command ships realized what happened and came over to compensate for the lost ship. Then Leon would have to do this all over again.

Leon brought the ship down and the aliens who weren't already in a fighting ship got aboard and huddled in the control room. They couldn't be sure the ship was clear of enemy aliens, so Willy stood guard by the door. Once everybody was on board, Leon took hold of the spherical steering wheel and began spinning it until the ship had risen, then set course for Europa. After that, Leon began looking for the button to send the ship into hyper drive. He tried a few spots which seemed like logical places to put the button, and after accidentally firing a missile and dropping a load of cargo from a storage room, Leon found the right button and the ship sped off using the ogelan in the engines which Leon hadn't crashed through.

CHAPTER TWENTY-NINE

While Leon was flying the command ship towards Europa, Gako and Lada were arriving at Sudokus's headquarters beneath the clouds of Jupiter. They brought Scott with them, and he was just beginning to wake up as they brought him into Sudokus's office.

"What about the other humans?" asked Sudokus.

"We were unable to locate Leon, and we had no time to search for anyone else," said Lada. "The engineer was the only one we managed to get.—and we grabbed his machine as well."

"I hoped you would've at least gotten Leon, but I didn't expect you to fully complete your assignment. After all, I've learned over the decades that if you set your expectations low, you can never be dissatisfied. Now take your money and be gone." Sudokus waited until Gako and Lada had left before turning his attention to Scott, who was still waking up from the sleeping serum Gako had injected into him.

"Do you know why you're here, Scott Winchester?"

"Where am I?" asked Scott.

"You know where you are," said Sudokus. "And you know who I am. Just peer into my eye."

Scott was then compelled to stare deeply into the shiny red eye planted in the center of Sudokus's face. Scott saw exactly what Sudokus wanted him to see, and Scott soon learned where he was and who this robot was. It was a strange sensation. Sudokus was a miracle by engineering standards, yet to Scott and all the other soldiers from Earth, he was anything but a miracle.

"This can't be Jupiter. No life or civilization can exist on Jupiter."

"Who told you that?" Sudokus's voice was devious. Even an innocent question like this had a nefarious intonation.

"No one told me, it's just a well-known fact. Life can't exist on Jupiter plain and simple. There's no water, no land to support even microbial bacteria. This just can't be Jupiter."

"What makes you think there is life here?"

"Robots can't build themselves."

"What if they could? And what if there was life on Jupiter? Really think about this—you're a relatively intelligent being. If Homo sapiens inhabited one of the moons surrounding this planet, you don't think that after thousands of years they would learn how to live here? The only reasons humans aren't here yet, is because they're too far away. The aliens are just like you humans in some respects. They'll look for somewhere else to live, hoping for a better chance in life. Maybe life didn't start out here, but it soon learned how to live here. Soon, there was a floor installed, made from the most durable moon metals. Then soil was imported and agriculture began. Now there are cities and billions upon billions of people living here. It's the same with all the 'uninhabitable' planets." Sudokus paused for a few moments. "And no, I didn't build myself. I simply arrived here and became the voice of power to a group needing a leader. And why not listen to someone who the less attractive parts of the mind hasn't bogged down. I don't have to worry about emotions. Emotions are what cause all problems— those and morals. For you see, murder is only bad if a majority of people say it's bad. So if I say it's not bad, then everyone can freely do it. That logic may not make sense to you now, but it will one day. The reason I tell you all of this is because I'm giving you a chance to become a citizen and worker in this domain and avoid becoming a casualty in the war like so many humans. You specialized in aerospace engineering. Why not continue to do it, except with purpose? Because, when you think about it, you had no purpose back on Earth. That's why you didn't particularly enjoy your job. But here, you could see what your hard work was accomplishing, and you'd always know why you were doing it."

"So, you're behind this whole war? Surely you must have someone controlling you though. Robots can't just function on their own. They need information input in order to produce any output. Unless you're a program. A simple robot with a simple goal to obtain. Yet, with the ability to evolve and adapt to meet the goal."

"I appreciate your thought Scott, but I am nothing like what you know. I have considered the possibility that I am a simple program—I considered that a long time ago—but I am not. I am not an imitation of life, I am a fully functional robot with a mind. I have no goal other than the ones I set for myself, and I have no simple commands that drive me forward. There are some things you will never know, and you have to learn to not question them. I am not a well-intentioned machine that went wrong, I am not an escaped experiment, and I am no one's puppet either. I am Sudokus." Sudokus's red eye penetrated Scott and burnt him. Not literally, but Scott could feel it inside of himself because of its intensity. It was something indescribable. The eye was the deepest red imaginable, yet it somehow went past color, even went past reality. "Now," said Sudokus slowly and calmly, "do you want to work for me?"

"No, no, I can't. I have to get back home. I wish for you to allow me transport, or I'd like to speak with someone who can help me." Scott desperately wanted to sound confident and in control, but the enormity and inescapability of the situation was sinking in.

"I don't think you understand. I have a mind, just like yours. I think. I make decisions. I am a leader. I am the person you talk to. No one is above me. I'm the only one who can help you, so I'll make it simple for you. You can work as an engineer, creating the robot soldiers, and thus saving lives, or I could kill you right here, and your life would be lost and your name would mean nothing. History would never speak of you again. Don't think for one second that your life is more valuable than the life of an amoeba. Do you think anyone besides the humans you talk to on a regular basis care about you? There are millions upon billions of galaxies out there, and each of them with life. Do you think any of them care about you? The choice is yours. Live or die."

Scott was silent for a few moments as the situation began sinking in. He tried to think of something to say, but in the end, all he could muster was, "I would like to live."

"Good, I'll take you to your work space then." Sudokus began walking down the hallway knowing Scott would follow. "This is the workshop you'll be working in. You'll be designing mechs: robots who can serve as security for the cities, and soldiers for the wars.

"This building is the safest place in the solar system. It is literally indestructible and no one gets in unless I decide to let them in. It's all very advanced technology. You'd be perfectly safe in this building and you'd have all the food and drink you could want. I will make sure you have anything a man could want here. Anything. All you have to do, is make robots."

"Can we at least negotiate this?" Scott figured he had nothing to lose, so he refused to be submissive although he knew his voice was shaking.

"Scott, there is no negotiation to be had. It's life or death. There is no escape from here. Now I'll ask you for the last time, will you work, or won't you?"

Left with no other options, Scott decided to agree to work. But secretly, he still thought Sudokus was just a robot, and he was looking for some switch to turn him off, and then he could run away from here. Was he really on Jupiter? Sudokus never said that, but his eye had said so. But there was no time for that now, because Sudokus began leading Scott into a different room where aliens were working on mechs. But every single one had a gaping problem, and every single mech that came off the assembly line needed incineration.

"This is why I need your help," said Sudokus. "You'd think all the mechanical engineers in the galaxy could work out a few problems. However, I know that you specialize in several different areas and therefore you're the perfect candidate for this job. I suppose I'll let you get to work now. One of my assistants will bring your machine out to you shortly, and if you have any other questions, someone will be around to help you." Then Sudokus walked away and left Scott to do his job.

PART III

CHAPTER THIRTY

Leon and Willy arrived back on Europa intact, but with their actual mission not fully accomplished. They left for two reasons, one was to join up with the rebel forces on Mars—which they did—but the other one was to get the machine. It was true the machine was more of a secondary objective, but it would have been of great assistance. Especially now, since it appeared half the army had left Europa. Willy was the first to notice this and decided to ask Cpt. Drew about it.

"Cpt. Drew, where is everyone?"

"It would seem we received some bad information," replied Drew. "Sudokus isn't where we thought he was. All of this was just a clever diversion. So, the new man I appointed to fill in for you decided to take the pilots on a search mission."

"Why didn't you stop him? You knew I was going to be back."

"You can't know anything for certain, Willy. You should know that just as well as anyone by now; you fought in the last war, didn't you? By the way, Willy, I couldn't help but notice you came back with a command ship. I can tell it's alien by the design, but how did you manage the feat of bringing something like that back."

"Don't give me the credit; it was one of my pilots, Leon. He came up with the plan and executed it. And he managed to load up aliens that want to help us. There was a whole rebel base there and everything."

"Friendly aliens? You can't be serious, Willy. If you're in a war, and it looks like the enemy, assume it is the enemy. I won't be having these aliens arriving here in that Trojan horse, no sir. Take it out of here this instant."

"I assure you those aliens are friendly. Their base even got attacked while we were there, injuring and killing a few of them. If they were saboteurs, would their own men try to kill them?"

"A valid point, Willy, but I still wouldn't trust them further than I could throw them. Be careful around them, and keep them well away from my men. That's an order, not a suggestion."

Willy walked away from Drew then, sensing the hostility. He didn't blame Drew for his cautiousness though, why should he trust these aliens? Especially since this was his first time seeing them.

At the same time, Willy didn't like something about Cpt. Drew. Drew was just like the rest of them—willing to keep his men in the dark just because *they* told him to. Who were *they*? Even Willy didn't know all of them, but they were the people who handed down the orders. They were like Gods, simply because they knew things other people didn't. Maybe that was the reason for all the secrets: they didn't want to become mortals. Their knowledge made them somehow greater than everyone else; they could somehow live forever through their secrecy. Willy didn't care though; he would give away their secrets without hesitation. If only he knew all their secrets. How much technology was really being stored away? With all the contact, all the diffusion, there had to be more than what was here.

Willy headed back to the command ship where he saw Leon walking around and stretching out his legs.

"You think it's time to let those aliens out yet, Leon?"

"Oh, hey Willy. Yeah, I was just about to open up the doors. I had just gotten out myself. It took a while to figure out how to shut off the engine."

Leon headed back to the command ship to tell the aliens they could come out. They all made a swift, but cautious exit, as they were unsure what would await them outside the ship. They wandered around for several minutes before people corralled into tents for the night. One alien stayed back however, and Leon soon realized it was the alien who had given him mental training. Recognizing the alien, Leon decided to try to initiate conversation.

"Did you have a pleasant journey?"

"I would assume you would know the answer to that, seeing as you were also on the ship," replied the alien.

"Yes, but I was flying it, and you were crowded in with all the other aliens."

"It was a smooth journey." The alien spoke calmly and had a soothing effect on Leon.

"I'm glad...ummm, I don't believe you ever did tell me your name."

"You wouldn't be able to pronounce if I told you. Human tongues are too weak. No fault of your own, just evolution"

"Try me."

"Tzkcarwyagnz. I suppose you could just call me Tzkc, for short."

"How about I just call you T?"

"It makes no difference to me. There are far more pressing issues. You realize what is going to happen to your friend now, don't you?"

"Not really, but I could guess. They'll probably try to torture him to get top secret military information, and when he tells them he doesn't know anything, they'll probably kill him, and he'll appear as another statistic of this war."

"No, little one. Getting information is much easier than that for Sudokus. He has spies everywhere that could've read Scott's mind. No, he wants your friend to work for him. Either that, or he's using him as leverage in some sort of hostage situation. But that's doubtful since Scott has a very small field of people who'd be willing to give anything up to get him back."

"It doesn't matter if the enemy has one man, or one-hundred men as prisoners, it's worth it to attack and get your own kind back. I can't go on knowing that we've lost one of our men."

"It won't be easy. He's probably with Sudokus now. You know who Sudokus is, right?"

"I've heard about him from those three small aliens—how he actually has a mind and can learn. I know what I'm up against."

"You think you know, but no one can completely fathom Sudokus. It's one of the mysteries no one has solved yet." Tzkcarwyagnz looked up to the sky then. "It grows late. You should get some rest. There won't be any time for resting once this war starts back up, so stock up now."

CHAPTER THIRTY-ONE

Leon awoke to see Willy entering his tent in full battle gear. "Why are you dressed so early?" asked Leon, still half-asleep.

"It's not that early," said Willy. "Also, we've decided to leave as soon as the pilots get back. It's not safe here anymore. Now go get some breakfast before it's gone."

"We have a kitchen now?"

"If you can call it that, it's just a room with some appliances for cooking. Did you know a chef was on the original command ship we brought?"

"Really? I thought it was just soldiers that came along." After a pause, Leon asked, "So when are the pilots coming back anyway?"

"Anytime now, just keep an eye on the sky. They said they wasted their time following up a dead lead, and they'll be back any time now. To be honest with you, I thought they would have found a way to get themselves killed up there, but I guess not."

Willy then left Leon to go prepare for the big move. The humans had been lead to believe that not only was Sudokus no longer Ganymede, but that he wasn't even near Jupiter. However, the humans had finally managed to get a reliable lead from talking to the alien rebels, and it turned out there was a vulnerable city back on Mars. It was several hundred miles away from the rebel base though, so there wouldn't be as many command ships hovering. The city was vulnerable because of a virus going around which seemed to affect only the city's guards, who were foreign to the planet. This left the city ripe for conflict, uprising, and, in this case, war.

Willy had questioned his higher-ups on why they were attacking this city, seeing as it wouldn't really bring them any closer to Sudokus, but the only answer Willy got was that it would be beneficial to have a stronghold outside of Earth for the soldiers to set up camps. Secretly, Willy believed this was just a way to vent some anger for the unsuccessfulness of this war and as a way to acquire more land for the human population, which was growing too large for the Earth and moon to sustain.

Whatever the case, Willy couldn't argue, so he just continued to prepare and watch the sky until he finally saw the pilots returning in full force. They landed down in the camp and joined in with everyone to help make the transition to Mars as smooth as possible. Of course they were surprised to see all these new aliens and the command ship, but no one really questioned it because they were too busy preparing for the next move.

Once it was just about time to go, Willy looked for Leon to see if he was ready to leave. He found Leon with all of his piloting gear on, but he was just standing near his ship, staring off into the distance.

"Got something on your mind?"

"I was just thinking about Scott. I know we didn't really have much time to talk with the war and all, but I liked him. He was a nice guy. I just hope he really is still alive and we can get him back. But he's smart, so I'm sure he'll make it easy for us. If he's really out there, he'll find some way to communicate with us."

"Don't concern yourself with Scott too much, Leon," said Willy. "People die in wars all the time, and you knew that when you signed up. There's no time to sulk now, you just have to use your emotions to fight even harder."

"Thanks, Captain," said Leon. "So where are we headed to?"

"Mars."

"Didn't we just come from there?"

"Yes, but we're going to a different part. And this time there's going to be more fighting. We're going to attempt to take a city. I'm not exactly sure what we'll do if we succeed, or if we fail for that matter, but we just have to take small steps for now and see where they take us. Now, get yourself focused and ready. Departure is in an hour."

As Willy was walking away, Leon could sense the three little aliens coming from behind him. He casually turned around to engage them.

"You guys seem like you know everything," started Leon sarcastically, "So when is this war going to start going in our favor?"

"Sooner than you might expect, little one. Sudokus has already made his first mistake. More specifically, Gako and Lada did, but since they were working for him, it is as if he made the mistake. Gako and Lada's mission was not just to take Scott; they were also supposed to get you."

"Why?"

"He is dealing with feelings out of his range of emotions. He doesn't know what you'll do, but forces from another universe have intertwined with your destiny and you now give off a certain energy he can detect. He only detected that energy by accident when you took in that alien you mistook for a man. That's the only reason he sent people after you, because he senses something that's beyond him. Sudokus not getting you was simply a mistake. Yes, it would've have greatly helped him, but no, Sudokus doesn't think anything of you. You clearly still have much to understand if you think Sudokus cares about you.. The mental training you underwent was merely the beginning for you."

"Well, tell me this," said Leon, a bit confused, "What's going to happen when we go to Mars?"

"We will catch them off guard, and we will have some success, but remember that Gako and Lada are always ready to do Sudokus's bidding."

"Do I know them?"

"They are the two assassins who most likely came and took Scott."

"Oh yes, that's right." After a pause, Leon added, "So you think two people will defeat the whole army?"

"You must stop trying to interpret what you do not fully understand, little one. Some things you'll just never know."

The aliens began hovering away to talk to Tzkcarwyagnz and Leon realized he was hungry. He decided to head down to the kitchen Willy had mentioned earlier.

Willy was right when he said this wasn't really a kitchen. There were some tables and chairs, and there were chefs in the back with cooking equipment, but it was obvious that all these things were just afterthoughts on a room most likely intended for storage. Leon was going to find his own table in the corner and wait to be served, when he heard a familiar voice say, "Leon, over here, comrade." Leon turned around to see Alexander sitting with a group of pilots.

"Welcome, comrade," said Alexander.

"Hey, what's up?"

"Not much, not much, comrade. We just came back from a scouting mission. Where were you by the way?"

"I was, uh, off on a personal errand. We needed some objects recovered from back home." Leon tried to be as vague as possible.

"Well, you did not miss much. I'm not sure what we were looking for anyway. I guess we were looking for a big sign reading, 'Sudokus's hideout'," said Alexander letting out a laugh. "But where are my manners, comrade? I forgot to introduce you to the comrade I met while on the last mission. This is Odegbula; he's both an elite fighter and an elite pilot."

They ate quickly after the server brought out their food, but Odegbula kept looking up at Leon. Leon would look down and take some food, then look up and meet Odegbula's eyes. He looked around the room, then looked at the other people around the room. Everyone else had their heads down, eating. Then he'd look at Odegbula, and Odegbula would quickly glance up at him before putting his head down. Leon was getting uncomfortable. Finally, Odegbula spoke and ended the awkwardness.

"Was your father an army commander in Uganda back during the last war?"

"Yes, actually, he was," said Leon, surprised.

"You look just like him. I worked with him back in the day. He was a great man you know. We had a saying back in my home country, 'The son should only be as weak as the father's greatest moment'. I can only hope that for you. I'm afraid I didn't catch your name."

"It's Leon Dudley, sir."

They finished eating the meal in silence and then headed off to their separate ships. Leon got into his ship and waited for the takeoff signal. This was a new ship for Leon. Since he destroyed his last ship flying it into the command ship's tailpipe, he had to use one of the reserve ships. However, at least upon first inspection, the ship seemed just as good as his last one, and he had no complaints about it.

As time passed, Leon got the feeling that he was forgetting something, but he didn't know what it was. Then, the three little aliens flew in front of his ship, and Leon let them in. Now he was ready for take-off.

Leon looked around at all the other ships that were near him as they began accelerating toward the darkness known as outer space. There were two command ships in the fleet now, and the homemade ship was slowing down the more advanced one. It seemed that everyone knew the dangers associated with trying to move a rebel fleet this big through Sudokus's kingdom, but the benefits greatly outweighed the risks in this case. In the future however, they would have to coordinate their movements better.

Leon began to relax himself and prepare for what appeared to be just a routine flight, when he suddenly felt tentacles in his mind. It was like a shadow falling on him, trying to overtake it by blocking out the light. Leon used the mental training he'd received and fought to block out the tentacles. After a few minutes, he felt the presence leave him and he returned to his normal self.

"What was that," he thought to the three little aliens.

"Maybe one of Sudokus's other hired hands."

"You think it could have been Sudokus himself?"

"No."

"How are you so sure?"

"If it was Sudokus, you wouldn't have to ask."

CHAPTER THIRTY-TWO

The rest of the flight was uneventful and the fleet was right on schedule as they neared their destination. They were just a few hundred miles away from Mars, just far enough to be out of view of any looming command ships.

The plan was to send in a few ships at a time along carefully planned routes. If they sent in too many at a time, the enemy soldiers would see them and shot them down before they penetrated the atmosphere. Leon thought it was strange that there was a way to sneak past the ships, but maybe the ships were for keeping people in more than they were for keeping people out.

Leon stuck together with Alexander and Odegbula and soon it was their turn to enter, which they promptly did. They were able to touch down on the surface without a hitch, and they were soon organizing with the others who had already landed. Most of the people were pilots, and some were ordinary soldiers.

They had to coordinate the siege of this city just right. They couldn't start opening fire until they had enough people on the ground. At the same time, if they waited too long, the guards would eventually stumble upon them while just patrolling their routes. For now however, they were unnoticed as they waited on the outskirts of the city. The little aliens, who were staying behind in the ship for safety reasons, delivered one last message to Leon before the battle started.

"Leon, tell the men to only attack the guards: not any civilians. The guards will be recognizable by the armor they wear; the civilians wear more casual clothing. Tell the men that the civilians will not hurt them as long as they don't attack them."

"You want me to tell them right now?"

"Yes, Leon. Tell the men before the battle starts; it will be too hectic during the battle to relay any messages."

Leon pushed his way to the front of the group to deliver this message, although he wasn't the type of person who'd normally attract this much attention to himself. Leon quieted down the crowd and gave them the message. Immediately afterwards, someone older than Leon stepped forward and said, "Hey, kid, I know we trained that way in target practice, but this is war. We'll shoot anything that looks ugly."

For a moment, no one said anything, but then Odegbula stepped into the man's face and yelled, "You heard the man, don't shoot any civilians." Odegbula was almost as intimidating a presence as Willy, and the man decided to slink back into the crowd. Odegbula could tell the soldiers were growing confused now, so he decided to take control of the situation by talking some more. "Men, today is the day we finally show the aliens that we're serious. Today is our first significant victory, and our first foothold. Now's not the time for second-guessing and hesitation, it's time for action. Now let's move out there, and do what we've all been trained for." Odegbula then turned toward the city and let out a battle cry. This riled up the group to follow him out into the streets. Leon questioned why he couldn't have given a speech like that on top of telling the people not to shoot civilians. After all, the little aliens said there was something special about him, so didn't that mean he should be able to lead and be important? But there was no time to think about that now, as he rushed out with everyone else into the streets.

For now, all they had to do was clear a spot for one of the command ships to land. Then they could unload more of the real soldiers. Lt. Bennett had trained the pilots in boot camp, but ground fighting just wasn't their specialty.

Since they didn't have time to scout out this city in advance, they made up the details of the attack as they went. At first, it was just a straight charge forward, firing at the guards. That was successful until the guards began using their surroundings to their advantage and ducking behind buildings and going into alleyways for cover.

The guards soon reemerged however, and began firing upon the soldiers. Some of the guards stood behind riot shields and others were on rooftops with strange looking sniper-like guns. The human soldiers all ran for cover into an alley between two tall buildings.

"Now what?" asked one of the soldiers with a hint of nervousness.

Leon was about to make up for his lack of a speech earlier by answering this question, but Odegbula once again beat him to the punch.

"Didn't you hear me back there, soldier? Now is not the time to second guess. We just need a plan, that's all. Half of you will go out the back of this alley, and the other half of us will go out the way we came in. I'll lead the half of you going this way, and Leon will lead the half of you going out the back. We're temporarily splitting up. Any questions?"

Leon was wondering why Odegbula would think him capable of leading a group of soldiers in battle, but he didn't question him and he still remembered enough from boot camp to do it.

One of the actual soldiers, realizing Leon was a pilot with only a side arm, gave Leon his gun. Leon accepted gratefully, only because he knew soldiers always carried two primary weapons in case they ran out of ammunition.

Odegbula (who carried standard issued ground soldier guns with him as a habit) charged out from the front of the alley and began firing upon the guards while ducking behind anything he could. There were some sort of wheel-lacking vehicles— similar to the hover cars on Earth, but different—lining the streets, which the soldiers were able to use for protection. Odegbula fought with a style similar to the Spetsnaz from the cold war era. He did a lot of duck-and-rolls and often times ended up firing couched with one knee on the ground. Yet, he was a very effective fighter, especially for a pilot.

The rest of the men with him fought with mixed styles, some would hide for a few seconds, then pop up randomly and start shooting for a few seconds. Others were jumping out from behind the cars, shooting, and then running forward to the next vehicle, steadily creeping closer to the enemy. Every now and then, a civilian would run out from one of the buildings onto the street; but apparently people listened to Odegbula, because none of the soldiers shot them.

Leon's men were able to move out more easily from the other side of the alley, seeing as the guards had positioned themselves for an attack at Odegbula's location and weren't prepared for an attack from this direction.

Leon's men took out the little resistance they faced, and then decided to walk a little ways down and circle around so they could sneak up on the guards from behind. The only problem was that there were more guards in the city, racing toward the battle and coincidently crossing the path of Leon and his men. Leon's men faced a group of guards with riot shields who were marching down the streets. The fighting went similarly to how Odegbula's fighting went, only Leon didn't do all the fancy rolls and flips Odegbula did, just a simple point and shoot.

As the fighting continued, it just so happened, through pure luck, that the space between Leon's men, and Odegbula's was just big enough for a command ship to land. The command ship's pilots just needed the soldiers to hold it a little bit longer while the ship descended.

However, the ship was having difficulty landing at the moment because an enemy command ship had spotted the fleet and engaged it in an all-out battle. Willy made the decision that the command ship stolen from the aliens should try to land on the planet, while the one created by the humans should stay back to fight. It would be a lesser loss if the aliens destroyed the homemade ship.

The fleet, which was missing many of its pilots due to the war on the ground, was having difficulty in the battle. The command ship the humans made was no match for the enemy's command ship. Combined with the rest of the fighter ships in the fleet though, it could provide enough cover fire for the other command ship to make it to the surface safely.

The alien fighter ships continued buzzing around the stolen command ship, firing away at it, but not doing any real damage. Eventually, the command made a safe landing and the next phase of the attack could begin.

On the ground, the fighting was so intense that neither side really noticed the ship landing. It was a tight fit, and the weight of the ship crushed some of the smaller buildings as it landed. Once it had come to a complete stop, doors opened up and both human and alien soldiers began pouring out onto the battlefield. They acted as the bridge between Leon's men and Odegbula's and soon there was just one large force attacking the heavily outnumbered alien guards.

The battle was soon over, with no civilian causalities. There was no time to rest for the pilots however, as they needed to head back to the sky to aid in the aerial fight. They headed to their ships on the outskirts of town and took off for the sky.

It was clear there was even less planning involved in this attack than there was in the last one. Ships were buzzing around everywhere, just hoping nothing hit them.

Leon began looking around for something to take down the command ship. He didn't want to lodge himself into the tailpipe again, because this was his personal ship now, not something expendable. Leon scanned the area until he saw something he'd never noticed before: a small meteor orbiting around the command ship. Leon quickly put the pieces together in his head to figure out that the ship was just big enough, and dense enough, to have its own weak gravitational field. Leon wouldn't have guessed the ship would have any sort of gravitational pull, but the evidence was right in front of him

Now, if he could somehow manipulate the meteor and shove it into the tail pipe he figured he could clog it. Then the pressure would build up in ship as the engines continued to run. It was a bit of a crazy plan, and it might not even work. But in order to even try it, Leon would have to ram his ship into the meteor at the right speed and angle.

His plan was to hit the meteor without causing damage to his ship. He was going to go full speed toward the ship, then quickly turn to the side at the last second so that just the side of his ship smacked the meteor. It would require perfect timing and since the meteor was orbiting slowly, he didn't know how long he'd have to wait to get his next chance if he missed his first.

Leon took deep breaths while he waited for the meteor to be in position. When it finally was, he took off. Leon was too focused to be nervous as he got closer to the meteor. He knew he had timed his departure correctly, now he just needed to time his turn correctly. Leon gripped the steering wheel tightly and then when the moment was right, he made a hard turn on his ship, smacking the meteor perfectly.

Leon could tell by the vibrations sent through his ship that he would have a dent after this, but it would be fixable. Leon looked behind him to see the meteor flying toward the ship's tailpipe. He waited to see what would happen as patiently as a golfer waiting to see if his putt goes in. Leon was nervous for a moment when he realized that the meteor was nearly the same size as the hole. He began thinking that the meteor was bigger than the hole. Would it fit?

To his relief, it did.

The meteor sunk into the pipe and Leon could hear it scraping against the sides.

"That was very skillful of you," thought the aliens, "But don't do that next time. Only do something like that if it is absolutely necessary. What if you'd wrecked your ship? Scott isn't here anymore to fix it. You didn't even take time to consider all the options."

"Well, I felt that was necessary, and if I waited to consider my options, I would have missed the chance. Please just trust me sometimes. By the way, where is Scott anyway, can't you read his mind or something?"

"We would read it, but Sudokus is protecting him. We've been trying to access his mind on and off since his disappearance, I assure you."

The conversation ended when Leon saw a flash of red streak across his windshield, a near miss from an enemy laser. Leon joined into the fight for a few more minutes, taking down enemy ships left and right.

Gradually, a noise became audible. It started at a relatively low pitch, but as the volume increased, so did the pitch. Soon, all the ships fighting stopped for a moment to listen. Once they began to realize it was coming from the command ship, even the aliens began fleeing the battle.

Leon took the most pleasure out of anyone in watching the command ship explode. First, the back part where all the fuel is stored went in flames, but less than a second later, the fire had spread to the rest of the ship. Soon the rear of the ship completely separated from the front and floated away from the battle. The ogelan-fueled fire was out within seconds, due to the lack of oxygen, but the damage was done. There was plenty of debris in the sky, and probably some alien bodies too, but nobody cared about the latter.

The alien fighter ships immediately began retreating from the battle. They were on their way back to Sudokus. They hoped that Sudokus would give them another chance, but Sudokus almost never gave anyone a second chance. Besides, with the mech project under the control of Scott now, there would soon be no need for any living soldiers anymore. Any aliens who lost from here on out would become food for Sudokus's pet, Jum-Jum, and that was all there was to it.

CHAPTER THIRTY-THREE

A few minutes after the battle was lost, a radio transmission informed Sudokus about what happened. While he wasn't satisfied to hear the news, he wasn't surprised. After all, the troops weren't machines and therefore they were bound to mess up no matter how much genetic engineering the bio-engineers devoted to them.

Sudokus stepped outside and waited for the defeated aliens to come to him. It didn't take long before a group of ships became visible, first as specks in the dark sky, and then as gleaming war machines. Then they began descending onto the surface. Sudokus waited until everyone had exited their ships before addressing them.

"What happened out there?" Sudokus's gleaming red eye gave the appearance that his was looking at all the soldiers simultaneously. "Doesn't anyone want to answer the question? It could be the difference between life and death."

Finally, one of the soldiers stepped forward to explain what happened. "That particular city had been vulnerable, sir, due to a virus affecting the guards there. Some rebels must've snuck past our command ship and taken the city, but before we could do anything about it, we ended up in a battle of our own. Hundreds—no, thousands—of ships surrounded us and the battle quickly got out of control. But the real reason for our defeat was that something happened to our command ship. It just exploded. There was nothing we could do at that point, sir."

Sudokus decided that moment to kill all the aliens, more out of an overall sense of dissatisfaction with how things were progressing than anything else, however, he decided to humor them before feeding them to Jum-Jum.

"Did any of you see what happened?" asked Sudokus. "No? No one wants to talk? I think I can hear Jum-Jum's stomach growling from here."

Sudokus suddenly got a vision of what happened. He saw Leon in his eye. He saw Leon flying around, and he knew then that it Leon destroyed the command ship. He didn't know how, but he didn't need to. He could sense Leon's power was slowly building, and he knew now that Leon definitely was a threat to him.

"Why should I let any of you live?" The aliens all stood around, stone faced, ready to face death. "So, you're saying I should feed you all to Jum-Jum?" They wanted to say no, but they knew it was all pointless now.

"Sir," started one of the aliens cautiously, "Some have suggested mortals like us learn from mistakes, and that all mortals make mistakes. So, perhaps, we would never make mistakes again since we've already made one and learned from it."

"Your theory is wrong. You are not a machine, and you are therefore doomed to always make mistakes. Well, maybe you're not always doomed; there is one way to end your mistakes I suppose." Suddenly, Sudokus grabbed one of the aliens out of the group and clasped down on his arm with his claw-like hand. Some thick, green goop started coming out of the cut Sudokus created. Then Sudokus twisted his arm until the bone inside broke. "I heard what you were thinking just now," said Sudokus to the alien he was holding, "You were thinking this is not fair. You were thinking I am a bad leader. How could you accuse me of being a bad leader, when I have the largest dominion in this galaxy? You dissatisfy me. Guards, take all of them and feed them to Jum-Jum," said Sudokus tossing the soldier down. "Death. Death is the way to end your mistakes."

Sudokus headed down to Scott's shop to see his progress on the mechs. Currently, there was a mech running an obstacle course. The mech was the same brown color as Sudokus, but about three quarters of his size. The robot seemed very bulky and cumbersome, but it was surprisingly agile. It had two sets of fully functional guns; one that fired lasers and one that fired metal. Both were extremely accurate and lethal.

"I knew I had gotten the right person for this job," said Sudokus.

Scott was still a bit uncomfortable around Sudokus, but he knew by now that Sudokus was really in charge, and if he had any hope of escaping, he'd have to get on his good side.

"The mechs are coming along nicely," said Scott, "Still a few glitches though. It's very difficult to make them resistant to damage and still aerodynamic in flight. We might just have to settle with them hovering rather than actual flight."

"I hope you're not giving up yet, I don't keep you around to settle you know."

"Oh, don't worry," said Scott. "I'll keep improving them until you tell me you're ready to deploy them. Even then, I'll still be looking for improvements. You know, making sure they don't malfunction. I wish I could give all these mechs the same mind you have, but no one, not even you, knows where that stuff came from."

"Well, one person knows where to find it," said Sudokus. "Whatever created me knows."

"You mean you don't know who—or what—made you? Surely there must be some way to find out."

"What makes you think I was made? Maybe I just always existed."

"Most humans live their lives searching for a meaning," said Scott. "Don't you care to find out what your purpose is? Don't you think your life has a purpose?"

"For me, there are no mysteries and there is no life," said Sudokus. "I can't die, so how can there be life without death? I don't care to find who made me. That's why I created the myth that I killed my creator, so people don't wonder about it. When you think about it, it doesn't really matter, now does it?"

"It might. What if whoever made you put a time bomb in you, and you only have a few more seconds of functioning before you explode?"

"I would know about it then, because I know everything about myself. I know how every little wire interacts with the thing next to it. I could take myself apart and put myself back together if I wanted to. I just couldn't make another me, because I don't know what substance composes my mind. It's the only thing that has eluded me for all these years."

"Well," said Scott, "If you know everything about yourself, then what is your energy source? You never sleep, nor do you recharge, yet you are still functioning at peak performance."

"My energy comes from everything. I could convert you into energy right now if I wanted to."

"But where does the energy, to do that, come from?" Scott felt as if he was on to something now, but he couldn't think about the path he was going down, lest he wanted Sudokus to know as well. He asked each question relying on instinct.

"I started off with some energy," said Sudokus, "And now I'm constantly pulling energy from everything: even the smallest molecules."

"So if you were sent out into the vacuum of space, where would your energy come from?" asked Scott.

"Don't you have some mechs to work on?" asked Sudokus, dissatisfied. "I'm not paying you to talk." With that, Sudokus exited the room.

Scott kept thinking about the conversation, and he began formulating some ideas for a possible escape.

CHAPTER THIRTY-FOUR

Leon and the rest of the soldiers from Earth were working on the Martian city during the weeks after the war. They had made an alliance with the inhabitants of the city and were using some of the aliens they had brought along with them to translate. They wanted to extract as much information from the city natives as possible without using force.

There was a division amongst the aliens between those that were happy about humans running their city, and those that weren't happy about it. The ones already bred to believe Sudokus was good were upset, and the ones who had a bit more free will were happy to not have the guards around any longer. However, none of them particularly liked the humans; it was a matter of choosing the lesser of two evils.

After a lot of work on the city, it looked just like a grand city on Earth. There were tall glass buildings, shrubbery—alien shrubbery, but nonetheless shrubbery—and even canals acting as rivers. Talking to the residents, they had discovered that the aliens did not drink water and that water could even kill them.

"That's two things now," said Leon. Leon sat in a room in a private hotel high above the sidewalks below.

"What's two things?" asked Willy. Willy sat not too far away from Leon in the same room.

"Insect repellent and water."

"What about insect repellent and water?" asked Willy irritated by Leon's vagueness.

"Insect repellent and water can kill the aliens. Well, the soldier aliens anyway. Remember when we used insect repellent back on Earth; before we went to the Russian base?"

"I remember now—those little aliens gave you the idea, right? We were pretty lucky to have them with us."

"Yes we were, sir." Leon paused then, and stared out the window.

"Isn't this view amazing," said Willy standing up to look out the window as well. Looking down they could see the other buildings around, the hover cars zooming below, and even the rivers glimmering in the sun, which, at this distance, was smaller than any human was accustomed to. There were dusty yellow streets in a grid formation around the city and even aliens selling alien fruits on the side of the road. Even further in the distance was a factory with smoke spewing out. Yet, even the smoke seemed somehow beautiful and natural, just like a cloud glowing in the light of the afternoon sun.

"Maybe this is the problem," started Leon. "We spent so long building this city, and now we're just looking at it. How long has it been since we last attempted to fight the aliens? How long are we planning to stay here? And if we spent so long building this city up, we'll have to leave some people behind to protect it when we leave. How can we make sure they won't lose the city?"

"You're getting way ahead of yourself, Leon. We are here for a reason. We're talking to the locals; we're also fixing up our command ship. Plus, think about; if we just go killing as many aliens as we can, does that make us any better than Sudokus? This war started because we needed to defend our moon. Then they came to our home planet and we decided that we'd need to take the fight to them to avoid any civilian casualties. But if we don't take some time to make sure we're actually on the right path to Sudokus, then we're killing innocent aliens, and then we might as well join Sudokus because we'll be just as wrong as him. We're not here to make hasty moves."

"Well if we're supposed to be learning, what have the locals taught us? Besides that water is deadly."

"I'm not supposed to tell you, but I will anyway. It turns out that the people out in the countryside are starting to become sick from all the smoke that comes out of the factories. Not like the factory near here, the blue smoke from the slave factories. Unfortunately, there are none nearby to investigate. The slave factories are apparently making some sort of blue liquid, but no one can say for certain what it is. Some speculate that it's some sort of liquefied energy. Unfortunately, no one knows what happens to this liquid after it's produced, but we assume it's going to Sudokus."

"Why does that matter, I mean are we supposed to free the slaves now?"

"I never said that. I figure we just have to find a way to keep the people from getting sick. That way they'll like us more. But if that means freeing the slaves, I'm all for it. Besides, the aliens also told us that most of the slave farms are poorly guarded, and it probably wouldn't be hard for us to liberate them."

"That might be important, but enough talk about Mars, Willy, what's Earth like right now? Something weird was going on last time we went there."

"John is seriously messing stuff up back home. Can you believe he's still trying to convince the people that we're fighting humans? And I know he's keeping alien technology from us. So are the other world leaders, but I don't know them as well, so I can't say for certain."

"What was John before he replaced Winston as leader?" asked Leon.

"He must have been something important, because there was no election like there usually is when a leader resigns. I don't know exactly who gets to takes over after an assassination. It's never happened until now."

While Willy and Leon talked, there was an alien ship approaching the city from space. It had special radar blocking technology making Earth's command ship unable to detect it as it entered. The ship was pitch black, and in the darkness of space, it was invisible.

Inside the ship were four similar looking aliens. They were about six feet tall with dark blue skin. They looked strikingly humanoid, but they were clearly not human. The aliens were apprentices personally trained by Gako and Lada to take over their job when they retired in some many decades from now. They even had the same types of guns Gako and Lada would use for a mission like this.

Sudokus knew he would've been better off just hiring Gako and Lada for this, but he had a feeling that he would need them rested for an even more important mission in the future; not to mention that their failure last time caused Sudokus to lose a bit of confidence in them.

The ship landed by a drainage ditch outside of town. The four aliens got out and surveyed the area. It was just as they had expected it to look from their extensive mapping out of the city. There was a pipe with a gentle stream of water coming out of it. The aliens walked alongside the ditch until they were near the pipe. It was just big enough for them to get through it if they traveled in a single file line. They simply had to make sure they didn't touch the water on the bottom.

The first alien jumped into the pipe and used his hooked nails to hold on to the top of the pipe as he slowly pulled himself along where it was dry. The other aliens did the same thing, following him through the main sewer system.

Eventually the aliens came to a manhole and pushed it out from the bottom. There weren't any civilians in the vicinity to see them sneak out of the sewer and duck into an alley.

The aliens had already coordinated a plan and they waited in the alley to work out fine details. Their ultimate goal was to reach the building Willy and Leon were currently in. Sudokus could care less about Willy, but they needed to eliminate Leon.

They had to be stealthy on this mission, and cloaking would do them no good. While they could disguise their bodies, they wouldn't be able to conceal their weapons in the crowded streets. With this in mind, the aliens all split up and went on separate paths.

One of the aliens headed out the back of the alley and went right. He was walking across relatively unpopulated side streets with his gun ready for anyone who crossed his path. So far, he hadn't needed to use the gun, but he wasn't close to his objective either.

The alien stopped by a river to check the positions of his teammates. They were all where he had expected them to be. Each of them had to know where the others were at all times so they would reach the building simultaneously.

The alien heard some voices and crouched behind a bush near the river. He pointed the tip of his gun so it was sticking out just a little bit, and prepared to pull the trigger. It was only some civilians passing by however, so he decided not to shoot and instead just waited for them to pass by.

Once the coast was clear, he continued on his way down the path. He was beginning to get into the more populated part of town, so he was always looking for the next hiding spot. He moved from spot to spot, always having to wait for all the people to pass before moving to the next area. Soon there would be too many people around for this strategy to keep working. By then however, the rest of his group would rejoin him.

The alien ducked into an alley as things were getting too crowded for him. He was at the rendezvous point, but he was early and he had to wait for the others. Looking through to the other side of the alleyway, he could see the target in the distance.

He checked the positions of his team to make sure they were also in position. They were all on schedule and they soon arrived into the alley. Now it was time for the guns. All the stealth in the world couldn't help them through this part of the city. As soon as one of the aliens moved, they all burst out in the streets, guns blazing.

"That's why I think we have to leave by tomorrow," said Leon.

"I see your point, but we have to work with what we have, and right now—" Willy was suddenly cut off when someone burst through the door with a worried look on his face.

"We have a problem. There's something out there. Aliens are out there, and they're shooting up the streets. No one knows where they came from, but they're headed in this direction."

"Stay here, Leon. I'll take care of it," said Willy.

"You want me to stay here? You have no idea what you're going to find out there, I'll go with you to help you out."

"Leon, I'm a soldier, not a leader. If I die out there, you could take my job and it wouldn't make a difference. If you die, I have no one to replace you. Yes, there are other pilots, but you have more knowledge about the aliens, and that's irreplaceable." Willy grabbed one of the biggest guns from the gun rack in the room. Then he added, "Besides, this is what I used to do for a living."

Willy got into an elevator and rode down to the bottom of the building. The whole ride down he was mentally preparing himself for what was going to happen out there. During the last war, he would've thought nothing of this, but now he was getting older and he wasn't sure how well he'd be able to do out there.

The elevator doors opened up and Willy stepped out. He was on the bottom floor of the building now and he could see people running into the building from outside. Willy stepped out of the door to see the aliens marching through the streets shooting at anything that moved.

Willy dove out of the way when one of the aliens saw him and started shooting. He rolled behind a large flowerpot on the side of the road. Willy poked his head out from behind the pot to see where the aliens were. Then he started looking at his surroundings. One thing he learned was always to know his surroundings. Willy observed that they were near a river. He knew this could be helpful because the locals said water was lethal. Willy also noticed there were several currently abandoned fruit stands lining the streets. Willy knew that those would serve as good protection.

Willy rolled out from behind the flowerpot firing at one of the aliens. Willy was using whatever he could find as cover, but the whole time he was making sure to place himself between the aliens and the building.

By now, the aliens were beginning to focus all of their attention on Willy. Willy saw one started to inch closer to where he was hiding while the others began making their way toward the door. Willy waited until the alien was almost on top of him, then he popped out and smacked the alien across the face with his gun before unloading a round into the aliens chest. This dropped the alien dead on the ground. To be sure it wouldn't come back, Willy kicked its corpse into the river.

At this point Leon was watching the battle unfold from the room. He had made sure to barricade the doors just in case one snuck past Willy. He also grabbed one of Willy's guns from off the rack. He saw what Willy's plan was, but he was unsure of whether it would actually work. He felt better after Willy had killed the first one.

Willy began running back toward the hotel's door, ducking behind one of the nearby fruit stands. He leaned around the side of it and began shooting at the aliens who immediately ducked behind a low wall on the side of the river. Willy took advantage of this and ran across the street to a part of the wall around the corner from the aliens. One of the aliens poked its head up to look for Willy thinking he was still by the fruit stand. Willy took advantage of the opening and shot the alien in the head. He hit a weak spot and the alien's head exploded the same way the head exploded on the alien Leon killed in one of the early battles of the war. Willy hoped he could get head shots on the other two aliens.

One of the aliens lifted its gun up over the wall and began blindly firing at Willy who had to duck back down. Willy started walking along the wall, staying crouched down the whole time.

One of the aliens ran from behind the wall and headed for the door. Willy had to make a quick decision on whether he was going to go for the one running, or the one shooting. He decided to go for the one shooting.

Willy quickly wrapped around the wall and in the same motion scooped up the dead alien body to use as a body shield. The alien was still blindly firing over the wall, so it took it a few moments to realize that Willy was now next to him. The alien began firing and Willy began firing, but Willy used the alien corpse to absorb bullets until he finally shot the attacker dead.

Now there was only one alien left, but he was nearly to the door now. Willy dropped everything that could weigh him down—most importantly the body shield and his gun—and began sprinting toward the alien. He was able to catch him just as he was opening up the door. Willy grabbed the arm the alien was using to hold his gun with one hand, and wrapped his other arm around the creature's neck.

Willy used his strength to drag the alien from the doorway back toward the river. The alien struggled with Willy, and was nearly as strong as he was. The alien finally managed to work his gun hand free, but Willy slapped it aside before he could get off a shot. Then Willy spun the alien around and pushed him to the ground. Willy jumped on the alien's back and got down on his knees, making sure to put all his weight on the alien. He then grabbed the alien's arm and began bending the elbow joint in a way it wasn't meant to go. The alien put up a fight, but eventually Willy reached the joint's threshold. He then made a quick jerking motion and broke the alien's arm.

At this point, he grabbed the alien's gun and threw it away towards the river. Willy then proceeded to pick up the alien and just began punching him. The alien tried to defend himself, but could not with only one hand. Willy slowly dragged the alien toward the edge of the river as he continued to beat him. Willy was now against the low wall on the bank of the river, still holding the alien. Finally, Willy simply dropped the alien over the side.

Willy could see the alien struggle to try and get out, but he was quickly swelling up with water. Soon, the pressure inside of him built up too high, and his skin began bursting open. A mixture of water and green blood came spewing out from all of the holes, and eventually the alien stopped struggling.

Willy hadn't noticed the group that had been gathering around the fight, but they now began cheering, grateful that Willy had saved them.

CHAPTER THIRTY-FIVE

Willy returned to the room tired. He put his gun back on the rack along with one of the alien's gun he'd brought back as a souvenir from the battle.

"I guess you're right then, Leon," said Willy. "We'll have to leave here tomorrow. They're on to us now, and it's not safe here anymore."

"Ya, but that was incredible. Why didn't you ever tell me how good of a soldier you were? You must've been ten times better in your prime. You'll have to teach me how to do some of that stuff."

"Teach you? How do you expect me to do that? It's not something I can just show you. It takes training and real world experience. I can attempt to show you, but it won't really sink in until you find yourself in a difficult situation and realize training is merely a foundation and it's up to you to know what you have to do," Willy paused, realizing he should at least try to help Leon. "Look, here's what I'll do. When we leave tomorrow, load your ship into the hangar of the command ship. I have a room in the ship where you can stay. During the trip, I'll show you a couple of techniques I've learned."

"Where are we headed anyway?"

"Not sure yet. I have to talk to a few guys and pull a few strings. I'll let you know as soon as I find out." Willy then walked out of the room to change into some clothes not stained with alien blood. Then he headed down on the elevator to the meeting room to discuss plans with other commanders.

Leon looked out of the window to see janitors lining the streets with sweepers, vacuums and other machinery Leon wasn't familiar with. They were vigorously working to clean up the dead bodies of the aliens.

Leon looked over when he heard the elevator coming up. It opened up and inside were the three aliens, hovering in their spacecraft.

"You guys take the elevator?"

"Well, it's not like we can teleport through walls, little one. How else are we supposed to visit you? Besides, you're not on Earth anymore, so I suggest you get used to the site of aliens taking elevators; it's not as uncommon as you may think."

"Do you need to talk to me, or what?"

"We actually do. We heard your thoughts earlier about saving the slaves. That's a very noble mission, little one. More than just being noble, it is also an effective method for war."

"Why is that?"

"Don't you see? That's the work force. No one else is doing work. So if you can liberate them, the society will collapse. Sudokus will either have to make the citizens do work, and then they'll resent him for it, or he'll have to let the society collapse."

"Either way he loses," said Leon.

"But only if liberation attempts are successful. We'll leave you alone to think. We still wish to explore the city more." The aliens then headed back to the elevator and were gone.

This left Leon alone in the room, contemplating everything that had been going on the last few months. One second he was working as a test pilot, the next he was signing up for a quick battle, and now he was in mars trying to find a robot named Sudokus. Everything was getting confusing and he still had no idea why those three little aliens were following him. He didn't even know where Scott was. For now, he just kept telling himself that Sudokus needed to die to prevent any innocent human casualties. Yet, he felt like there were other reasons for this war too.

Leon decided to get back on the elevator and head down. There was no point in staying in this room when he still had to get ready for the departure tomorrow.

Once downstairs, Leon could see people bustling around in the lobby. Out of the corner of his eye, Leon saw Alexander and Odegbula approaching him from across the room.

"Hello there, comrade," said Alexander, "How's your stay in this glorious city been?"

"About as good as it can be in a war."

"Point taken, comrade. So are you aware of whether or not you will be partaking in the journey to Neptune yet?"

"Neptune, is that where we're going? Yes, I'll definitely be there."

"That's good, comrade. I think almost all the pilots are going from what I've heard, myself included."

"Do you know why we're going to Neptune?"

"There are two reasons for Neptune," started Odegbula, "The first is that it is the furthest occupied planet from the sun—the final planet in the solar system, if you wish. We figure that we can start at the end and work our way up. The other reason is that we've received information from some of the aliens that Neptune is more of an unsettled territory than a functional unit in the kingdom. This means it will be less guarded, and easier to work in."

"Well, rest up now, comrades. We'll be leaving tomorrow."

With that, Leon continued on his way outside. He watched as the clean-up crew placed the final alien in a body bag and loaded it into a truck. Leon noticed there were guards in the streets now—the classic reaction of trying to improve a flawed system only after it fails.

With no dead bodies left in the water, all the civilians cleared out. Leon also walked through the streets with them, not going anywhere in particular. While he was walking, he felt normal. For the first time in a long time, he was able to be a normal person for a few hours.

CHAPTER THIRTY-SIX

The next day, all the pilots who were leaving for Neptune had loaded their stuff into their ships and were beginning to arrive in the Martian hangar for the final time.

Leon didn't feel quite right being inside the command ship instead of his own ship, but he knew that it was better this way because this was the only way Willy could teach him.

Leon made sure to bring the three little aliens with him onto the command ship. They tried to stay out of the way while on board as they explored the ship a bit.

Leon headed into Willy's room, which was currently unoccupied. The room seemed about as makeshift as the rest of the ship was. There was a slim mattress tied to the floor for a bed and a bathroom in the corner of the room with just a toilet and a sink. Other than that, the room was barren. Willy entered the room shortly after Leon had. He was wheeling in the gun rack Leon had seen yesterday.

"I have a feeling this is going to be a long ride," said Willy.

"How fast does this thing go?"

"Not fast enough. I'll start your training as soon as we take off. I'm just warning you, it won't be easy to learn these techniques. Mimicking them is easy enough, but when you find yourself in an actual battle, instinct just has to take over."

The command ship built by Earth would be the only one of the two command ships to continue the search for Sudokus from this point on. The other command ship would defend cities like the one on Mars. Earth's command ship was not as big, or fast as most command ships, but it would still be vital to them in any space battles and it was the best means of mass transportation.

Leon and Willy couldn't see what was going on outside, since there were no windows in the room, but they could feel when the ship began to rise for takeoff. It was a very shaky rise, which made Leon think the ship might fall apart at any second. However, the ship didn't fall apart, and they were soon in space, comfortably cruising.

"Well," started Willy, "We took off. That means it's time for your training. Let's start off with some gun work." Willy spent the next several hours showing Leon how to handle a gun, avoid enemy fire, and fight in hand to hand combat. Leon tried his techniques on Willy with some success, but he was nowhere near Willy's skill level.

Leon spent countless hours working with Willy over the course of the day-and-a-half flight. He was a bit disappointed that he didn't really get to practice in real life situations; for although Willy could teach Leon how to avoid gunshots, he couldn't actually shoot at Leon and have him avoid gunfire.

Alas, the training ended when an announcement came that scouts had spotted an enemy command ship near the outer limits of Neptune.

Leon headed out to find his ship in the hangar located at the bottom of the ship. He got into his ship and waited until the door opened up on the underbelly of the ship creating a vacuum and sucking all the ships out into the battle. Out in space now, Leon saw the enemy command ship looming in the distance with fighter ships surrounding it. Leon sped away to rejoin with the other pilots who were already in the heart of the battle. It was clear that this planet was of less importance to Sudokus, because there weren't as many fighter ships as there usually were.

The battle carried on for hours with Earth gradually gaining an edge. The pilots began realizing that, at this rate, eventually the only ship left would be the command ship. The intensity of the battle picked up gradually, until with no warning, the aliens began pulling out. Then, in the bleakest moment of the battle for the aliens, all the ships, including the command ship, retreated from the battle, heading back for Jupiter.

With the battle over, the command ship from Earth touched down on the surface of Neptune with the rest of the pilots. They set up a camp to discuss attack plans and rest up. The space suits' built in heating systems kept everyone warm on this frozen planet. Leon had been resting for an hour when Tzkcarwyagnz woke him.

"Why are you sleeping at a time like this?" asked Tzkcarwyagnz.

"I've been awake and active for the last seventeen hours. I need to rest."

"The word has been going around that you have talked about freeing slaves. That is a wise strategy and the sooner you start the better. In case you didn't realize it yet, this planet is loaded with slaves. Not here, however. You'll have to go look for them elsewhere."

"Can it wait until tomorrow?"

"I suppose, Leon, but the sooner the better. Also, you'll have to be secretive about this. If you bring a whole army with you, you'll scare the slaves away to the next plantation. Try to travel in a small band of soldiers. Lastly, you'll be able to identify a slave field by the blue smoke which comes out of the pillars of the nearby factory."

"I'll see who I can get to help me, but tomorrow. I need rest and tomorrow is only a few hours away."

Leon slept for another two hours before waking up again. He wondered what time it was, but from this far out, Leon couldn't even see the sun amongst all the other stars. Leon decided he should probably start rounding up people to help him out. It didn't take long before he realized he only knew pilots. He needed soldiers, but he didn't know any besides Willy. Leon decided to pay a visit to the Captain to see if he could offer assistance.

"Hey, Willy," said Leon. "The aliens from Mars think it would be a good idea to liberate some of the slaves out here. The only problem is that I need a few elite soldiers to help me out seeing as it'd be too dangerous to do on my own. So I was just wondering if you knew anybody or knew where I could find somebody."

"Don't Leon, it's too dangerous. Someone else will take care of it."

"I don't trust anyone else to take care of it."

"You have to. If you don't trust anyone else, at least trust me. I'll give you my word that I'll take care of it. I've also been thinking about this lately. I can see the logic behind it, and I think it will give us a big boost towards victory: a boost we can't win without."

"Who will do it though? And when will they do it?"

"I don't know. All I know is that we can leave as soon as we're sure we have this area under control. The ultimate goal however, is to build a city here, just like on Mars. I'll make sure it's done before then."

"Why would we build a city out here? No one would ever go to it."

"It's just temporary, until this war is over. I do agree though, it is a waste of resources to try to build anything out here. The one on Mars makes sense, because we can visit it when we please. Out here, we just need an outpost. You know, a few buildings and a way to get food. Just enough stuff so that if we ever needed to come back here, we could meet all of our basic needs. None of that concerns you however. We'll most likely be gone in two or three days. Just try to get some sleep in that time, alright?"

"Will do, Captain."

Leon left to head back to his tent where he saw Tzkcarwyagnz waiting.

"Someone else is going to take care of it," said Leon. "The whole slave thing I mean."

"Excellent. This will deal a huge blow to Sudokus. As for you, you should rest." Tzkcarwyagnz gestured with his arm towards the tent and then left.

Leon lay down in his tent and looked out of the opening in front. Out here, there was no day and night. Everything was night—or day, depending on how you wanted to look at it. The point was, it never got very bright outside. Leon didn't even know where the sun was amongst all the other stars and constellations.

In the distance, blue smoke rose in the air. Leon wondered what could be making blue smoke. The blue smoke was as mysterious as Sudokus. The blue smoke and Sudokus. Could there be some connection there? Something useful? Before Leon could even give it a second thought, sleep overwhelmed him. He was overwhelmed with fatigue, and it was the second time he slept that day.

As Leon slept, Willy got busy with the slave problem. He grabbed his communicator from his pocket, but then paused. Who should he call? Who else would be accepting of this? Yet, he couldn't go off by himself either without risking his job and status in the army. He came too far to get in trouble now and lose everything he'd been working towards. Willy looked at the blue smoke in the distance as a sense of hopelessness overwhelmed him. He hadn't felt this hopeless since Uganda. Then the answer hit him, he would call Odegbula. He knew him from Uganda, and he was a good fighter. It wouldn't be difficult at all, and there wouldn't be too much resistance here since it was such an unsettled territory. Even if his own men caught him, he wouldn't mind going out with Odegbula. It would still be painful to lose it all this far in, but if it was going to happen anyway, it should be with Odegbula.

Willy used the voice command on the communicator to call Odegbula.

"Odegbula, get your gun and meet me at the canteen. We have to take care of something. It will be just like old times."

Then he hung up. He didn't want to reveal any information on the communicator and risk anyone tracking his conversation.

Odegbula met Willy, and Willy explained the plan, the risks, the benefits—everything. Odegbula agreed to go along with it, just as Willy anticipated, and then they headed out, following the blue smoke.

The guards assigned to protect and watch-over the slaves weren't much opposition. They were large green blobs with two tentacles hanging out from either side; no distinguishable features at all. It took a lot of bullets to take them down, but once they were gone, the slaves were easy to corral. They were always looking for someone to follow. The slave guards had never experienced any threat, so Willy and Odegbula were easily able to liberate slave farm after slave farm. They just had to follow the blue smoke.

After they had over a hundred slaves following them, they headed back. They didn't walk through town though, they walked on the outskirts of town to avoid detection. Eventually, they found their way to the command ship. They loaded all the aliens into a storage room and then closed the door. They were unraveling Sudokus's society one worker at a time. If nothing else went right, they could at least be proud that they tried.

CHAPTER THIRTY-SEVEN

From here on out, a pattern began to form for the humans. The fleet would head to a planet to battle the alien fleet, then the command ship would land and some soldiers would get off to begin work building a functional town. Then Willy and Odegbula would sneak off to let more slaves loose in unpopulated areas, which not only stole away Sudokus's labor force, but also kept people from seeing the slaves. Then, after a few days on one planet, the command ship would leave for the next planet with all the pilots, leaving some soldiers and aliens behind to continue to build and defend the city.

Sudokus took note of the apparent ease at which the humans managed to move from planet to planet, weakening his dominion with each visit. He watched day after day as his soldiers failed miserably at trying to stop the humans. He knew now, more than ever, that he needed to eliminate Leon. At first it was just a feeling, now he could see Leon as a threat. And at the rate the humans were moving, they'd be on Jupiter before the next moon cycle.

Sudokus had never experienced this problem before, but it wasn't long before he thought of a solution. Instead of going after the army, he should go after the planet. If the humans really wanted to resist him, they'd have to save their home planet first. It'd be easy since nearly all the soldiers were concentrated on him and almost none were back for defense.

There was one problem however. Sudokus had tied up all his soldiers with defending his galactic territory from rebels, and it would take too long to clone a big enough army to send to earth. It was clear to Sudokus that for this job, living beings would not work. It was time for the mechs.

Sudokus went back into the engineering room where Scott was running some more mechs through tests. Every time he saw one of Scott's new designs, it was better and more battle-worthy than the last. Even the machine Scott used to turn sketches into actual parts impressed Sudokus. It was a piece of technology Sudokus had never seen before; his library of knowledge grew every day.

"How is the work going?" Sudokus asked Scott.

"If these last few tests work, then they'll be up to your standards."

"Excellent, because I think it may be time to use them."

"There is still one issue. I haven't yet found an efficient energy source for them. They'll have to recharge themselves regularly as it is, but I'm sure there's something out there that will last the length of a war."

"Mass produce whatever you have right now. Or use the blue energy from the factories. I won't have you stalling to look for some energy source that doesn't exist. I'm sending them to Earth now and if they're successful, I'll let you visit too. I know how you living creatures like to attach a nostalgic value to things."

Sudokus walked out of the room then to plan the attack. He had to do something soon, because he was beginning to feel the impact of the missing slaves. He wasn't feeling it directly, but his people who so strongly supported this war, were now beginning to oppose it due to a lack of food and supplies that the slaves normally supplied to them. Sudokus was feeling the effects of the universal truth that everyone only supports a war in the beginning.

What was directly burdensome to Sudokus however, was that the slaves did indeed create a liquefied form of energy used to create things, and now the production was waning. The substance they created was like no other material on Earth. Imagine something that was almost pure energy. More unstable than anything else, but so easy to use, and in its liquid state, anyone could mold and tamper with it to create matter, or use it to provide a power source. Without that liquid, the energy to keep everything running smoothly would have to come from somewhere else, but there was nothing else as cheap or effective.

Scott stayed back in his shop, preparing the prototype for mass production. It pained him to do this, but he knew that Sudokus would not hesitate to kill him if he showed signs of trying to rebel. He looked for every way possible to create some flaw in the mechs, but he knew that his innermost thoughts would give him away if he tried anything like that.

Scott just needed a way to try to talk to Leon one more time before the attack. Or better yet, he needed the army to come here and save him. Yet every time it seemed they were getting closer to figuring out where he was, one of Sudokus's double agents threw them off the trail.

Scott could build a communication device, but there was always the worry that Sudokus would find out about it. It all came down to whether he was willing to sacrifice his own life to better the lives of others. One day, Scott figured he would lose all hope and be willing to do it. For now however, he'd just have to do Sudokus's bidding.

CHAPTER THIRTY-EIGHT

The army had just finished their work on Saturn, when Willy received an urgent message. The message said that there had been an attack on Earth. It didn't say who or what had attacked, it just said that the army had to stop whatever they were doing and come back home to defend because the navy branch wasn't having much success.

Cpt. Drew had gotten the same message and he told his soldiers as Willy was telling his pilots. No one particularly liked the news, because this meant that Sudokus was still out there and they might never discover where he was. This only added to the thought the soldiers had that Sudokus was somehow invincible. After all, they had been fighting this war for months now, and nobody had so much as seen him.

Leon didn't like the news for a different reason. He still needed to find Scott, and this was slowing him down. The three little aliens were able to determine that Scott was not with Gako and Lada, but they couldn't pinpoint his position.

However, Leon couldn't worry about Scott right now. This war was really to defend Earth and its inhabitants, and that's what they had to focus on now. There would be other times to fight the army at its source, now they had to take care of the immediate threat.

The day after receiving the message, they landed back at the Russian base. It was the first time most of the soldiers had been back on Earth since they'd left, and it was only because of the invasion that the world leaders allowed them back on Earth; until very recently, the ban on soldiers returning was still in effect.

The first thing everyone did was to head to their respective rooms to gather up anything that they'd left back there. While they were doing this, the chefs at the base were setting out bear meat for the soldiers to eat. Everyone arrived to the kitchen at different times, and therefore finished the meal at different times. They then waited in the kitchen for further instruction. It wasn't long before Drew entered into the room to deliver those instructions.

"Men, today is a big day," began Drew. "Today we must defend this planet of ours. If we lose today, it could be over for us. If we win," Drew paused, then continued, "just know that we can't risk a loss today. I'll lead my men out, and the rest of you can follow your respective commanders. We'll be heading to the last reported location of the invaders. It's due south of our location. Soldiers, there's a caravan ready to transport you out there. The rest of you can hold tight here until you're told where to head."

At that point, about half of the room cleared out and Willy entered. He ordered all the pilots out to the hangar to board their ships. The command ship would stay behind not only because it was too big, but also because it needed repairs.

The pilots would have to wait in the hangar until they got the call that the soldiers were ready for them. An attack like this had to be perfectly coordinated to work.

The navy—who'd been waiting back at Earth just for this moment—traveled to their destination following transportation canals. The canals weren't frozen because it was summer now in Russia, and the snow had melted. They didn't know whether they'd be of much use, but they'd be on the lookout from their shorelines.

The soldiers marched out, hoping they'd be ready for whatever they'd encounter. Unfortunately, there was no way for them to prepare for the mechs. The mechs were a war machine the likes of which the galaxy had never before seen. The soldiers arrived on the mechs location to see neatly aligned rows and columns of robots. The command ship the mechs arrived on was somewhere off in the distance, in a thicker part of the forest. The soldiers unloaded from their vehicles to stare down at the mechs. No one was quite sure what they were, but there was something about them clearly not alive, even from a distance. Just the coldness of them, and the way they just seemed to be there. No real purpose, other than to kill and conquer.

It was impossible for the soldiers to tell how many robots there were, because they stretched back so far. There could have been tens of thousands. Simultaneously, the robots got up from the resting crouch position they were in, and aimed the guns built into their arms at the soldiers. The soldiers instinctively ducked behind anything that could hide them as bullets began flying out toward them and the mechs began marching forward.

Cpt. Drew knew immediately that they were outmatched and didn't hesitate to call in the pilots. Leon was just in the middle of one of his mental conversations with his three little aliens when he heard the signal for departure. He knew that this was a bit earlier than anyone had expected the call, but he didn't think anything of it.

When the pilots arrived at the battle, it was a sorry sight. All the humans were hiding and steadily moving backward as their weapons had seemingly no impact on the mechs and the mechs marched forward relentlessly. The planes came in firing lasers and dropping bombs on the mechs, but the mechs armor was impenetrable and even if an explosion knocked a mech down, it just got back up and kept marching.

Eventually the mechs, who viewed the planes as one might view a housefly, began flying up to confront the aircraft using rocket propulsion on their feet. Leon had to make a hard turn to avoid crashing into one of the mechs who had flown up in front of him. Another mech flew right up in front of Leon, but this time he didn't have time to avoid it. Leon smashed into it and his ship went spinning out of control and crashed into a tree—the mech only got a dent.

Luckily, Leon had landed behind the cluster of mechs, so they were heading away from him and ignored him. That was at least one design flaw they had; they were too goal oriented, and not flexible enough. Not a single one so much as turned around to look at him, they all just marched forward.

"I know," thought Leon to three aliens as they got out of the ship. "I could've gotten all of us killed; but did you see the way that thing popped in front of me? How could I have avoided it?"

"We did not see this coming," thought the aliens. "It appears Sudokus has disturbed the natural balance in this part of the galaxy. These mechs shouldn't have appeared for a few more years."

"So you're saying water and insect repellent aren't going to help us anymore?"

CHAPTER THIRTY-NINE

Leon walked through the forest for a while, making sure the mechs didn't see him as he made his way back to the caravan. By the time he got there, the battle was over and the mechs had already marched on towards their target. Most of the vehicles were gone too, but since so many men had died, they hadn't needed as many vehicles to leave as they had to arrive. Leon was able to drive one of the vehicles back to the base to rejoin the dejected men already there.

Leon headed to his room and lay down on his bed. He decided to grab his journal and his pen. It had been months since he'd written anything in here. Leon opened up to the next blank page and began writing.

They had told us that World War Four was the war to end all wars. They never told us that only meant the end of wars between humans. Worse yet, this war against the aliens doesn't seem to have an end in sight.

Now we face a robotic threat. I'm sure the aliens are closely connected with these robots, but I'm not exactly sure why the robots are here or what they want. I also don't know how to stop them because their armor seems resistant to everything. Their mission may just be to kill enough soldiers so that we can no longer oppose them. Then they would move onto all the cities that we established on other planets. Once we lose our influence, Sudokus will have won.

But I don't think that will happen. The reason is that I am almost positive Scott designed these robots. It's not coincidence that shortly after Scott goes missing, these robots pop up. Even though Scott is a great engineer, he'd never build an indestructible robot to wipe out the human race. I suppose Sudokus could force him to, but I know Scott must've designed some failsafe. There has to be some easy way to stop these robots.

What if Scott didn't install a failsafe in these robots though? What if Sudokus forced him to make them indestructible and unstoppable? Then I imagine Sudokus would be stupid, because if the robots are unstoppable, they could kill Sudokus. Maybe that's the key; get the robots to kill Sudokus. But how could you do that unless the robots malfunctioned? I highly doubt anyone but Scott or Sudokus can control these robots, that'd be too obvious for Sudokus to overlook.

I also wonder if anyone can destroy Sudokus. If he's survived this long ruling like a tyrant, someone must have tried to stop him. If they couldn't stop him, can anyone? I'd have to say yes, because Sudokus is just a machine when you think about it, and every machine needs an energy source. If I can find what that energy source is, and then take it away, then maybe he'll just run out of energy.

So I guess what this really all comes down to, is that I need to find Scott soon. I know he can stop these robots. I just need to figure out where Scott is. Maybe I can figure this out using a little bit of logic and reasoning. If I were Sudokus, where would I hide? Maybe I would think everything revolves around me and go to the sun, or as close as I could get. That'd probably be Mercury. At the same time, he might just want to be somewhere in solitude. That could be on any moon. Or, he could go somewhere big, so even if someone knew where he was, their odds of finding him would still be low. That'd be Jupiter. Jupiter also has many moons, which means more places to flee to if we found him. Those are all the possibilities I can think of right now, which doesn't help much. Hopefully I can get some answers over these next few days. Those three little aliens seem to know so much, yet they don't know where Scott is. But if Scott is with Sudokus, and they know where Sudokus is, then maybe...

Leon stopped writing to go talk to the little aliens who had gotten out of their space ship for the first time in a long time, and were walking around on the drawer next to Leon's bed.

"I haven't seen your faces in a while," said Leon. "I had forgotten what you looked like."

"That's funny," thought the aliens, "We did not forget what you looked like. You were thinking loudly back there, and we couldn't help but hear your question. You want to know where Sudokus is because you think Scott is with him. Seeing as how we can't find Scott's mental frequency, that is reason in itself to believe he is with Sudokus. Who else would go to such lengths to hide him? Yet, we don't know where Sudokus is, only where he is not. You see, we've searched for his mind everywhere, and it has turned up nowhere. There is, however, one area of nothingness on the fifth planet. By that, we mean no mental frequencies escape from that particular spot. However, this area is quite large, and would require extensive searching. Not to mention the dangers associated with trying to locate Sudokus directly. You shouldn't go there unless you're ready to die, that's why we've never mentioned it before. Besides, there's no guaranteeing Sudokus will be there anyway, it could be a diversion."

"Sudokus has to be there. I know Scott has to be with him, and if you can't pinpoint either of them, they must be in that block."

"If you truly want to go there, it'd be a suicide mission. Unless you could convince the whole army to just abandon their mission of defending the planet against the mechs to come with you."

"What about the Ginyu guards, they could take over for us, right?"

"Most likely not. They're even less equipped for the mechs than your soldiers are. They might be able to slow down the mechs, but that's about it."

"What are the mechs trying to do anyway?"

"They want to rid this planet of all resistance and force you to become part of Sudokus's empire. They're going to kill civilians as well as soldiers until they get what they want."

"I'll go myself then. You said no one should go to the block until they're prepared to die, and I think I am. The way I see it, I can either die trying to save Scott, or I could stay here, and die in vain. It's obvious we have no way to stop those mechs anyway and I could've even been killed today."

"Think this out carefully, little one. You say you don't want to die in vain, but if you go alone, you will die in vain. Make sure that whatever you do weakens Sudokus's power. Your mind was already strong, and this new realization of the value of your life has only increased your mind's strength. Therefore, we cannot tell you what you should do. You are wise enough to know, and we're sure you'll do what is right. Of course we'll stay here to help you out, but you won't need us."

Leon already knew what he was going to do. This was a rare moment of absolute decisiveness. Leon reached into his desk drawer and pulled the schematics for his ship that Scott had given him a while back. He considered how lucky he was that Scott had given this to him. Now he could give it to one of the other aerospace engineers and have them recreate his ship.

Leon headed up to ground level to show the design to the engineer who was currently over there. Leon showed the engineer the paper and he looked at it, nodded in approval, and then headed deeper into the room to grab his tools. Leon then headed back downstairs, trusting the engineer to finish in the next few days.

Until then, he'd either have to join the navy or the ground forces so that he wouldn't be sitting idle. Sitting idle was just as bad as going AWOL. Leon decided it would be better to join the navy, where there wouldn't be as much action and he could think about rescuing Scott.

Leon made the call on his communicator to join the navy once he'd arrived into his room. He'd be sent out tomorrow to a sea ship which hadn't seen a battle since World War four. He wouldn't need any real training to join this naval platoon since they would just assign him to clean up the ship between battles. It was an easy job, all he'd have to do was mop the floors when there was smooth sailing, and not die in the unlikely event of a battle. Leon would just have to trade his space suit in for a sailing suit temporarily.

Leon had to wait at least a day before he'd know for sure whether the navy would accept him. The wait seemed to drag out for Leon. There had been so much action over the last few weeks, that Leon didn't know what to do with this one day off. He was so used to being on edge and being ready to head out for battle at any moment, that he couldn't relax now. Eventually, he found himself sitting in his room, alone, and he began to wonder if he should tell anyone about his plan to look for Scott once his ship was back in working order. He eventually decided he should at least tell one person, so if he died, they'd know what happened to him. Leon decided he should go to sleep, and hoped that the answers would come to him in the morning.

However, Willy used his universal key card to enter Leon's room and cut his slumber short. Willy stood over Leon's bed and shook him awake.

"Leon, are you awake? What's this I heard about you transferring to the navy? You don't want to go back into space or something?"

"No," said Leon, "It's not that. It's just that I wrecked my ship last battle and I want to do something while it's being repaired."

"Just be ready to come back to us when we're ready to head back out again. We need every man we can get, but especially you."

"I don't know if I'll be rejoining you guys. Not because I like sailing better than flying or anything, I just don't know what the future holds for me. You see, Captain Willy, I'm going off to find Scott once my ship is repaired. I think Scott is the only one who can stop the robots. I just don't know if I'll come back. I hate to say it, but I've decided that saving the lives of the other eight billion people on this planet, is more important than my life. I'd rather die trying to do something meaningful, than die fighting a fruitless battle. Death would be better than a life under the control of a robot."

"I respect the fact that you've found a cause you're willing to die for, but you're crazy if you think I'd let you go alone on a suicide mission. You're doomed to failure if you rush in. If it was easy, if it was even possible, someone would have done it by now. You have to have a plan. It would literally take an army to bring down Sudokus, but I think it's worth it. If what you said is correct, and Scott really is the only one who can stop these things, then we may have no other choice."

"So, you're suggesting we bring all the pilots? I was thinking stealth might be more important here."

"No, someone as powerful as Sudokus would have too much protection for you to try and be stealthy. We must overwhelm the defenses before we can attempt to locate Scott. I wouldn't even bother to leave anyone behind for defense. The way things are going now, defeat is inevitable. You should hear some of the conversations we have during our meetings. Supplies are running low, we're losing soldiers all over the place, support for this war is declining—it's just not a good situation. I know things may have seemed like they were on the upswing a few days ago, but they never were. The fact that we even made as much progress as we had was a miracle. Now, do you have an idea where Scott may be?"

"According to the little aliens, Sudokus is on Jupiter somewhere, and it's probable that Scott is with him. They know the general area, but it might take a little bit of searching. I'm sure Sudokus will be under the largest cluster of fighter ships, or something obvious like that."

"Here's the plan then; we're going to go, and we're going to bring as many people as we can with us. But we can't tell anyone else about this until it's time to go. I'll tell you what, just let me take care of all the coordinating, you just relax and prepare yourself."

Willy left the room the same way he'd entered. He quickly checked the time—which his communicator digitally displayed—and realized he was late for a meeting. He quickened the pace of his walk as he headed toward the elevator. He got onto the elevator, pressed the button for the first floor and anxiously waited as the elevator made its descent. The doors opened up and he found his way down the hallway and to the meeting room. He opened the door and joined the discussion, which was already in progress.

"Nice of you to join us," said Cpt. Drew. Willy could sense a hint of animosity in his voice. He had always suspected the others of disliking him for his behavior, because even though they didn't know for certain that he divulged nearly all of their secrets, he knew they suspected him of it. Now, not only could he feel their distrust, he could hear it too.

"I was just talking to one of my pilots. The conversation went a little longer than I had planned."

"And what exactly were you talking to him about?" persisted Drew. "Were you—"

"Cpt. Drew, that will be enough," said one of the superiors cutting him off. The superior, whose name is unimportant, was dressed in a dark blue business suit, and had buttons and medals pinned on his sleeves throughout their lengths. "Do not question someone on your same level. If anyone will question him, it will be me. Now is not the time for questioning however, we're already behind schedule. Let's continue.

"We obviously have a problem here. The question is, what do we do about it? As I've already told you, we could call a truce with the aliens at any time. We interlinked our economies years ago, and we could just give them a lump sum of money and possibly some land here on Earth to end this war. Another option is to finally reveal to the public that we are in fact in the middle of a war with aliens and just begin integrating some of their technology with our technology to increase our chances of winning. The final option is just to continue fighting this costly war as we are."

"You know what my opinion has always been," said Willy, "Tell the public everything we know and then we'd be free to do whatever we needed to."

"Willy," said Drew, "How many times do we have to tell you? If we tell the public everything we know, it will cause mass panic. People would begin to question things they needn't be concerned with and the very fabric of society would unravel."

"Then why," started another man, "Didn't we just tell them when we first made contact? Then they'd be just as surprised as us."

"Because," said another, "We made contact long before any of us were born. The incident you were referring to was just the time when mutual contact was made."

"Don't all talk at once here," said the superior, "Let's have an orderly discussion. Let us have a vote; how many of you agree with Captain William and think we should tell the general public what we know?" Willy and one other person out of the fifteen people there raised their hands. "Let it show that the motion to tell the public has not passed. Now, who thinks that we should continue this war?" Six people raised their hands this time. "Let it show that the motion to continue this war did not pass. One more vote left: Let's hope we reach a conclusion. All in favor of trying to call a truce and end this war?" Once again, six people raised their hands. "Someone here did not vote," he paused, and no one else raised their hand, "but let the record show that the motion to truce did not pass. So, what do we want to do if none of the original options are desired?"

"I believe a truce would be most favorable," said Drew, "But we don't know if that's an option anymore. We used to interact with the aliens before Sudokus had control over this territory. We don't know who we'd be dealing with if we tried to communicate with them now."

"That's where you are mistaken, Cpt. We have made contact with Sudokus." People in the room began murmuring with astonishment with this last remark. "It was very limited contact, but still contact nonetheless. We do know what we're dealing with, and it's nothing good. He will want to be appeased, so maybe surrender is in order."

"I don't understand you guys," said Willy, "Why are you making this more complicated than it has to be. We have the technology to at least try to fight the robots out there right now, why don't we just use it?"

"You still don't understand, do you?" accused the superior. "We can't do risk revealing that aliens exist. We can't give into the conspirators. If we do that, it's just a matter of time before anarchy ensues. Before you know it, society will collapse. Religion will collapse as people start confusing aliens for angels as other conspiracy theories start to gain power. Religion creates a set of moral values that laws never could. I mean, honestly, just think of it: how can you just reveal something like that with no warning. If you think these robots marching through the town right now are dangerous, imagine how dangerous the people will be when they start demanding jet packs, and ray guns, and all the absolute crap they read about in their science-fiction books, which they mistake for science-fact. We can't. Not now anyway, maybe not ever."

"Don't you have any trust in people to not destroy themselves? Either we destroy ourselves, or the robots outside destroy us. Who knows where the robots even are right now? They could be on their way here, or they could be at a major city, burning down buildings and killing innocent civilians trying to flee. Humans have survived for thousands of years, and revealing this one secret won't change that. Now we can either sit back and talk about how to peacefully succumb to Sudokus's commands, or we can put up a bit of a fight. The choice should be a simple one; you can be cowards, and live in a society ruled by a machine, or you can act like living creatures, and do what's necessary to survive."

"Willy," said the superior, "You may excuse yourself from this office and you may surrender your title effective immediately. You've been causing trouble since day one and it's clear to me now that you don't have the experience needed to be a true leader. You may leave and take your liberal non-sense talk with you. We'll be sure to find someone competent to fill your position."

"I see how it is," said Willy. He was calm, which surprised the people in the room although they didn't show it. Willy had known for a long time that this day would eventually come. "You guys can stay here and enjoy your meaningless conversations. Just continue to sit around doing nothing, and thinking that you have some sort of power. As if the title on your badge will mean anything when this planet is burning from the fires of this war. If this is what I signed up for, I'm glad I'm leaving. I'm sure Sudokus will thank you for letting him take Earth without much of a struggle. Sudokus will probably love you, in fact. But me, I want Sudokus to hate me." Willy ripped the badge from his shirt, and walked out of the room closing the door calmly behind him.

This sudden loss of a job changed everything for Willy. Now he had things to do before Leon got his ship back. He'd be traveling with Leon, and so would the rest of the pilots; it would just take some considerable effort on Willy's part—lots of effort, and a bit of forced cooperation from the people around him.

CHAPTER FORTY

Sudokus sat back in his chair and saw in his eye the destruction his mechs were causing on Earth. He watched as the mechs began marching into towns and eventually cities, leaving behind a path of destruction. They marched in rows and columns, slowly and menacingly, with the single purpose of conquest and domination. People would stare at the mechs as they approached, and then begin to run away once the mechs began shooting at them. Some people escaped, and some did not. Sudokus could've watched all day as the mechs lay waste to people and infrastructure, but he had other important business to attend to. Everyone in the kingdom was now feeling the effects of the decline in slave labor, and now Sudokus would have to address the people. He'd have to make a speech to restore confidence in his people.

Sudokus decided to talk to Scott before giving the speech, to get all his facts straight about the mechs. His people would wait patiently for him because they loved him and depended on him. He'd convinced them that there was nothing more to life than gaining power, and he could give them that power. Of course, the individual would remain weak, but they could be a part of a powerful empire, and that was enough for them.

Sudokus arrived in Scott's workshop to see Scott was working on something other than mechs. Sudokus didn't recognize the device Scott was working on, so he decided to question him about it.

"What do you have there, Scott?"

Scott looked up quickly, caught off guard at Sudokus's presence. "Nothing, lord Sudokus. Nothing important."

"Don't lie to me. I know that ever since you arrived here you've been looking for a way to escape. Don't lie to me now and tell me that what I just saw in your hand was nothing important. I'll give you another chance now, what were you working on?"

"Really, it was nothing. Just a little experiment."

Sudokus, still not believing Scott, walked over to him and snatched the object away. Sudokus did not recognize it, but he thought it looked similar to a communication device. To air on the side of caution, Sudokus crushed the object in his claw-like hands until it was just frayed wires and scrap metal.

"Now don't let me catch you working on anything other than the mechs again, or I'll feed you to Jum-Jum. I have my reason for keeping you around, but don't think I won't still kill you if you give me even an inkling of a reason. I have a speech to give now, and I have to get some facts straight. How soon do you predict it will be before the mechs can fully conquer Earth?"

"If they all work at their maximum potential and the resistance from Earth doesn't increase, then they will have destroyed every major city in exactly two months and three weeks. But that's only if everything goes perfectly."

"Why wouldn't things go perfectly?"

"No reason, my lord. Everything is right on schedule and there's no reason that should change."

"Excellent. Anything else I should know about these mechs?"

"No, but there is something I've wanted to say. I just want to go back to Earth after the mechs have finished there."

"I don't recommend that. There's usually a lot of turmoil on a planet just after its takeover. You know how creatures are so reluctant to change. If you want to be close to Earth, I recommend Mars. It's been under my control for nearly a year and you can see Earth when both planets' orbits come near each other."

"Thank you for the suggestion, but I'll still take my chances going to Earth. I wouldn't expect you to understand, but just seeing Earth isn't the same as actually being on it. As soon as you're done with this game, I'm going home."

"Foolish human, this is no game—and it's not going to be over any time soon. I wasn't going to tell you now, but I guess there's no point in waiting—seeing as victory is imminent. Once I have this solar system, I'm going on to another system. Once I have that one, I'll move on to another and another, until I have control over an arm of the galaxy, and eventually the entire galaxy. Do you know why I want to do this? It's because all of the universes are death traps, and I refuse to die. You see, one day the sun will burn out, and that would kill me. That's why I must leave this solar system. But one day, this whole galaxy will destroy itself either through a black hole, or through simply sucking itself into its own gravitational center. That's why I must leave this galaxy. Yet, even this universe would eventually kill me. One day our universe will shrink back down to the size of an atom, and I'd die along with everything else. Either that, or it will grow so large that it bursts. However, I can escape death. I can go to a different universe, one that is growing, rather than shrinking. You see, in a growing universe, new galaxies and solar systems are always forming, so I can restart this whole process, thus securing my immortality. I merely need control of this universe so that I can get to the next one. You see, I've planned it all out. I already found a universe with life, and I've communicated with them. I can go to that universe, for a cost. I can get that money if I control this universe."

"Since when is money required for inter-dimensional travel?"

"It's not. Yet despite my infinitesimal knowledge, I cannot get to another universe on my own. I contain energy inside of me, and energy cannot transfer from one universe to another. I still do not fully understand how the transfer will occur, but I know it will, for I've read stories of creatures who have done it before." Then, as if he needed to further prove to himself that the transfer would work, he added, "I will never die."

"You're plan will never work. There's no way you can live forever. Some force in the universe will stop you. You're evil by nature, and evil will always be stopped."

"I'm not evil, foolish piece of meat. I am no different from any other being, living or otherwise, in this universe. If you consider me evil, then you must also consider your fellow humans evil."

"You're more evil. You kill innocent beings, and force slaves to do hard labor with no reward. You send soldiers to war and kill them if they fail. You take hostages and you lie to your people. You're the embodiment of what's evil."

"Do not humans do the same things? Don't innocent people die all the time during wars? Have humans not for thousands of years had forced slave labor? Aren't defeated soldiers treated poorly back on Earth? Isn't there always some hostage crisis? Don't your political leaders lie to you, even during this very war? Doesn't corporate money and lobbyists control your politicians? The people on your pathetic planet still do not know I, or any other alien, exist. They don't know they've been in a war for the past few months—or at least they don't know whom they're fighting. By your definition of evil, humans are evil. And if they're evil, some force must stop them, right? Is the force you're referring to not some sort of deity? Well, I am that deity. I am the force in the universe that stops evil. I am who you meet when you die. Human religion is merely an attempt by simple creatures to explain things beyond their knowledge. Now, I suggest you reconsider everything you've been thinking these past few days. You can't escape from me, there exists no force in the universe destined to stop me, and you have no reason not to enjoy being in my jurisdiction. I have a speech to deliver now, and I suggest you just listen to it, and get those ideas of escape out of your mind."

Sudokus walked up a flight of stairs to the upper part of his spherical building. He then walked out a door to a balcony high above the ground. Below him, a group of aliens waited anxiously for him to deliver his speech. There was a lot of nervousness emanating from the aliens below, and it rattled Sudokus's dissatisfaction receptors.

Everyone was wondering which problem Sudokus would address first. There was the problem of what to do about the sudden decrease in slave labor, then there was the status update on the war, then there was the problem of pollution from the slave factories.

Sudokus had carefully thought of which one he should address first. He knew as a rule of thumb, it was always a good idea to end on a good note, but in this case, he had a surprise to turn two of these problems into good news.

"My good people," started Sudokus, "Let me first quickly address a bit of bad news. New research shows that the pollution from slave factories has worsened. Some of you have become ill from this blue smoke. Rest assured that this illness is just a growing pain, and some of you will become adapted to the smoke.

"Now, let's move on to more uplifting news. This war, which has seemed an eternity to you, is about to end. You have been here for satisfactory and dissatisfactory times, and watched as we eliminated our rivals. Now, I am satisfied to inform you that the end is in sight." Sudokus paused to allow the crowd to cheer. "I predict that within the next three months, victory will officially be mine. Of course, I mean it will be yours as well, for what's mine is also yours. I would also like to inform you that the mechs are a success. Not only does this mean we will never lose a battle again, it also means no more lives will have to be lost due to war." Again, Sudokus paused for cheering. "Furthermore, the mechs will be the security of the future, thus eliminating crime one-hundred percent. As we speak, the mechs are tearing across Earth's surface, slowly bringing us closer to victory. Three months until victory is secure, I promise you. Then, we'll have the golden age you're all waiting for. A time of political stability, peace, a prosperous economy, and advances in science and technology.

"Now, I must also talk about some troubling news. As many of you have heard, there has been a decrease in slave labor recently. This has led to a scarcity of certain foods and products you have been enjoying since the formation of this kingdom. Rest assured, life as you once knew it will return very shortly. Slaves are not living creatures, not in the way you define life. They are merely test tube creatures, genetically engineered to do manual labor. We can, and will, recreate them in labs until their numbers are as large as they were before. Then we'll make more, so we'll never encounter this problem again.

"Now, for the most satisfactory news of all. Our most hated enemy, Leon Dudley, is walking into a death trap as we speak. I have seen it in my eye, and his days are numbered." Sudokus waited while the crowd cheered again. It gave him satisfaction to know that his propaganda against Leon, the E-poster and all the denouncements against him, had worked. While he was waiting for the cheering to die down, he signaled for Gako and Lada—who had arrived behind him a few minutes after the start of his speech—to come out onto the balcony with him.

"Leon will be travelling here by his own free will," continued Sudokus, "And then he will be taken care of by my two most reliable employees, Gako and Lada." Lada raised her hands to the people below and they cheered for her. "Do not be worried that the enemy is coming here. I have planned this all out carefully, and I am the one who let him know where I am. Leon thinks he is smart for discovering my location, but he is unaware that I know now that he is coming, and I am ready for him. The assassination will be live, and all will be able to see it. When Leon's head is detached from his body, you will know victory is ours.

"I leave you with these parting words: stay strong for these next few months, and all of this will be over. I am greatly satisfied with your support during this entire war, and that support is about to pay off. The end of this war is in sight."

Sudokus walked away with Gako and Lada while the people below cheered wildly. They cheered blindly too, for they had no idea if anything Sudokus said was true or not. No research had shown that the people would soon adapt to the blue smoke and stop becoming sick, Sudokus had no idea if any of them would die or not. Telling them that they would be fine made them feel better though.

Scott heard Sudokus walking back down the metal stairs and put away the communicator he was working on. Scott had successfully fooled Sudokus for the time being. He intentionally let Sudokus see him working on what looked like a communicator earlier and tried to be vague about it, knowing Sudokus would destroy it out of suspicion. What Sudokus actually destroyed was just some scrap metal pieced together in the shape of a communicator.

The real communicator was still intact, and Scott planned to use it to try to get through to Leon or anyone else from Earth who would listen. If Scott were careful, Sudokus would never find the communicator, because he was sure he'd already destroyed it, even if he still had a lingering feeling of dissatisfaction about it.

CHAPTER FORTY-ONE

The wait on the sea ship seemed like a long time to Leon. The navy had accepted him, just as he expected, and he wound up cleaning the ship, also as he had expected. The only thing he hadn't expected was the amount of people on the ship that were just there to avoid fighting. Somehow, these people knew they wouldn't be of use, but it gave them an excuse to escape from whatever their lives were before the war. Leon didn't actually talk to any of the people—other than some small talk—but he could see it in their eyes, and the casual way they acted, they hadn't done any fighting, and they didn't plan to either; they certainly didn't want to.

During the three days he was on the ship, there was no action. There were only radio reports constantly updating the crew on the progress of the mechs. "Mechs have marched 40 miles east in the last four hours." "The mechs have besieged the city of Tobolsk," and so on. Eventually a small transport ship, which ran back and forth between the base and the sea ship, arrived and Leon hopped aboard to head back.

The transport ship traveled fast, but it was crowded with other sailors headed back to the base for a host of different reasons. While aboard the ship, Leon pulled out his communicator to talk to Willy.

"Willy, I'm coming to get my ship now. Be ready to leave in half an hour."

"Half an hour? Will do. Just a heads up, when you get here, it might be a bit hectic, so make sure you find your ship right away and you're ready to go." Leon was unaware that Willy lost his job, and also unaware of what Willy now planned.

Willy had half an hour to do what he needed to do. He needed to convince all the pilots they were on an official mission to Jupiter, but only his replacement could give those instructions. The only problem was that his replacement was one of *them*, and would never side with Willy, or even listen to him.

Willy knew his plan was risky, but he didn't question it because he didn't have time to. While Leon was relaxing out at sea, Willy was studying the man who replaced him. Willy had to sneak everywhere now because he technically wasn't even supposed to be at the base anymore. The Ginyu guards didn't really take notice of him because, subconsciously, they still thought he belonged at the base, and he wasn't causing any trouble to bring any attention to himself. Even if he wanted to leave, he couldn't since the mechs were outside.

From what Willy had learned over the past few days, his replacement enjoyed hanging out in his new office. This was perfect for Willy, because there was a microphone in that office which could make announcements. Right after Willy had gotten the call from Leon, he grabbed his gun and began heading off to the office—he was allowed to keep his gun since it wasn't government issued. He knew he'd encounter guards on the way there, but he also knew it was worth the risk.

Once Willy had reached the outer door to the office, two guards protecting the man on the other side stopped him.

"Sir," said one of the guards, "I'm going to need you to step back and put the gun down."

Willy considered his options in this scenario. He was outnumbered, but he still had his gun. He eventually decided the best course would be diplomatic.

"I don't think you understand," said Willy. "I have official business to take care of with the man inside."

"Do you have paperwork?"

"As a matter of fact, I do." Willy reached into his pocket and pulled out an old crinkled up piece of paper. Willy handed the paper to one of the Ginyu guards. Before the guard could even realize the paper was blank, Willy grabbed him to use as a body shield as he gunned down the other guard. Willy then wrapped his arm tightly around the still living guard's neck. With each passing second of constricted arteries to the brain, the guard began to fade from consciousness until eventual he collapsed, alive but unconscious. Willy then opened up the door—the soundproof door, which prevented the man inside from hearing the gunshots—and burst into the room with his gun aimed right at his replacement's head. The man was defenseless as Willy inched closer and closer to him, closing the door behind him with his foot, and ultimately grabbing him in a headlock.

"Now," said Willy, "I need you to make an announcement to all the pilots out there, understand?" Willy's heart was racing and sweat beaded on his forehead.

Outside, the pilots were all walking around the base enjoying one of their few days off when the announcement came ringing through the speakers. It caught everyone off guard.

"Attention all pilots." The man spoke, but Willy whispered in his ear exactly what he needed him to say. "There has been a change in plans for today. Set your coordinates for 5.024.233. Departure will be in ten minutes."

Willy tore the microphones cord in half then, rendering it useless, and then set the man down in the room and kept the sights of his gun aimed at him to prevent him from moving. Keeping one hand on the trigger of the gun, he opened the door, and then shut it once he had exited the room. He then piled the guards' bodies up outside the door to prevent the man from opening it up and getting out. The guards themselves weren't that heavy, but the armor made it so that the man couldn't push the door open while two of them blocked it.

Willy knew he would only have a couple minutes at most to make it into one of the ships in the hangar before all the guards started pursuing him—assuming they weren't doing so already. So he went sprinting through the base with his gun ready until he reached the hangar. He found Leon's ship and jumped in, cramming himself behind the pilot's seat to avoid detection.

Willy also knew that back in the room, the man who had replaced him simply had to make one call with his communicator and all the guards would know what just happened. The situation became more perilous with each passing second.

Leon arrived at the base to find that it was a hectic scene just like Willy had warned. Guards swarmed around everywhere, and pilots ran around looking for their ships.

Leon was surprised when he entered into his ship and found Willy crammed into the back, but with all the other craziness around him, he didn't question it. Leon signaled with his mind for the three little aliens to come to the ship, and once they were inside, he closed the hatch.

The ships all took off before anyone found Willy. No one knew it, but they were heading into the final battle of this war, and the fate of the solar system now rested in the hands of a group of pilots who weren't even supposed to be going on this mission, and a soldier who was getting too old to keep fighting.

CHAPTER FORTY-TWO

All the ships headed off for Jupiter, leaving behind some furious commanders as well as the command ship, which was still in the repair process. Willy almost hoped he wouldn't return from this, because if Sudokus didn't kill him, his superiors would.

"You comfortable back there?" asked Leon.

"Ya, I'll be fine. Being here is better than being down there at the base."

"Where are we headed?"

"Jupiter," replied Willy. "I don't know where on Jupiter, but I figure that if we get close enough to Sudokus, his army will confront us and we won't have to worry about finding him."

"When we find Sudokus, what's the plan?"

"I was hoping you'd know that part."

"I need to find Scott," said Leon. "So I could just head out to look for him while you guys serve as a distraction."

"I don't think it will be that simple. I hate to say it, but we're just going to have to play this by ear. Whatever happens, happens."

"I guess that's the way it will have to be. I'm going to go into hyper sleep now and try to get some rest before this starts."

Leon pressed a button and a mist of sleeping gas poured into the ship as Leon and Willy fell into an induced sleep, and the ship sped ahead for Jupiter.

A radio transmission awoke them some time later, saying that enemy ships had been spotted near the destination. Neither side fired shots as the humans crept closer to the alien ships. Leon sat up straight, ready to shoot at any time as tensions mounted. Finally, when it seemed the ships were too close not to confront one another, somebody fired the first shot and the battle began.

To the humans, it seemed like a normal battle, but they didn't realize that the alien ships were steadily moving away, and dragging the humans with them. The humans unwittingly followed the alien ships until they were directly above Sudokus's headquarters. Being so close to Sudokus triggered something in the three little aliens, and they could detect Sudokus's presence below them.

"Leon," thought the aliens telepathically, "He's somewhere down there."

"Who's down there?"

"Sudokus. Directly below you. We can sense him. His presence is overwhelming."

"Is Scott down there as well?"

"It is difficult to tell. Sudokus is so powerful that we can't detect anything else."

"I'm going down there then."

Leon prepared himself to head down, but before he actually made the move, Alexander and Odegbula found him.

"There you are, comrade," said Alexander through the radio, "How do you always manage to separate from us just before we take off?"

"Sorry, Alexander, but I can't talk now. I've got some business to take care of on the surface."

"If you're going down there," said Odegbula catching up to them, "Then we're going too. We all have to look after each other."

Leon didn't want to endanger Alexander and Odegbula, but he also knew their assistance would be too beneficial to pass up, so he told them to come with him.

Leon headed down to the surface and cruised low enough to see the millions of aliens gathered below him. Alexander and Odegbula followed. Lines of aliens stretched out for miles, all there to witness the Leon's death.

"Keep going, Leon," said the little aliens, "You'll know where Sudokus is when you see a building. Sudokus would never wait out in the open, he's sure to be in a big building somewhere around here."

Leon made sure to keep his distance from the carpet of aliens below him. They all reached their arms out towards him, as if they were hoping he'd dip down too low and then they could swallow up his ship.

At last, Leon saw the spherical building staring him down in the distance. As he got closer to it, he slowed down, to look for some way to get inside of it. Leon couldn't help but notice how strange the building was upon observing it. Just the shape of the building would've been an architectural nightmare back on Earth. On top of that, tubes and pipes crisscrossed wildly at the base of the building, with no symmetry whatsoever. The sheer size of the building was also strange to Leon. It was as tall as a fifty story building on Earth, yet it was the only building in sight for miles.

Leon pulled his ship up to fly over the top of the building. He circled around it looking for some sort of an opening, or a platform to land his ship. Leon eventually saw a rather large, flat piece of metal protruding out of the side of the building. Leon's ship and the others were easily able to land on it.

Leon checked to make sure his oxygen box was in and then got out of his ship. He was surprised at how loud the crowd's cheers were outside. They all seemed to be staring at Leon as he walked forward on the platform and made his way over to a door. He opened the door and stepped through to the interior of the building. Alexander, Odegbula and Willy followed him closely. Odegbula was the last one in, and he closed the door behind him, blocking out the sound of the crowd.

Leon looked around the room they were currently in, to try to figure out where they were. It was a large room with a conveyor belt cutting through the center. The conveyor belt carried metal parts while robotic arms were grabbing the parts and connecting them before putting them back on the conveyor belt. They then passed through an array of laser lights, which ensured perfection of the parts. The good parts went through, and the faulty parts went into a furnace to be recycled. The parts that continued on went through a hole in the wall to a different room.

Leon also noticed that it was cold in this room, and he remembered when Scott had used the parts making machine, it had cooled down the room. Leon figured the machine was somewhere nearby, and he knew if it was, then Scott was nearby as well.

Leon continued looking around for a way out of the room as he searched for Sudokus. There was a door on the other side of the conveyor belt, and a staircase off to the right. Leon decided to take the staircase since it was closer. Everyone followed him without questioning, because they had no idea which way to go either.

When they had reached the bottom of the staircase, they were in a room where there were giant glass cylinders hanging on the walls. Inside these cylinders were creatures Leon thought looked familiar. Leon walked up to one of the containers and peered into it. Inside, he realized, were slave aliens forming and growing. The creatures didn't have life yet, because they weren't fully developed, but judging by their size, Leon knew they were close. Leon had never seen the slaves before, but he recognized them through the three little alien's telepathy.

Leon turned around to leave and again faced the same choice as last time: a door or the stairs. Leon was about to choose the stairs again, but he thought he heard voices down the stairs, so he headed toward the door to avoid conflict.

"What exactly are we looking for?" asked Odegbula.

"My friend is somewhere in here," said Leon, "And he's the only one who can stop the robots back on Earth." Leon didn't know that for certain, but he wanted to convince everyone, including himself, that it was true.

Leon opened up the door and entered into a room that appeared to be the end of the assembly line they'd seen a floor up. Lifeless, but complete, mechs entered into this room where they received an electrical zap that activated them. The activated mechs were then carried somewhere outside of the room. Even here they looked menacing.

Leon walked up to a large window in the room and looked through the glass to see another room a level below this one. He saw Scott in the room standing nearby Sudokus. It appeared Scott was talking to Sudokus, but Leon was too far away to know with certainty. Not wanting Sudokus to see him, Leon backed away from the window.

"Listen up guys," said Leon, "Scott is just past this window, but he's with Sudokus. We'll have to find a different way to get to him."

"Which way do you propose we take, comrade?"

"Well we have to go down one level, but taking this set of stairs would be too obvious, so I say we take that door and see where it leads us."

"Hold on, Leon," said Willy. "Don't you think it's strange that there are no guards patrolling the building Sudokus is in?"

"It is strange," said Leon, "But what can we do about it? Just make sure you guys all stay behind me, in case we do run into a trap. I'll walk slowly, and you guys run the other way if you see something happen to me."

Everyone drew their weapons as Leon prepared to open the door. He cautiously opened it and they walked into a room that smelled of death. As for the looks of the room, it was plain— almost too plain.

Leon made each of his steps slow and deliberate as he inched forward. He looked around constantly, expecting a trap to open up at any moment. The room was basically just a hallway, and on the other side was a doorway Leon hoped to reach. Leon kept looking around the room as he slowly walked. The room smelled so bad, yet there was nothing in the room. Leon was almost to the door when something finally caught his eye. Next to the door was a big blue button.

Leon got a bad feeling about the button and was about to turn back around, but it was too late. Lada suddenly slithered her way into the doorway from behind the wall at the far end of the room and pressed the button. Meanwhile, Gako had snuck up from behind and stood at the doorway on the other end of the hall and both of them had their guns out and poised to shoot, forcing everyone to freeze.

The button Lada pressed caused the floor just behind Leon to start to shimmer. It began shimmering faster and faster until it disappeared and everyone standing behind Leon fell through. Leon hesitated on whether or not he should also jump through the floor, but his decision was made for him when the floor shimmered back into a solid.

Leon looked back up to see Lada slithering toward him with her gun aimed right at his head. Leon stepped backward to try and keep some distance from her, but he ended up bumping into Gako who grabbed him with his massive arm. Lada led the way up a flight of stairs and Gako followed with their prize in hand.

CHAPTER FORTY-THREE

Willy, Alexander, and Odegbula fell through the floor and ended up landing in the basement with Jum-Jum. No one had fed Jum-Jum in a while, and she had built up an appetite by now.

Jum-Jum was slow to stir when she first realized the next meal was here. The dim lighting made it difficult for the men down there to see her, but eventually their eyes adjusted to the lack of light and they could see her rising up.

She took a step forward and began staring down the men as they backed away from her. It soon became apparent to Willy that this beast would try to eat them, and Willy began shooting at it. Metal bullets had never hit Jum-Jum before, only lasers, so this new sensation was a shock to her. However, the combination of her shell and thick, tough skin, made it so the bullets could only penetrate into her an inch at most. Soon the other men were shooting at the beast, but their guns were even less effective.

It quickly became apparent they'd need a plan. Willy looked around for a temporary escape and he eventually saw a small, cave-like crevice in the wall, which he directed everyone to run into. They were just able to make it to the hole before Jum-Jum closed in on them.

Inside the hole was horrific. There were skeletons of aliens who had tried the same thing littered everywhere. The smell was the same awful smell they'd smelt in the hallway, and there was a damp and sticky feeling in the air.

"I don't think our training back in Uganda prepared us for this, Willy," said Odegbula.

"Everything you do can prepare you for something, we just have to think this through carefully. Look around the room and figure out what's in here that can help us."

The men looked around for something. Every now and then, Jum-Jum broke their line of sight trying to fit her beak-like mouth through the hole.

After careful observation, the men were able to notice a complex working of wooden scaffolding was supporting the ceiling. They also noticed there was a button on the wall near the ceiling that looked just like the button Lada had pressed. It was near enough to the scaffolding that if they could find a way to climb up without Jum-Jum eating them, then one of them could press it.

"Alright, men," said Willy, "I only see one way out of here, and it will be dangerous. See that button up there?" Willy pointed to the button as he asked the question. "One of us will need to press it, and if my assumptions are correct, then we'll be able to get out of here the same way we came in. The only question is, how will we get up to that button without first getting eaten?" As if on cue, Jum-Jum once again shoved her beak against the hole.

"This beast must have some weak point," said Alexander.

"I was just thinking about that," said Odegbula, "And I believe its weak points are its eyes. It seems protected everywhere, but its eyes are just as exposed as any other creature's."

"Yes," said Alexander, "But who wants to go out there and shoot it? The only way to get an angle at it is to stand at the edge of this hole. But then the beast's jaws would be all over you, comrades."

"Here's what we're going to do," said Willy, "There are three of us here; Odegbula and Alexander, you will run out of the hole and head right. I will head left. Whoever it turns towards, you start shooting at it: aim for the eyes. The other person, or people, will start climbing up the scaffolding and try to hit the button. Just be careful because—," Willy was cut off by Jum-Jum sticking her head into the hole and letting off a roar. The sides of the hole were chipping away each time she stuck her head in and each time she was getting in a little further. "—Be careful because we don't know what will be past the ceiling."

Jum-Jum poked one of her eyes in the hole for a second, and then pulled back. Then she stuck her hand through the hole, and skewered Willy's space suit with one of her claws. Willy managed to work his way loose before Jum-Jum could pull him out of the hole, only suffering a torn suit—he could survive this because the suits were multi-layered.

"You all know what you're doing," said Willy, "Let's head out, now!"

Odegbula let out one of his war cries and they all sprinted out of the hole. This caught Jum-Jum off guard, and by the time she lunged out at the men running below, they were out of range.

Now they had to wait and see which way Jum-Jum would turn. They all pulled out their guns and aimed them towards her until she turned towards Willy. Willy had hoped Jum-Jum would turn towards him because he knew he had the best gun to handle the beast.

Willy began firing toward her eyes, but as soon as he landed a hit, she retracted her eyes close to her skull, and sealed her thick eyelids over them. Willy kept shooting, but the only benefit at this point was that Jum-Jum would not open her eyes back up unless the shooting stopped. The down side was that Jum-Jum now led a blind charge forward forcing Willy to dive out of the way.

Willy looked over at the scaffolding to see Odegbula leading the way up and nearly to the button. However, the wood-like material was old, and some spots were weak, which was causing Odegbula to test each piece before he used it to pull himself up.

Jum-Jum did another blind charge to where she thought she had heard the men go. Jum-Jum consequently brushed against the scaffolding, causing it to shake a bit. This caused Odegbula to lose his footing and he slipped down a few inches. He got another foothold, but a piece of material underneath his left foot cracked and fell down right on top of Jum-Jum. In response, Jum-Jum turned around and charged into the scaffolding, causing part of the structure to collapse.

In reality, the collapse only took a few seconds, but Odegbula felt the whole incident unfolding in slow motion. He knew that he was nearly in range of the button, so he reached up to the next piece of wood with his arm and pulled himself up as the scaffolding was tilting and falling. He then gave a strong push off from the woodworking and soared toward the button. Maybe it was all the adrenaline pumping through Odegbula's veins, or maybe the collapsing scaffolding had given him an extra boost of momentum, but Odegbula somehow overcame the strong gravity of Jupiter and hit the button, thus opening the ceiling. Unfortunately, he landed on Jum-Jum's neck and had to hold on for dear life.

"Odegbula!" shouted Willy, "Shoot down its throat! Fire a shot down its throat, Odegbula!"

Odegbula pulled out his gun, but fumbled it and it began plummeting toward the ground. Thinking quickly, he reached over the side of Jum-Jum's neck and grabbed the gun in mid fall. This caused him to lose his grip on the neck and he ended up holding on with his legs hanging upside down.

Jum-Jum turned her head to try to get her mouth at a better angle for devouring Odegbula. She opened her mouth and let out a roar that splattered sticky spittle over Odegbula. Odegbula didn't let this distract him, and he began shooting down the beast's throat. Soon, Jum-Jum was coughing up blood and making choking sounds. It was a grotesque scene, to see the death of such a creature, but within two minutes, she collapsed to the ground.

Odegbula jumped off as all the men sprinted to the part of the scaffolding that was still standing and climbed their way to safety. Willy hit the button on the top side and the floor began shimmering back into existence. Just before it totally sealed off, they heard the scream of Jum-Jum mixed with the gurgle of blood—the last sounds she ever made.

CHAPTER FORTY-FOUR

While Sudokus couldn't have counted on the men escaping Jum-Jum, everything else was going according to plan. The audience had been anxiously waiting, and now the main attraction was here. While Jum-Jum was keeping the rest of the group occupied, Gako had carried Leon out to a platform where millions were waiting below for just this moment. They seemed to be ready to catch Leon's head, should it come off. The platform was just large enough so that Gako and Lada could have a little fun shoving Leon around, but Leon had nowhere to run.

Gako held Leon up in front of the people below. They cheered as he pushed him to Lada, and Lada shoved him back. That went on for a minute before Lada pulled out some rope-like substance and tied Leon's hands behind his back.

Lada then pushed Leon back to Gako. Gako pulled his gun out and held it up to Leon's head, but he didn't shoot. The crowd cheered more vivaciously than ever. Gako smacked his gun up against Leon's head, causing Leon to collapse to his knees, and then he spit on Leon.

Leon was helpless. He wanted to fight back, but Gako was more powerful than he was. He still had his gun, which they didn't bother to confiscate because they knew he wouldn't dare shoot one of them knowing the other would kill him instantly if he did. Leon just assumed Willy and the other men were dead and it was all up to him to get Scott. Eventually Gako and Lada tired of playing around with Leon. After all, they were assassins, not jesters, and the only reason Leon wasn't already dead was because Sudokus was paying them extra to toy around with him. Gako pushed Leon into one of the corners and smacked him across the face once more with his gun to ensure that he stayed down on his knees.

Lada had positioned herself in the opposite corner of Leon and aimed down her scope at Leon's head. She made Gako stand just a few feet away with his gun aimed at Leon's head as well, just in case. Lada made a few adjustments, and then she was ready to fire. Leon tensed up, although he knew it wouldn't help. Just before Lada pulled the trigger, she heard Sudokus's voice bellow out and she stopped.

"The time is now," said Sudokus from a balcony above Leon's. "This is how we shall win the war. You've witnessed this happen time and time again: a rebel leader desperate to keep his planet from joining our satisfactory empire. How does it always end? Just like this. Now without further ado..." Sudokus motioned his hands to signal for Lada to take the shot.

If Sudokus hadn't given that insignificant speech, if Sudokus hadn't paid Gako and Lada to toy around with Leon, if Leon had done something to provoke Gako or Lada to shoot him, if Willy had taken a few seconds longer to devise his plan, if Odegbula hadn't been able to press the button, if Jum-Jum had pounced on the men quicker, then things might have turned out differently. Things would be completely different.

But everything did happen like it did, and because of that, Leon lived.

Leon lived because, just at that moment, just before Lada was able to pull the trigger, Willy burst through the door onto the balcony. If the crowd noise hadn't been so loud, maybe Lada would've heard his footsteps and shot Leon sooner, but she never heard it coming.

Willy's sudden entrance distracted Gako and Lada just long enough for Leon to swing his arms under his legs and get his hands in front of him. Leon then jumped onto Gako, wrapping his arms around him and using the rope-like substance to choke him. Willy shot and killed Lada right there on that balcony. Leon struggled with Gako for a few moments until Willy shot and killed Gako as well with one well-placed shot to the head.

The crowd was silent for a few seconds, and then they started screaming again, but this time, the screaming sounded different, more fearful. During all the commotion, Sudokus managed to escape back inside the building.

Willy and Leon ran back inside as well and closed the door behind them. Willy then pulled a combat knife out of his pocket and cut the rope off of Leon's hands.

"How did you guys get out from underneath the floor?" asked Leon.

"That's not important right now," said Willy, "What is important is that we do what we came here to do. We're not leaving until we find a way to shut down those robots and the only way to do that is to find Scott."

"Willy," said Leon, "Remember that I saw Scott in that room earlier. We should head over there right now to see if he's still there."

"What if Sudokus is there too?" asked Odegbula.

"Then we fight him," said Leon. "We can't keep backing down from him. We have to end this right here, and right now. For all we know, Sudokus could be running away from here right now with Scott. We have to move quickly and make sure we find at least one of them. Stick together, and move quickly." As Leon had uttered that last sentence, he remembered that he had left the little aliens behind. "I have to head back for something," said Leon, "But it's not too far away from where we're headed. Head down the stairs, make a left, head straight down the hallway, through the door, through another door, and then up a flight of stairs. Then we head back down the stairs, and see if Scott is in the room behind the window. Let's go."

The group headed back the same way they came until they finally reached the platform where they'd landed their ships. The noise outside was deafening. Everyone was terrified: Leon, Willy, Odegbula, Alexander, the crowd outside, none of them knew what was going to happen next. Leon opened the hatch on his ship and pulled out the spaceship with the three aliens.

"Sorry about that, guys," thought Leon. By now, Leon was comfortable with mental telepathy.

"Why did you leave us in there? We figured out by all the shouting what was going on over there, and we know we could've saved you from Gako and Lada."

"Maybe, but you could've also been captured along the way. They say everything happens for a reason."

"Who are they?"

"I don't even know anymore. Now let's find Scott. I have an idea where he might be, but we may need your help."

Leon closed the hatch back up and then the group rushed back down the stairs and through the doors until they reached the room where the mechs received their electrical zaps into life. Leon looked out the window, but the room was now empty.

"Shit, he's not here," said Leon. "Where else could he be. He has to still be here, right?"

"Not necessarily," said Willy, "Sudokus could've taken him anywhere; he could be dead for all we know."

"No," said Leon, "He's still out there." Leon consulted the aliens to try to figure out where he was. "Do you guys sense him anywhere?"

"He's definitely still out there, but the signal is constantly being scrambled."

Suddenly, the building began trembling. Everyone braced themselves as the floor began shaking more and more.

"Where's that shaking coming from?" Leon asked the aliens.

"Directly to the left on the other side of the building. Only something big could create this shaking. It seems like...a command ship."

"I know where Scott is," said Leon to the group, "But we have to hurry."

Everyone began sprinting through doors, down stairs, and through corridors until they reached a room that looked like a loading dock. This was the final destination for the mechs. A conveyor belt carried them into the storage compartment of a command ship. The command ship, which was parked outside, was just as big as the building they were currently in.

The ship was causing all the shaking by starting up its engines in preparation for takeoff. Leon saw Sudokus several yards away walking into the ship, dragging Scott along. Sudokus headed towards a small, open door.

Leon and Willy led the charge as they sprinted toward Sudokus. Sudokus passed through the door just a few seconds before they reached it, but Leon and Willy managed to make it on board as well before the door completely closed. Unfortunately, they were the only ones who made it. Leon got on in plenty of time, and Willy had to dive through as the door began closing up. The rest of the men and the three aliens could only watch as the massive ship began to take off for the great beyond.

CHAPTER FORTY-FIVE

Leon and Willy found themselves on the very same command ship Sudokus and Scott were in. They heard someone banging on the door outside, trying to get in—either Alexander or Odegbula—but the ship soon went airborne and the banging stopped.

Leon and Willy both had their guns out and ready to fire as they navigated their way through the command ship. Adrenaline had distorted their sense of time, yet they still found it perplexing that Sudokus had managed to get out of sight so quickly. They had seen Sudokus get aboard the ship only a few seconds before they had, yet there was no trace of him now. They kept expecting him to pop out at any moment.

After they passed through the atrium of the ship, they found themselves in the engine room. This was the room they would have needed to find if they could've infiltrated the command ships during their battles. If you destroyed the engine room, the whole ship would deactivate and plummet. However, the engine room was hot and humid and they were glad when they moved past it.

They found it strange that they were able to navigate their way through this ship without once encountering an enemy. Nevertheless, they continued their way through the ship, winding around corners and down hallways, until they finally realized they were lost.

"Haven't we already passed through this part of this ship?" asked Leon.

"I don't know, Leon," replied Willy.

"I think we're going in circles. There has to be a logical layout to this ship, we're just doing something wrong. I think if we head that way, then—," the sound of static through Leon's communicator cut him off. Leon pulled it out of his pocket and listened closely as the signal faded in and out of clarity.

"Is someone there?" asked Leon. "Hello, is someone out there?"

"Hel...Who is...Le...It's Sco..."

"Who is this? There's a lot of static."

"Leon, is that...It's me, Scott."

"Scott, it's really you? The signal is getting better, try talking now."

"Leon, where are you?"

"I'm on the command ship with you, but I don't know exactly where you are and I'm a bit lost myself."

"I was locked inside of this...room by Sudokus. I'm not exactly sure where I am in relation to the ship, but there's a window in here and I can see...circular room where Sudokus is. It's almost like he's waiting for you, but it's got to be a....He's just too...for this...his hiding place." It was difficult for Leon to make-out what Scott was saying. He seemed to be whispering even when there wasn't static, but maybe he needed to whisper.

"What's the last room you remember passing through, Scott?"

"We went through this room where there were a...mechs standing around, and just before that, we were in...long hallway. I'm not exactly sure where we were before that."

"Don't worry, we'll find you, Scott. We are on our way right now." Leon put the communicator back into his pocket. "Come on, Willy. We have to look for a long hallway somewhere."

Leon and Willy once again began walking through the deserted ship, on the lookout for a long hallway. After a few minutes of walking, Leon turned a corner and found himself staring down a corridor so long, that he could not see to the end of it.

"Willy, I think we found the hallway. Just be careful once we reach the other side, because Scott said there were mechs in a room at the end."

"But if there are mechs," said Willy, "What would stop them from walking into this hallway and shooting us while we're in it? We'd have nowhere to run and it'd be like shooting fish in a barrel. Pardon me for any images that expression may have created."

"We'll just have to hope that doesn't happen I guess. Even if it does, there'll probably be a side hall that we can duck into. There's no way that this is just one continuous hallway with no side corridors."

Leon and Willy walked down the hallway, their legs shaking nervously with each step. They walked for minutes, with the end of the hallway still not in sight. They took it step-by-step, always looking straight ahead with their guns clutched tightly at their sides. Everything looked the same; it was as if they weren't even walking since there weren't any fixed points for them to be able to see their progress. They could've been walking on a treadmill for all they knew.

Finally, the end of the hallway stopped being a vanishing point, and became a reality. This gave the duo more inspiration as they continued to march ahead. Finally, they reached the end. It was a sense of relief to finally be somewhere.

Leon peered around the corner to see the room filled with mechs. The room was also filled with crates labeled, "Spare Parts". He quickly pulled his head back to keep them from seeing him. Then he slowly peered back to try to see what was past that room. Just as Scott had said, it was a big round room.

"I have a plan, Willy, but I'm afraid it'll be a suicide mission for both of us."

"Just getting onto this ship was a suicide mission," responded Willy. He was sweating and breathing heavily, yet something about him looked calm, as if he'd just now accepted death. "Just think about it this way, Leon, we can't leave the ship, and we don't even know where we are in space right now, so let's just do what we need to. If we don't make it out, then that was probably our fate anyway. There's no retreat."

"Alright, here's the plan," began Leon in a whisper, although he wasn't sure if the mechs were sound sensitive. "One of us has to distract these mechs, and the other has to get Scott from Sudokus. Which job do you want?"

"These mechs have the guns, so I'll handle them. You just go after Scott and use what I taught you if Sudokus tries to get in your way."

"No, no, you're the master at hand to hand combat, Captain. Going against the mechs is more of a suicide mission, so I'll do it."

"Leon, I'm getting too old for hand-to-hand combat. I saw how you restrained Gako. I know you have a better chance than I do, now go get Scott. I'll head out for the mechs. Wait a few seconds until I have a chance to get all their attention, then go." Willy didn't wait for any sort of acknowledgement of this plan from Leon, he simply charged out into the room.

Leon watched as the mechs turned toward Willy. At first, no one shot. Willy ducked behind one of the many crates in the room and waited to see what the mechs would do. Leon waited anxiously to see what would happen as well. He could see the doorway he needed to reach, but he had to wait for the mechs to do something. Willy finally decided to be the aggressor and fired a shot at one of them. That's all it took to get them started.

During the commotion of gunfire, Leon walked into the room and snuck around behind the mechs. Leon then entered the circular room and was surprised to see a door automatically close behind him. Leon didn't know how long Willy could survive by just hiding behind the crates in the room, but he hoped that he could find a way to shut down the mechs before they got him.

Leon gazed around the room. He knew Scott was in or near here, but he'd somehow managed to elude him. Leon looked up towards the ceiling. It wasn't a very tall room, and in a window on the wall near the ceiling, he could see Scott. Leon began walking toward Scott, although he couldn't reach him from the ground because he wasn't tall enough.

Unbeknownst to Leon, Sudokus waited just behind him. He had pressed himself against the wall as Leon entered. If Leon had looked directly to his right upon entering the room, he'd have seen Sudokus standing there with his big red eye glaring at him. But he hadn't done that, so he hadn't noticed Sudokus.

"Excellent work," said Sudokus from behind Leon, not caring to take full advantage of his stealth. Leon whirled around to see Sudokus now standing just a few feet away from him. "This has been a laudable effort on your part. I've seen a lot of rebel leaders try to challenge me before, but they've never made it this far. I mean, really think about where you are now."

"I'm no rebel leader," said Leon confidently.

"You're not? Well, you do a good job of acting like one. You were one of the first to join this war and you're the one who is here right now."

"There's someone else here with me as well."

"No there is not. You and I are the only ones in this room. Willy is outside and Scott is up there."

"How did you know my Captain's name?"

"The same way everyone finds out information: telepathy, mind-reading, whatever you'd like to call it."

"I don't have time for games right now, stand down and let me speak to my friend or I will have to restrain you with force."

"Why would you want to talk to Scott? Think about where you are right now. You're on a safe ship, on a pleasant journey through the solar system. No one is going to hurt you unless you provoke it."

"I may be safe here, but what about everyone back on my home planet, are they safe?"

"Why do you care about some humans back home? You don't have any family there. No dependents or loved ones. Why

should you care how many people my soldiers kill on their way
to take control of the planet? Allow me to show you something,
Leon." Sudokus walked over to the side of the room and slid
open a panel on the wall. "Look out of this window, and what
do you see?"

"Mostly darkness, with some stars strewn about."

"Look right here; look at that pale blue dot. Do you know
what that is? It is Earth. Do you see how insignificant it is? Do
you realize that if you condensed the history of this universe into
one year, then relatively, humans have only been around for ten
seconds? Are you beginning to realize your insignificance? So
what reason do you have for caring for that pale blue dot out
there?"

"I hope to return there one day. Get back on with life, do
things normal people do, and I don't want a mindless machine
controlling my everyday life."

"Mindless? I have more knowledge than any other being.
My mind can read other's minds with its power."

"Yes, but you have an artificial mind. It can be easily
replicated. That's why no one has ever read your mind, because
you have none. Because inside peoples' minds, lives a conscious.
And if you had one, you'd realize how wrong everything you do
is. It's not right to genetically engineer slaves, or kill people just
to increase your own power."

"Says who? What right do you have to say what is right and
wrong? Besides, don't pretend like humans wouldn't do exactly
what I am doing if they had as much power and knowledge as
me. Don't even pretend like they don't try to imitate me exactly
right now."

"Maybe they would—maybe they do—but it's still wrong,
so they'd fail just as you will. You'll fail because there's a force in
the universe. Some say that there is a God. Some say Allah, or
Brahman, some call it Dao, but people dating back thousands of
years have believed in an all-powerful, omniscient presence
which sets a code of ethics, and that's why what you do is
wrong."

"But I am all powerful and omniscient, so that means that I can decide what is right and wrong. Besides, this force you speak of, only exists on your planet for beings not intelligent enough to explain things that would otherwise be mysteries. Your friend, Scott, tried spewing that talk on me earlier."

"Look, I don't have time for this. I have two people—no, a whole planet—counting on me, and I'm wasting my time talking to something that has no mind and isn't alive."

Leon was finished talking then, and pulled out his gun. He hesitated for just a moment before pulling the trigger. He wondered if his bullets would actually do any damage, then wondered why the humans couldn't have advanced to lasers for everything yet, but then he stopped wondering and decided that even if they were useless, he should try anyway.

The bullets merely bounced off Sudokus, and Leon had to take a few steps back. Leon whirled around and shot the window Scott was behind. The window shattered and Scott was free. Although Scott didn't leave the room at first, because he didn't want to get caught up in the middle of the fighting below.

Before Leon could turn back around and confront Sudokus, Sudokus grabbed Leon from behind and flung him to the ground. He kicked the gun out of Leon's hand and then stepped on Leon's chest and pinned him down to the ground.

"You are a foolish human. I could've saved you, even let you join in my conquest; but some intangible code of ethics is more important to you. The only things that are real are palpable. But that lesson is learned too late for you, I fear."

"It's never too late for anything," said Leon to no one in particular. "I came here for one thing and I'm going to do it."

"No you're not, you won't do anything." Sudokus picked Leon up and flung him against the wall. Then he walked back over to him and kicked him again, breaking one of his ribs. But between bouts of extreme pain, Leon managed to talk.

"Scott, you have to stop those mechs. Do it now while—" Leon stopped as Sudokus picked him back up and threw him across the room again. "While you can. I'll hold him off a little longer, just stop the mec—," Sudokus picked Leon up again and threw him to the ground, stepping on his chest again with even more malicious intent than last time.

Scott had always been waiting for an opportunity when he knew Sudokus was preoccupied and he could switch the mechs programming. Now that time had arrived, but all the stuff he needed was back in the shop. He had nothing, absolutely nothing—except for the communicator. A revelation hit Scott then. Scott knew that if he could find the correct frequency the mechs operated on, then he could use the mechs' voice recognition system to switch their programming. Scott began searching desperately for their frequency, but only got static. He was helpless to Leon's beating below and the constant torrent of bullets Willy was taking outside.

Leon might have just let himself die there at the hands of Sudokus's grasp; but Willy had trained him better than this, and Willy had asked him to use that training. So as Leon lay on the ground, watching Sudokus approach him, he managed to lift himself up and got into a fighting stance. Leon's chest was bruised and bleeding both inside and outside, multiple ribs were broken, he had fractured his elbow, and his ankle was broken; but, there was no retreat.

"Ah, now you want to put up a fight," said Sudokus. "I'm very much satisfied when they try to put up a fight."

Sudokus lunged forward at Leon who ducked out of the way and stuck his leg out to trip Sudokus. Sudokus stumbled, but managed to stay on his feet. Sudokus turned around to see Leon still standing in the same spot in his same fighting position. Sudokus reached out his arm in an attempt to grab Leon, but Leon dodged and quickly followed it up by reaching forward, grabbing Sudokus and attempting to pull Sudokus down to the ground with no success. Leon let go and retreated as Sudokus quickly popped turned around to face Leon again.

Sudokus lunged forward once more at Leon and this time he made sure to grab a hold of his arm with one of his claws. Leon struggled to work his way free, but he could not. Sudokus just kept increasing the pressure of his grip, cutting into Leon's arm as the blood started dripping out, and then rushing out.

Soon Sudokus would sever the arm, but he was torturing Leon with the pain before that happened. And he kept staring at Leon with that big red eye. Everything about Sudokus's face seemed to be mocking Leon, and the big red eye just stared through him. The longer Leon stared at the eye, the bigger it seemed to get. Soon, it was all Leon could see: it was hypnotizing him, paralyzing him. It seemed like it was seeing inside of Leon, and analyzing him, as if there was some formula it could use to solve him. The eye seemed all knowing, it seemed even greater than the most intelligent mind. Leon couldn't take any more of the eye. He pulled his arm back, and slammed his fist straight into it. The eye shattered, leaving glass everywhere. A red light glowed out from the hole where the eye once was. Sudokus pulled away from Leon in shock.

Just at the moment Leon broke Sudokus's eye, Scott had found the frequency for the mechs. He was able to give them a new program. Their job was now to destroy Sudokus, and then self-destruct. This didn't just apply to the mechs on the ship, even the mechs on Earth immediately stopped killing people, and began heading back to the command ship which they'd come here on. Even the mechs back on Jupiter were searching for a way to reach Sudokus.

Willy was in a corner behind a crate, had run out of ammo, and the mechs were only a few yards away from him when they suddenly turned around. Willy watched as they approached the door and began trying to open it. Soon, the mechs stepped back as a spin-off of the mech model came down the long hallway and into the room. This mech looked exactly like the other mechs, except it had a missile attached to its back. The mech tilted forward to aim the missile at the door, and then fired off a shot, blowing the door wide open. Willy waited until all the mechs had entered, and then he rushed into the room to see if Leon or Scott were still alive.

To Willy's surprise he saw them both still alive. Scott had jumped down from his room and was standing next to Leon. The three of them were trying their best to stay out of the way as the mechs did what they could to try and destroy Sudokus. However, all of their bullets just bounced off his hard metal outer casing. Sudokus knew that he'd have no way of defeating the mechs, so he ran to the opposite side of the room and pressed a button that opened up a hidden door. He went through the door and was gone.

"We have to get out of here now," said Scott.

"No," said Leon, "We have to destroy Sudokus."

"Don't worry about that, Leon. I programmed those mechs to destroy Sudokus for us."

"They will not succeed. Sudokus will simply run away from them until he has a way of destroying them. You can't send a machine to do a job like this."

"Leon, we've done what we came here to do," said Willy, "Now we have to start searching for a way out."

"You guys can look for the controls of this ship, or some escape pod, but I'm going after Sudokus. That way we can all do what we have to do and we'll get home just fine. Now I need to start going after Sudokus or I'll never catch him." With that, Leon left.

"I'm sure Leon will be fine," Willy said to Scott. "But he's right, we need to find out how to control this ship and land it back on Earth."

"Or find escape pods."

Willy and Scott headed one way, while Leon headed in Sudokus's direction, following the mechs and pushing his way past them. He eventually tracked Sudokus down to a room where, ironically, there were escape pods. Leon wished Willy and Scott were here; then they could just leave on these pods. Leon might have changed his mind about killing Sudokus, and left while he knew he could, but he wasn't going to leave without telling Scott or Willy.

Leon had to make sure he stayed out of the way of the mechs line of fire as they shot toward Sudokus. Bullets as well as lasers were flying towards Sudokus, and every now and then, one of the bullets would embed itself into a weak point in his joints, or become stuck in the open part of his chest. As more bullets stuck into Sudokus's leg joints, he collapsed, and soon he was crawling. Leon looked ahead to where Sudokus was heading, and saw a strange, swirling blue portal. Leon had never seen anything like it before, but he could tell it was something powerful and important. It seemed to sink into the wall, and Leon couldn't find the source of the portal, but he wanted to find some way to destroy this thing before Sudokus could use it for himself, but he couldn't get near it with all the stray bullets flying around.

Just then, Willy and Scott entered the room through a different door after taking a wrong turn and going in a circle. Leon used his hands to usher Willy and Scott closer to him so they could hear him talk over the sound of the mechs.

"Take the escape pods over there and get out of here!" he shouted over the noise around him. "I have to make sure Sudokus is properly destroyed, and then I'll join you. Just don't wait up, go!"

"No, we're going to stay with you to make sure nothing happens," yelled Willy. "We came in together and we leave together."

Leon, not wanting to waste any more time talking, headed over to Sudokus's crawling body. He couldn't get near it yet though, because of the constant flow of bullets pelting it. So Leon just watched as the crawling got slower and slower, and eventually came to a stop. Once that happened, the mechs stopped firing and just began analyzing the remains of Sudokus, except for one mech who'd arrived late. It was the mech with the missiles on his back. The extra weight had slowed it down and it was just now arriving. Leon heard it as its poorly oiled joints struggled to aim the missile toward Sudokus. Leon began running away from Sudokus, knowing that the blast range on the missile would kill him if he wasn't far enough away.

Leon signaled with his hands for Scott and Willy to head to the escape pods. Willy and Scott were much closer to them than Leon was, so they were able to make it in, but Leon wasn't so lucky. The missile fired off and hit its target. The blast didn't get Leon; the hole the blast created did. Although the humans could never penetrate the command ships from the outside, the metal linked together in such a way that it was penetrable from the inside. The part of the hole created by the missile overlapped the blue portal Sudokus had been attempting to reach, yet it didn't destroy it. It only created the effect of a vacuum behind the portal, which began sucking everything into it. Leon tried his best to grab onto something as he was pulled towards the blue portal, but there was nothing.

Leon could see the portal getting bigger and could tell it was going to suck him into it. As he entered the portal, he could just barely see what was going on inside the ship. He saw pieces of Sudokus flying towards him. Some missed the portal and went into outer space while others went into the portal, forever scattering his individuals parts throughout and the galaxy and even further. The same thing happened with the mechs who were self-destructing now that Sudokus was dead. The last thing Leon saw were the escape pods Scott and Willy were in, flying away from the command ship, which was now collapsing in on itself.

After that, a tremendous pain overwhelmed Leon. The portal was actually a teleportation portal, but no one had ever dared to use it to transport life, merely to transport materials. Furthermore, no coordinates were set for the teleporter, so where Leon would end up was anyone's guess.

A pain, which encompassed Leon's whole body, knocked him out, and his vision became blue for a moment as the portal sucked him in deeper. Everything eventually went black as he entered a pain induced slumber.

Maybe if Leon hadn't been in such incredible pain, his last emotion would've been happiness. He, the insignificant mortal that he was, had managed to save the inhabitants of this solar system, and maybe the entire universe, from living in a society of the machine known as Sudokus. For, even though Sudokus may not have been evil, morals and mortality can never restrain a machine. The intangibles are what are really important in life, and a machine could never begin to understand the value of one pale blue dot, in a sea of dots and stars.

EPILOGUE

Leon woke up in a hospital surrounded by humans. He was receiving treatment for wounds he'd received during his ordeal. They also needed to stabilize his vital signs after going through that portal. The doctors ran around frantically grabbing different medicines and I.V.'s.

"Come on," said one of the doctors, "this is the most crucial part of the process."

One of the doctors inserted a liquid into a bag hooked up to Leon's arm and Leon fell back asleep. He woke up again later, although he couldn't tell how much later. Now, all the cords were off and the only thing left from the operation was the hospital patient clothing. After a few basic tests to ensure everything went smoothly, Leon received a change of clothes and permission to leave.

As Leon left the hospital however, he couldn't help but realize he had no idea where he was. At first, Leon thought it was nighttime, but when he looked at the sky, not only was it a dark green color, but a purple sun shone brightly. Leon pinched himself to try to wake himself out of his dream, but this was no dream. Leon thought maybe the hospital had given him some drugs that were messing with his vision, so he started heading back there to correct the problem. Before he got to the door however, someone grabbed him and dragged him behind one of the many trees.

"Leon, you are not where you think you are," said the woman who grabbed him.

"Who are you? Where are Scott and Willy?"

"Scott and Willy are safe on Earth. Maybe safe isn't the right word, but they'll be fine. Leon, you are not on Earth."

"I am on Earth, you are all humans and I can breathe without an oxygen supply."

"The portal you went through, do you remember it? It's a teleporter, but since it wasn't set, it could've taken you anywhere, and it took you here"

"It took me to Earth, you mean. There is no other planet in the solar system like this."

"That's the thing, Leon, you're not in your solar system, or galaxy, or universe for that matter."

"You lie, now let me go," exclaimed Leon.

"Aren't you at least curious to know how I know your name, Leon Dudley?"

"Hardly anybody knows my last name, who told you?"

"Leon, think back to when you first went to the Russian base. Remember that television show you watched? What was it about?"

"No…Those were just theories, there's not actually such things as…"

"Yes," said the woman, "You're in a parallel universe, Leon. As you can see, I look the same as you; or at least I look human, but there are differences. Look at the sky, and at the sun. It's the same set-up, but different colors. You're on the parallel planet of Earth."

"You never answered my first question, who are you?"

"I am Nella Vervolg, but that is not important. Your identity is much more important. You are the one we've been waiting for. Sudokus was just a test to see if you were capable. In fact, those three aliens you grew fond of, they work for us. We sent them out to help train you. They guided your destiny to make sure you ended up here when you did. Well, not exactly, but it can all be explained later."

"So, I'll just pretend you're not crazy for a moment and ask you this question: what do I have to do to go back home?"

"That's the thing. We need you to solve two problems before you can move on."

"Bring it on," said Leon sarcastically.

"The first and foremost was Sudokus. The second is that there is a man out there trying to steal energy from a different universe for us to use. As you probably already know, this would destroy our universe since technically, energy cannot be created nor destroyed in a closed environment and each universe is its own closed environment. He's trying to steal energy because we have a problem. Unlike the universes surrounding us, which are growing, we are shrinking. The shrink is exponential and within a few decades, or centuries if we're lucky, we'll be the size of an atom. This has caused more problems than you might think, but that is a discussion for a different day."

"Earlier, you said that Scott and Willy may not be safe, why is that?"

"Willy made some bad negotiations early on in the war to convince the other superpowers to aid him. Now his sector is in debt and the other sectors want what is rightfully theirs. Not to mention he's one of the most wanted criminals in the world. Also, instead of there being peace after the war, there is just another war. Plus, with Sudokus being dead, the planets are all open for the taking. The situation is ripe for upheaval in that whole solar system."

Now, with all the introductions done, Leon started to calm down and he realized that Nella was actually an attractive woman. In fact, he hadn't seen a woman since the beginning of the war. Leon had the feeling he'd be spending a lot of time working with her while he was here, and he was looking forward to it.

Nella led Leon to a building, which, upon first entering, looked like a building for carrying out official business—an embassy or something similar to that. They rode an elevator up and Nella showed Leon his room. It was even more luxurious than any house he had called a home back on Earth.

This may not have been Earth, but as Leon kicked his shoes off and settled into his bed, he started to feel at home. He turned on the television and then started to drift to sleep. It was the best sleep he'd had in a while.

ABOUT THE AUTHOR

Justin Smith is a fifteen year old living in Buffalo, New York with his loving family. This is his first novel, but he hopes to write many more, including a sequel to this one.

Made in the USA
Charleston, SC
23 December 2011